a familiar ring

······················· a novel

a familiar ring

.... a novel

rk terry

Covenant

Cover image, by © Digital Vision Collection/Getty Images.
Cover design copyrighted 2003 by Covenant Communications, Inc.

Published by Covenant Communications, Inc.
American Fork, Utah

Printed in Canada
First Printing: September 2003

10 09 08 07 06 05 04 03   10 9 8 7 6 5 4 3 2 1

ISBN 1-59156-261-9

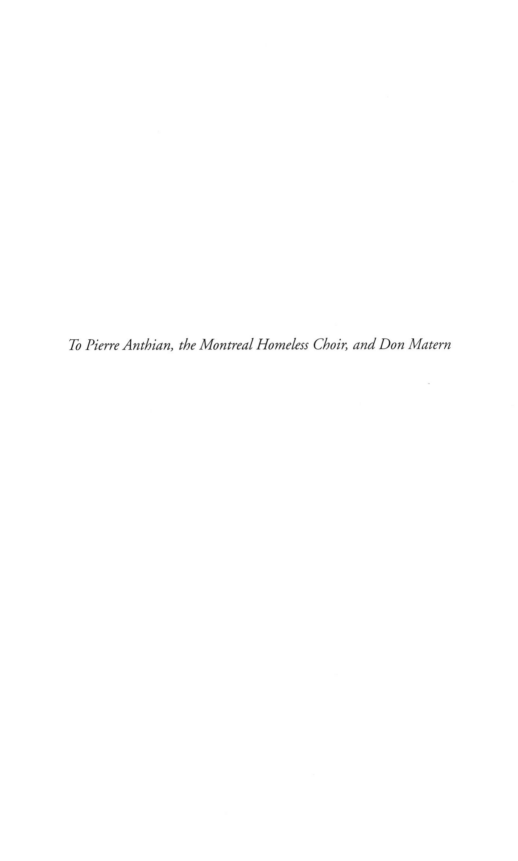

To Pierre Anthian, the Montreal Homeless Choir, and Don Matern

first christmas

....

Jerry

Five days before Christmas, unseasonably mild weather drifted into Salt Lake City from the West Coast. Only a few piles of dirty snow on the north sides of buildings remained from the previous week's storm. For a couple of days, the city's children had built snowmen, waged snowball wars, and generally assumed the ten inches of white stuff covering grass and shrubs would last through the holidays. But suddenly the jet stream fled north, warm air flooded the valley, and now it looked as though any hope of a white Christmas might have to wait for next year.

Not that the shoppers minded. They were out in droves, rushing from the ZCMI Center to Crossroads Plaza in light jackets, a few even in shirtsleeves, seemingly unable to part with their hard-earned cash fast enough. The local economy was booming—sales up ten percent over last year. Regardless of the weather, the retailers were going to have a green Christmas.

Jerry Carlson didn't mind the warm weather either. He shuffled slowly along South Temple Street in his usual attire of stained, threadbare jeans; a dirty blue parka; and a droopy stocking cap. Strains of "Joy to the World" wafted by as he passed what used to be the Hotel Utah. The Church of Jesus Christ of Latter-day Saints had remodeled the antiquated landmark and renamed it the Joseph Smith Memorial Building after the religion's founder. Now the posh lobby boasted a two-story Christmas tree and a high school choir belting out sophisticated arrangements of ordinary Christmas carols for anyone who happened to wander in. Jerry didn't, although on a colder day he may have stepped inside for a moment or two to warm himself and let the cheery notes bounce off him like pebbles tossed against a stone wall. Today he simply drifted on past the ex-hotel, past the ramp to the underground parking garage, past a wide flower bed—mostly dormant despite the balmy weather—past the crosswalk to the ZCMI Center, and finally sat down on the low, granite ledge of a planter box.

Setting his backpack on the ground, he unzipped it and pulled out a plastic cup from a fast-food joint and a rectangular piece of cardboard. He put the cup on the ground by his feet, rested the cardboard on his lap, and promptly began his daily routine of not looking up at the passersby. On the cardboard in black magic marker stood the single word, *homeless.*

The lunch hour was approaching, and Jerry spent every lunch hour here. Unless Freddy showed up. Freddy had a music box and played the same three songs over and over, and when he came, the trickle of coins that usually found their way into Jerry's cup ended up in Freddy's. Jerry's pathetic sign couldn't compete with Freddy's screeching renditions of "Jingle Bells," "We Wish You a Merry Christmas," and "Rudolph." But when the Music Man was busking elsewhere, the planter box by the ZCMI crosswalk was as good a spot for handouts as any in the city.

If Jerry turned his head to the right and looked up at the sky, he would see the twenty-eight–story, off-white, vertical stripes of the Church Office Building, where hundreds of everyday Toms and Marys handled the everyday business of The Church of Jesus Christ of Latter-day Saints. Most Mormons, Jerry had been told, were tight-wads, perhaps because most of them had large families and somehow still managed to fork over ten percent of their paychecks to the Church's tithing coffers, but he had discovered a little secret: stereo-types always make room for exceptions. When noontime rolled around and the COB disgorged a stream of hungry, middle-aged workers, many of them wandered over to the ZCMI Food Court, and more than a few dropped coins in his cup while they waited for the light to change.

Jerry wasn't necessarily grateful for the donations. He was far beyond any such tender emotion. Besides, the way he saw it, he *earned* the few dollars that landed in his cup. It wasn't easy work sitting there on frigid, windy days in his inadequate coat and thin gloves, nor was it pleasant on blistering summer afternoons. And even in balmy weather it wasn't easy to abase himself and beg for spare change. Somehow it made him feel less than human, lower than a dog who receives a home and food and affection just for wagging his tail, being a loyal companion, and greeting his master with unbridled joy.

No, Jerry wasn't capable of gratitude anymore. According to the strange slant on social mathematics rattling around in his head, he figured these well-employed folks owed him something. And a few of them apparently agreed. Although many of them silently despised his kind, Jerry suspected others felt guilty for reasons they couldn't articulate. The cruel calculus of large-scale social economics was perhaps beyond their grasp, but still, the idea of someone in their fair city being homeless troubled them, as if it were in some way their fault. They couldn't tell you why, but they felt responsible. Most put blinders on their guilt and refused to look at him—pretending perhaps that what they didn't see didn't exist—but a few couldn't eat their lunches in good conscience until they put a coin or two in his cup. Maybe now and then someone gave him money not out of guilt but because of some higher and holier emotion, but Jerry didn't even entertain this possibility. He'd grown too cynical, or at least too apathetic. All he knew was this: without these lunchtime penance payments, he would have either starved or frozen by now. Since moving to the crosswalk between the COB and the ZCMI Center, he'd been able to bring in enough change to buy a tarp and two blankets and to eat fast food. He hated the thought of standing in line for up to three hours to land a hot meal at the Downtown Mission.

On warm days he didn't mind sitting there. He sat and stared off into space and thought all kinds of strange thoughts while people either ignored him or bought him lunch. Some days he thought about food—all the delectables he had savored before his street life. Other days he pondered certain people he had known. And once in a great while he thought about his old job. But most of the time he tried to not think at all, because every trail of memory inevitably led to Brenda, and Brenda was the one image he tried to avoid. Even now, this image and this image alone could still cause him pain.

Like most homeless people, Jerry had his regular routine. But unlike most single homeless men, his routine didn't revolve around alcohol. As a rule, especially in winter, the men on the street—and some of the women—were a wretched crowd who drank to stay warm. And they didn't sleep at night. During the cold, dark hours, they would walk the streets to keep warm, then in the morning, a few hours before the Downtown Mission opened, they would line up for breakfast. After breakfast they would find a corner to sleep in, and after a short nap they'd wait in line again for lunch. Then they'd go beg for spare change. With their take, they'd walk to the State Liquor Store and buy enough "antifreeze" to get them through another night. The Mission would let any who could find a warm corner stay and sleep until the supper dishes were all washed and the volunteers were ready to leave. Then the good Reverend Del Greco would regretfully turn out all who didn't have cots, which he reserved primarily for women with children. The outcasts would find a quiet doorway or a deserted bench where they could drink their "antifreeze" until the cold drove them out again to tread the dark, empty streets.

Jerry, on the other hand, didn't drink unless it was bitter cold, and he tried to keep the same hours as "normal" people. He'd found a secluded hollow in the foothills above Salt Lake, and he slept there most nights, even though it was ten degrees colder than down in the city. He left his tarp and blankets there during the day, hidden behind a rock and covered with tree branches. His other belongings he carried in the old backpack. Early on in his street existence, he had hunted the city for nooks and crannies where he could stash his possessions, but no matter how well hidden they were, someone always seemed to find them and steal them. Later on he discovered if he just left his pack lying out in the open, even for days, nobody would touch it. If stuff was left lying around, people apparently assumed it was worthless. If it was hidden, then of course it must be valuable. Unfortunately, before he learned this bit of street psychology, he'd lost his driver's license, his Social Security card, and anything else he might have used for identification.

Up to that point he had maintained a mental link between the present and the past. As long as he could prove it to somebody else, he was still the Jerry Carlson who used to live on the corner of

Garfield Avenue and Eighth East. But when these substitutes for identity were gone, it was as if someone had stolen his soul, and he became another person, a nonperson, a cipher, a drifter, a vagrant. But that was fine, he supposed, since he really couldn't ever go back. The past was gone forever, and with it went the future too. So he lived minute to minute, day to day. And somewhere in the back of his mind, he knew just how fragile the present was when it had no past to anchor it and no future to give it direction. Some night, he supposed, the temperature would plunge too far below zero and he would freeze to death, or he would catch a cold and it would progress to pneumonia and he would not get better. But he held these thoughts at bay. They had no meaning in the present, so he didn't torture himself with them.

* * *

Max

On this particular day, five days before Christmas, with the warm sun shining in his eyes, Jerry found it easy to drift off into the bright, yellow void and ignore everyone and everything. The patch of sidewalk six feet in front of him now had him fully mesmerized, and only the occasional clatter of coins in his cup brought him almost to the brink of conscious thought. Time no longer had any hold on him. Minutes, hours, days, weeks, years all blended together into one giant, placid, mindless pool, wide as eternity, deep as death. But quite suddenly into the black hole of Jerry's silent oblivion came a jarring, jangling, grating noise. He tried to ignore it, but it wouldn't go away. Finally he focused on the world around him and found several pedestrians standing, staring right at him. And the noise became more insistent.

"Well, are you going to answer it?" asked a tall bald man in a double-breasted, black blazer, obviously annoyed.

Jerry nodded his head slowly, stupidly, as if climbing out of a deep sleep, and began hunting around for the source of the strident sound. And there it was, in the bush behind him. A cell phone. Someone had obviously dropped it there earlier, and now it was ringing. He picked it up and stared at it. He figured if he didn't answer it, the caller would eventually hang up. But it kept ringing.

"Well, man," said the impatient pedestrian, "are you going to answer it or not?"

Jerry stared at the phone again, and a new thought took shape. Maybe the owner was calling his own number, hoping some honest soul would hear the ring and answer. Jerry wasn't sure he fit that description, but he was self-conscious with everyone staring at him, so he scanned the buttons anyway and pushed one. The phone stopped ringing, and almost immediately the small crowd dispersed. *Funny*, Jerry thought, vague memories stirring, *how a ringing telephone rules people's lives.* He put the device to his ear and said hello.

"Well, it took you long enough, Jerry," a voice said.

A puzzled look worked its way across his face, then Jerry said tentatively, "Who are you?" The voice sounded vaguely familiar, but he couldn't place it.

"Who I am doesn't really matter, Jerry. You can call me Max if you'd like, but listen carefully—"

"Max?" Jerry interrupted. "Do I know you?"

"Listen," said Max, ignoring his question, "this is your lucky day, Jerry."

"What makes you say that?" He was still trying to figure out who the voice belonged to. He didn't know any Maxes, but the voice was familiar—an echo, perhaps, of some long-lost memory.

"Your life's about to change," Max announced.

"Is this *Candid Camera?*" Jerry asked, suspicion creeping into his voice. He looked to his right, then to his left, scanning the street for any sign of a hidden camera.

"Oh, no," Max laughed. "This is much better than *Candid Camera.*"

"Who are you?"

"I told you," said Max, "but that's immaterial. What's important is that this is your lucky day."

"I'll decide that when it's over," Jerry suggested. "I'm listening."

"For starters, Jerry, the phone is yours."

He pulled it away from his ear and stared at it for a moment, then spoke into it again. "Fine, but I don't have anybody to call."

"Oh, you will."

"Who are you?"

"There are three rules regarding the phone," Max explained, once again ignoring Jerry's query. "First, you have to keep the phone turned on the whole week before Christmas every year. I'll call during that time."

"Just once a year?"

"I'm very busy, Jerry. By the way, you'll find a spare battery and a charger in a bag near where you found the phone."

Jerry fished around in the bushes, and sure enough, he discovered a paper bag. "Okay," he said, "what's number two?"

"You can use the phone all you like, but you have to pay for the minutes you use. You'll get a bill in the mail each month."

"Fine," said Jerry out loud, but to himself he thought, *Who is this idiot? Where are they going to send a bill, anyway?*

"Third," Max continued, "you have to do exactly as I say."

"And if I don't?"

"Then I'll never call again."

"Is that supposed to be a threat?" Jerry laughed.

"I'll leave that up to you, Jerry."

Something in the tone of Max's voice made Jerry pause. Maybe this wasn't a practical joke.

"Okay, Max. So what do you want me to do, rob a bank?"

"Glad you've not lost your sense of humor," said Max, his voice betraying a hint of annoyance. "Look in the bag, Jerry."

Jerry took his glove off and reached into the bag. He pulled out a cell phone battery, a charger, and two crisp one-hundred-dollar bills. His eyes almost popped out of his head.

"Max," he whispered. "There's two hundred bucks in there."

"Merry Christmas, Jerry."

"What's the catch?"

"I already told you."

Jerry opened his mouth as if to say something, then shut it again and stared at the crisp federal reserve notes.

"Now, let me tell you what to do with the money."

"Shoulda known," Jerry muttered. "Go ahead."

"First, go to the barber shop on Third South between Main and State and get a shave and a haircut. Then go buy yourself some new clothes, including a new coat. If there's any money left, go get a decent meal."

"And if I don't?"

"I hate repeating myself, Jerry. That's one thing you need to know about me."

"Sorry."

"Good luck, Jerry. Don't let me down."

Jerry didn't answer. He was still weighing the options, wondering what he might lose out on if he never heard from Max again.

"Remember," Max was saying, "keep the phone on every year the week before Christmas."

"Okay," said Jerry.

"Oh, and Jerry, I almost forgot—there's a fourth requirement regarding the phone."

"Yeah?" *And ten more next time you call, I bet.*

"You can call me three times."

"Three times?" Jerry asked. "Three times a month? A year?"

"Three times," Max stated. "That's it. Three times in your entire life."

"Max?" Jerry said.

"Yes?"

"Why would I *want* to call you?"

"I'll let you figure that one out, Jerry. Who knows? Maybe sometime you'll need a favor."

"What are you, some kind of high-tech genie or something? Instead of three wishes, I get three phone calls?"

"Don't you wish. Now get a piece of paper and a pencil out of your pack."

Jerry unzipped his backpack, wondering how Max knew he carried a pencil and paper in it.

"Write down these two numbers. You can reach me by calling 555-6789. And the number of the cell phone you're holding is 694-3434."

"Got it."

"Jerry?"

"Yeah?"

"Talk to you next year. Remember, get a haircut. Good-bye."

"Bye, Max," said Jerry as the line went dead.

He looked at the display screen, and the number listed was 237-5511. He dialed it and got a recording from U.S. West Customer Service.

Jerry took off his frumpy stocking cap and scratched his head. He'd made a conscious effort the past few years *not* to think, so he was a bit out of practice, but the more he thought about what had just happened, the less sense it made. *Some guy named Max calls me on a cell phone he's stashed in the bushes, gives me the phone and two hundred bucks, and wants me to get a haircut.* Jerry laughed out loud, then pinched himself, but he knew this was too weird to be a dream. He looked at the two bills again, then at the phone. "What have I got to lose?" he said with a shrug. He put the bills back in the bag and stuffed the bag into his backpack.

* * *

The Mirror

Ten minutes later he stood in front of Marty's Barbershop. The storefront could have used a new coat of paint, but the two striped barber poles were spinning almost as fast as Jerry's brain. He stared at his reflection for a moment in the window. He hadn't seen the inside of a barbershop in three years, and he looked it. His hair was tied back in a shaggy ponytail, and his beard was unkempt and scruffy. He looked exactly like what he was, and the barber eyed him suspiciously as Jerry pushed the door open and stepped inside. There were no customers at the moment, and Marty was sitting in one of the padded red chairs with a magazine on his lap.

"Help you?" he asked without getting up.

"I'd like a haircut and a shave," Jerry stammered, avoiding the barber's eyes.

"Can you pay?"

Jerry fished around in his pack and pulled out one of the bills, waved it in the air, then put it back in the pack.

"Have a seat," said Marty. "How would you like it?"

"Cut it all off," Jerry answered.

"You want a buzz?" the barber asked.

"Nah, just give me a regular haircut and a shave. Make me look like, oh, John Stockton, but leave the mustache."

"Can't make you look like Stockton," Marty answered. "You're hair's blond, not black, and it's wavy, but I think I catch your drift."

He went to work and didn't say three words the whole time Jerry was in the chair. When he finished, he spun Jerry around so he could look in the mirror.

"Well?"

Jerry stared in wonder at the transformation. He hadn't looked anything close to that in three years. Memories came flooding back so fast they almost flattened him, but he took a deep breath and managed to bottle them up again. He hadn't looked himself in the eye for months. When he washed his hands at public rest rooms, he treated the mirror almost as a vampire might. When he accidentally caught a glimpse of himself every now and then, he saw a stranger staring back from the glass. But now he studied his reflection intently. Yes, that was the old Jerry peering back, except for the mustache—and the eyes. In his eyes was written everything he'd endured in the past few years: the pain, the loneliness, the rejection, and the utter, irreconcilable inner annihilation of identity that inevitably maimed the strangers and pilgrims of the street.

"Looks great," he said finally, tearing his gaze away from the eyes in the mirror.

He stepped down from the chair and followed Marty over to the cash register. Jerry handed him a hundred dollars, but the barber just held it in his hand and stared. "Do I know you from somewhere?" he asked, puzzled.

"I doubt it."

"I could swear I've seen you just recently."

"Not like this, you haven't," Jerry laughed.

Suddenly a light went on somewhere behind the barber's eyes. "I know where it was," he exclaimed. He rushed over to the shelf behind the chair and grabbed a large envelope. "A guy came in here a couple of days ago and gave me this. He said to give it to you."

"To me? You haven't even asked my name."

"No. He showed me your driver's license. Said to return it to you when you came in."

Jerry's face was a study in confusion. "What?"

"Here, look for yourself," Marty said, and handed him the envelope.

Jerry took the envelope, and inside was a wallet. He opened the wallet and found a driver's license. He studied it carefully. The name on it was Jerry Carlson, but everything else was wrong. The photo was of him, but not as he had looked the past three years—and not as he had once looked before the streets had swallowed him. The photo looked exactly like the image in the barber's mirror—short hair and a mustache. It didn't make sense. He'd never had a mustache in his former life. But the license was dated just a few days ago, and the address was one where he'd never lived. He shook his head. He'd been on the street for three years, but he hadn't lived in a cocoon. He knew it was possible to electronically alter photographs and do practically anything to the human face. Still, why would anyone bother? What was he but human trash discarded by society?

He looked inside the envelope again. There, folded in half, was a single sheet of paper. He took it in hand and read it.

JERRY, the note announced in bold capital letters, *welcome back to humanity. Go tomorrow morning to the address on your driver's license. Your new job is waiting for you there.*

He staggered as if he'd been hit between the eyes with an unexpected left hook.

"You all right?" Marty scrutinized Jerry's face. "You look like you've seen a ghost."

"I'm fine," said Jerry in a daze. He headed slowly for the door.

"Hey, buddy," Marty yelled. "You forgot your change." The barber hurried over and handed Jerry some bills and coins, which Jerry stuffed into his backpack as he walked out into the warm winter air, still staring at the paper in his hand.

Half a block up the street, he stopped dead in his tracks and closed his eyes. His brain was still frozen from disuse, but it had thawed sufficiently in the past few hours for him to figure this much out—Max's idea just wouldn't work. What was it they said about get-rich-quick schemes—if it sounds too good to be true, it is? Well, this apparent stroke of good luck, Jerry knew in his heart, was no different. No matter who this Max was, even if he *was* for real, he'd missed one tiny detail. His plan for Jerry, whatever it was, was pie in the sky. Jerry wouldn't get hired. When he'd left his former life behind and disappeared into the streets, he'd also left about thirty thousand dollars of debt—ten on his Discover card and twenty on the Visa he had through his employer, not to mention unpaid rent and utilities and income taxes. No matter where he went, unless he worked for cash and never filed a W-4 or had taxes withheld, they'd catch him, and who knew what would happen then. He assumed his old employer would come after the missing twenty grand. But how long do cash-only jobs last? About as long as a bag of Doritos at a Superbowl party. He'd be back on the street before he could even get his feet warm.

The only way he could ever really escape the streets, he figured, was through crime, but the mere thought scared him to death. He'd heard stories. Some of the homeless committed minor offenses when it was too cold or when they were starving just so they could have regular meals and a warm bed for a while. But they paid a price. Some were missing teeth. Others had crooked noses and fingers. Still others refused to talk about it—memories so black they didn't want to dredge them up. No, Jerry was basically a coward. The last thing he wanted was a run-in with the law, which was exactly what he'd risk if he followed Max's instructions and went searching for the pot of gold at the end of the rainbow.

This was a difficult decision—hopeless, he was sure, but difficult nonetheless because his curiosity about this Max character gnawed at him like an ulcer. He'd need to sleep on it or at least stew over it until morning and consider all the angles before he closed the door on it completely. In the meantime, he had most of the two hundred dollars burning a hole in his backpack, and he figured he ought to go get some new clothes, just in case he lost his mind and decided to jump off Max's proffered cliff in the morning.

* * *

Decision

A couple of hours later, Jerry found himself sitting at a table in an Italian restaurant on West Temple, sipping hot soup, dipping bread-sticks, and anticipating a plate of steaming pasta. An Italian vista painted on the wall and dozens of frizzy indoor plants clashed somehow with the view out the bank of windows to his left—traffic hurrying by on Second South—but he didn't mind. It felt good to be indoors, eating something other than fast food and wearing something other than his old rags. He had on stiff new Levis, a comfortable denim shirt, and a pair of shoes with no cardboard in the soles to keep his feet dry. Hung on the back of the empty chair across the table was a nice-looking ski parka, warm and stylish. The old stocking cap had retired to the bowels of his backpack since the haircut. He'd ordered the all-you-can-eat soup and pasta special, and he ate slowly, savoring every bite, and when he finished his pasta, he ordered dessert. Jerry couldn't remember the last time he'd eaten in a restaurant, let alone enjoyed dessert.

When he finally couldn't swallow another bite of pie, he stood slowly, heaved a contented sigh, left a twenty percent tip on the table, and made his way to the exit with ten bucks still in his pocket. For some reason, he didn't want to go back to his hollow in the hills to sleep. He had a feeling he wouldn't be sleeping much that night anyway, so he walked over to Trolley Square instead, bought a movie ticket for the late late show, and wandered around the square window-shopping until midnight. Then, slipping into the rear of the theater, he sat contentedly immersed in the warmth and noise, surrounded by the smell of popcorn. He sank down deep in the plush chair and dozed through the first half of a movie he had no interest in. When he came to, he kept his eyes closed and tried to figure out what to do when daylight arrived.

Who is this Max? he asked himself. *Probably some rich do-gooder,* he speculated. *Thinks he's clever the way he planted the cell phone, I bet.*

So what does he want?

At this thought, Jerry scratched his head and pursed his lips. *Either he's cheating on his wife and feels the need to make up for it somehow, or he's setting me up for something bad.*

Nah, probably just some naive nut who doesn't know the can of worms he's opened.

Jerry thought about his debts. Anybody who did even a cursory background check would toss him to the sharks. But then another thought crept into his mind. He'd tried to keep it out all evening, but now he realized he actually wanted to think about it.

What if Max is filthy rich? What if he knows more about me than I think he does? What if there really is a job waiting for me? What if? What if? What if?

No. There's no way. He slammed the door on this blind hope. But it kept prying a side window open and creeping back in.

What if? There's no way you'll know if you don't check it out. Besides, you can always just walk away. You'll be safe on the street. They won't come looking for you if you don't have anything they can take.

And so he finally decided to follow Max's instructions. But it was curiosity more than hope that tipped the scales in Max's direction. *Besides*, Jerry told himself, *what do I have to lose?*

The flick ended, and Jerry walked out with the odd assortment of lovers and losers who frequent midnight movies. It was two o'clock, and he had the rest of the night to kill. Facing the choice between wandering the streets for six hours or finding a quiet corner and trying to get some shut-eye, he flipped a coin in his head, watched it come down tails, and headed for Memory Grove. On the way, he picked up the shopping bag he'd stuffed his old clothes in. No one had touched it, of course, since he'd left it on the sidewalk in plain view.

Memory Grove was a narrow strip of grass and trees convenient to downtown and straddling City Creek. In summer Jerry wouldn't have dared sleep in Memory Grove. Too much chance of running into either a bunch of high school kids out looking for trouble or the cops who'd inevitably come to break up the party. But tonight all was quiet. He searched out a secluded patch of grass at the far end of the park and stretched out on the ground, throwing his old parka over the top of his new coat for added warmth. And somewhere in the still of early morning, when Orion was tipping into the west, Jerry went to sleep.

* * *

A. J.

Jerry gripped the seatback in front of him with both hands. The bus was relatively empty at 8:30, since he was traveling against the flow—most commuters lived in the suburbs and worked in the city—but the address on his driver's license was fifty-two blocks west of Main Street and forty blocks south of South Temple. Jerry had no idea what he would find when he got to the mystery address, and this made him all the more nervous. What if it was all a cruel joke? What if a good job really was waiting for him? Would the disappointment be overwhelming when he had to turn it down?

Then an even more disturbing thought crept in. What if it was a police sting to catch indebted deadbeats who had run from their creditors? Not likely, he knew. They had better things to do with their time. Chances were Max was just a rich Samaritan who hadn't done his homework. Like a pitcher facing Barry Bonds, Jerry was well aware of the potential disappointment awaiting him, but an annoying spark of hope still burned in the back of his mind. *What if I get him to swing on an outside curve? What if he grounds into a double play or pops up? What if there really is a tooth fairy? What if Max is telling the truth?* The thought nearly drove him crazy, so he was glad when the bus finally stopped within a block of the address on his license.

He stepped out into the still unseasonably balmy December air and marched slowly toward his destination, checking the addresses as he went. Fifty-second West was a main road of sorts. He passed a day-care center, a fast-food joint, a veterinarian's clinic, an insurance agency, and a convenience store before finally stopping in front of an aquamarine, eight-foot-high cinder block wall topped with razor ribbon. A heavy, black gate with sharp, wrought-iron teeth grinned in the center of the wall and opened by command of a keypad mounted on a sturdy, waist-high shaft of heavy-gauge pipe just outside the gate. The place looked like a prison, but the sign next to the gate read, *A. J.'s Storage.* Not ten feet from the gate was a single metal door the same color as the wall with a smallish, square, eye-level window. Below the window was stenciled the word *OFFICE,* and below that, *PLEASE COME IN.*

Jerry stared at the door for a few minutes, trying to work up the courage to turn the knob. While he was standing there, a low-slung El Camino pulled up to the gate, the windows close to exploding as the radio emitted seismic waves somewhere in the middle of the Richter scale. Jerry could feel the music more than hear it, almost like a second heartbeat. A tinted window slid down to reveal a young man with a shaved noggin, diamond ear-studs, two silver rings protruding from his neck, and a tattoo advertising "Pit Bull" on his shoulder. Thunderous, throbbing swells of heavy metal escaped the cab, and Jerry gained a sudden appreciation for what the universe must have been like a split second after the Big Bang. The skinheaded driver punched in a string of numbers, and the gate slid open with an irksome screech. The El Camino disappeared into the storage complex, trailing billows of stereophonic pandemonium.

His fears frightened away by the noise, Jerry reached for the knob and opened the door. He stepped inside and found himself in a small office. No one was there at the moment, but he noticed a button on the desk next to a sign proclaiming, *Push here for office manager.* He pushed the button.

From the hallway at the rear of the office came a faint "Just a minute." A couple of minutes later, a fortyish man in coveralls, a paint-splattered baseball cap, and scuffed work boots appeared. He took off the hat to reveal a head of shaggy black hair flecked with white. He had gray eyes, a prizefighter's nose, and a crooked grin.

"Hi," he said. "Just been paintin' the bedroom for the new office manager. Can I help you?"

"Well, I don't know," Jerry answered, suddenly unsure what to say next. "Max sent me here to look for a job. Am I in the right place?"

"Oh," exclaimed the man, "you must be Jerry. What was your last name again?"

"Carlson," said Jerry, a puzzled look stealing across his face. "You've been expecting me?"

"You better believe it. I haven't got time to baby-sit this place. 'Bout time you got here."

"I'm sorry," said Jerry, now totally confused, "but you've lost me."

"You're Jerry Carlson, aren't you?"

"Yeah."

"Well, your buddy Max called. I've checked you out. The job's yours if you want it. You do want it, don't you?"

"Sure," Jerry said, then paused. "Exactly what job is it we're talking about?"

"Manager, of course. It's your room I'm paintin' back there. I've got an application with your John Hancock on it."

"Can I see it?" Jerry asked.

"Sure," the man said. He walked to the desk, fished around in a drawer for a few seconds, then handed Jerry the form.

He looked at it carefully. Everything was accurate—his former address and jobs, his current address (none), his Social Security number. All this was typed, not handwritten. He turned the form over, expecting to see a forged signature, but what he saw, as far as he could tell, was his own handwriting. He scrutinized it. It looked genuine. Hard to say for sure, though, because he hadn't signed his name in at least two years.

"Yeah," he said with wide eyes, "that's my signature."

"Name's A. J.," said the man, extending his hand. "A. J. Harper."

Jerry shook A. J.'s hand, then stood there awkwardly, wondering what to do next. He was sure the whole arrangement would fall apart as soon as A. J. found out the truth, and he was determined to get it over with sooner than later, so he said, "What did Max tell you about the past three years?"

"Said you'd been on the road, some kind of personal trek, living by your wits, camping out a lot. Sounded like quite an adventure, at least the way Max described it."

"Oh, it was," said Jerry. "You have no idea."

"You'll have to tell me all about it sometime."

"Sure, sometime," Jerry agreed. Max, it appeared, was in advertising or public relations, a regular master of spin. "Did you run a credit report on me?"

"Yeah," A. J. answered. "In fact, Max insisted. Wanted you to have a copy too." He rummaged through the desk again and came back with an envelope.

Jerry took it and opened it. Not a single debt. No back taxes. It listed his credit cards. The last payment on the company Visa had been two months after he'd hit the street—$20,147.67. The Discover bill of $9,965.43 had been paid the next month. He shook his head in disbelief. What on earth was going on? Two hundred bucks for a haircut and some new clothes was one thing, but thirty thousand dollars put Max in a whole different category of either totally nuts or ridiculously wealthy—or perhaps both. And this had happened almost three years ago. To say the least, Jerry was confused.

"How soon can you start?" asked A. J.

"Right now," Jerry answered. "Got nothing better to do. Maybe you can tell me about the job while I help you paint."

"Sounds okay," said A. J. "We can fill out the paperwork later."

"One more question," said Jerry. "You talk like you know Max. Tell me about him."

"Never met him," A. J. confessed. "I thought he was a friend of yours."

"Well," Jerry hedged, "I've been on the road for a while, you know."

"I understand," A. J. said. "Your friend Max just called on the phone, same day Bennie quit. Bennie was the old manager, you see. But this Max fella said he'd heard I needed a new manager and he had just the guy. He described you, said you'd been on the road so long you'd jump at the chance to stay put for a while. Also said your funds were running a bit short. He was very convincing, so I figured 'What the heck.' Save me one big pain in the neck."

"One more question," said Jerry. "If you've never met Max, how'd he get this application form?"

"When he called, he said he picked one up from Bennie the day before. Bennie musta told him he was movin' on, and Max thought about you."

"How long ago was this?"

"Couple a weeks. He said you'd be here before Christmas and he'd send the application in the mail. It came about three days ago."

Jerry took this in and mulled it over for a minute. In addition to PR, Max was apparently adept at forgery also.

"So you took the word of a voice on the phone, somebody you don't even know?"

"Like I said, he was very convincing, and you don't know how hard it is to find good help. Anyway, you're here, aren't ya? You want the job or not?"

"Let's go paint."

* * *

A Christmas to Remember

So Jerry found himself off the street for Christmas. One would think—in fact, Jerry himself thought—such a stroke of luck would have him turning cartwheels, at least in his mind, and reveling in the depths of gratitude to his mystery benefactor. But truth be told, for some reason he felt utterly bereft of emotion. Yes, it was nice to sleep in a warm bed, to have his own shower, his own toilet, his own kitchen. It was comforting to know he'd be earning a regular paycheck again and could begin living what most people considered a normal life. But he knew any semblance of normalcy would be nothing more than a thin sheen of water on the surface of a frozen pond. Beneath the surface he was still as cold and unreachable as the dark side of the moon. He had suffered too much for too long. Maybe in time, winter would pass and springtime would creep into his heart and set him free, but for the present—and the foreseeable future—the remaining fragments of whatever had once made him a unique individual were as frozen in place as molecules in an ice cube. The hopelessness of homelessness still governed his heart and would do so forever, he feared.

In the meantime, he had a new routine to get used to, new motions to go through while he pretended to be alive. A. J. walked him through his various responsibilities the first couple of days, then left him on his own.

"Call me if you have any questions," he said, but Jerry knew he would have few. His brain was engaged again—not fully yet, but sufficiently to recognize he could easily handle the ins and outs of managing two hundred storage units. First and foremost, he had to man the office between eight in the morning and six in the evening. And he had to be on the premises until ten, when the gate automatically shut down for the night. Six days a week. On Sunday the office was closed and the gate shut down at six. A. J. would give Jerry five vacation days the first year, but he wouldn't start earning them for three months.

During the day A. J. expected Jerry to patrol the facility periodically, pick up trash, padlock units of tenants who hadn't paid their rent, evaluate any items left behind when people moved their belongings out and donate them to either the Salvation Army or the landfill. He also had to plow the snow between the rows of storage units if it accumulated more than a couple of inches. A. J. kept an old pickup with a rusty plow attached to the front bumper in an out-of-the-way corner of the compound, and he allowed Jerry to use it for personal errands, but he couldn't be gone for long during office hours—just a quick trip to the hardware store or Wal-Mart in case of an emergency. He had to take care of his own shopping after six, preferably after ten.

Then there was the paperwork. Jerry was to mail out invoices, about 170 of them in an average month, and record rent payments on the computer. The actual books were kept by A. J., who in addition to being an amateur painter was also an accountant of sorts. "Why pay somebody to do something I can do myself?" he would say. "Never been audited," he would then add with his fingers crossed.

Managing the storage units was a job Jerry could do with half a brain tied behind his back, which was a fairly apt description of his mental state at the time. After three years of staring at sidewalks and avoiding any thoughts more complicated than survival required, Jerry's brain had atrophied to the point where prolonged concentration wore him out. He was slowly recovering, but his mental reflexes were not what they had once been. All in all, it was a perfect job for him, and the more Jerry thought about it, the more he convinced himself Max was no dunce.

If one defining characteristic of the homeless was mental deterioration from disuse, Jerry knew the other was solitude. Contrary to what many people assumed, the homeless were not members of a secret fellowship holding each other up in their collective misfortunes and sharing a special camaraderie outsiders could neither fathom nor participate in. The people of the street, with few exceptions, were among the loneliest, most solitary individuals on earth. Like Jerry, they were outcasts whose feelings of self-worth had been ground to powder and blown away by the winds of misfortune. They viewed each other with suspicion, as competitors for the scarcest of resources—not food and shelter, but human kindness and generosity. What they garnered instead was pity, and more often, scorn. Consequently, they were not social creatures, and Jerry was even more of a loner than most. Had Max tossed him a job requiring him to interact constantly with others, it likely would have overtaxed his meager emotional reserves, and he would have failed miserably.

But managing the storage units was perfect, lying as it did on the far pole of the employment world, as distant from such activities as network marketing and teaching high school as Lapland is from the Sahara. An occasional customer wandered into the office each day to pay a bill or lease a unit, and Jerry ran into a handful of others on his appointed rounds, but these were fleeting contacts, brief and painless. And yet they obviously served a purpose in Max's grander scheme of reclaiming the life of Jerry Carlson. These customers treated Jerry if not as an equal, at least as a real human being, not as an unwanted crust torn from the loaf of society.

Jerry started working for A. J. on December 21, and by Christmas Eve he was on his own, A. J. having fallen behind in his other responsibilities during the two weeks he had managed the storage facility and waited for Jerry to return from his "personal trek." A. J. was basically a collector of mortgages. He owned apartments, small office buildings, the storage units, a dental clinic, and a couple of rundown storefronts. He made his living running himself ragged, maintaining and cleaning his properties during the day and keeping the books at night. Only the apartments and storage units were watched over by on-site managers. A. J. wasn't wealthy yet—too many loans to repay—but he would be someday, he assured Jerry, as soon as the mortgages started to fall like dominoes. He had it all planned out. In the meantime, he had no time to worry about Jerry. "You'll be fine," he told him as he said good-bye on December 23. "It's really not a tough job, if you don't mind being alone a bit and tied down during the days."

"I'll survive," Jerry assured him. "Don't worry about me."

"Who's worrying?" said A. J. as he climbed into his battered old van. "Merry Christmas."

"Merry Christmas," Jerry echoed. He couldn't remember the last time he'd said those words.

* * *

Christmas Eve was a hectic day at A. J.'s Storage—not for Jerry, but for the tenants. Jerry figured at least half of them showed up sometime during the day, probably to pick up Christmas gifts they'd stashed in their units. A. J. had posted a sign on the gate explaining that the facility would be closed on Christmas Day.

After making his rounds on Christmas Eve for the last time before the gate shut down for the holiday, Jerry undressed, climbed into his warm bed, and turned on the TV, a luxury he'd not even missed in his years on the street, except for maybe the occasional chance to watch an NFL game. He channel-surfed for a minute and found *It's a Wonderful Life* on KSL, the local NBC affiliate. In short order, he was caught up in the misfortunes of George Bailey. When George finally recovered his real life and Clarence had his wings, Jerry was surprised to find tears coursing slowly down his cheeks. He couldn't remember the last time he'd cried. He'd been numb for so long.

He was surprised, however, to realize that George's plight had made him suddenly contemplative, even introspective, another luxury he'd not indulged in for days beyond count. George Bailey had received the rare gift of seeing what the world would have been like without him. A rare gift indeed, but as Jerry thought about his own life, it occurred to him he'd received the same gift, only the revelation was different. When George dropped off the face of the earth, hundreds of lives went to Hades in a handcart. But Jerry Carlson, unlike the fictitious George Bailey, had quite literally dropped off the map, and to his knowledge not one life beyond his own had been affected. No one had even missed him or wondered where he'd gone. Certainly no one had come looking for him, not even his creditors. Just Max.

Jerry turned off the tube and clutched a pillow to his chest. It was Christmas Eve, and he knew with a fair degree of certainty that ghosts were coming to visit him—not the ghosts of Christmas past, present, and future, but the ghosts of his own past, a past he had shoved into the shadows of forgetfulness. Suddenly Jerry heard a knock on the door, and he about jumped out of his skin. He half imagined Jacob Marley floating in through the kitchen. But the sound of a key in the lock followed the thumping on the door, and soon a voice echoed from the outer office.

"Jerry!" It was A. J.'s voice.

Jerry jumped out of bed, tossed the pillow down, and scrambled to put some clothes on.

"Be out in a second," he called.

Still buckling his belt, Jerry marched out to the kitchen, where he found A. J. sporting a large grin and toting a carton of eggnog and a fruitcake.

"I thought you were celebrating with your sister and her family tonight," Jerry said.

"I thought so too, but my nephew came down with the flu. They didn't want me to catch it, so I went out to dinner, and then I got thinking about you. You said you didn't have plans for the evening, so I figured you could use some company—and some goodies."

Soon they were seated at the little table, staring silently at two glasses of eggnog and a plate of sliced fruitcake. Jerry was a bit uncomfortable, but after the movie he didn't want to be alone. Something had started stirring inside, and he didn't want to shut it up again.

"You said you'd tell me about your travels sometime," A. J. said. "I figure now's as good a time as any."

"Oh, there's not much to tell," Jerry answered.

"Then tell me about yourself," A. J. insisted. "We've spent quite a few hours together since you got here, but you haven't told me ten words about Jerry Carlson."

Jerry shifted uncomfortably in the hard, wooden chair and looked down at the table in silence for a moment. He knew the ghosts would come anyway, either now or after A. J. left. Maybe it would be less painful to just let them in now and get it over with. In a way he wanted to talk, to let out everything he'd kept bottled up inside for so long.

"Okay," he said finally. "Just promise me one thing."

"Sure," said A. J.

"You won't fire me when I'm done."

"Now why would I do that?"

"I'll let you decide," Jerry answered. "Just promise me."

"Okay, I promise," said A. J., raising his hand for effect.

Jerry paused for a moment, then cleared his throat.

"I was born and raised out in Sandy," he began. "I guess I had a fairly normal childhood. Little League baseball, school. I was an average student; no report cards worth either framing or burning. There were summer vacations, fireworks on the Fourth, picnics on Labor Day, a paper route at twelve, a job stocking shelves at Andy's Corner Market at fifteen, driver's license at sixteen, first car at seventeen, first kiss in the first car somewhere up on the bench below Lone Peak that same year, first broken heart not long after the first kiss." Jerry laughed quietly. It was a sad but sweet memory.

"I went to college at the University of Utah," he continued. "Bachelor's degree in business after four years and a couple of extra quarters." His face twisted into a wry grin. "The extra quarters were to make up for grades I earned during my 'Greek' phase," he added. "After graduating, I got my first real job as a salesman for a commercial lighting company, Lumenescent, Inc. Then came the first hurdle in my rather ordinary life. The second year after college, my parents died in an automobile accident, a one-car rollover on Dimple Dell Road."

"I'm sorry," A. J. said. "How'd it happen?"

Jerry sighed as the memory of his parents' faces slipped back into his mind. "They were coming home late one night after bridge at Harvey and Ada's," he told A. J., "and if the cop who investigated the crash was right, my dad was blinded by headlights on the narrow road and missed a turn. So Sam and Carma Carlson ended their mortal journey down an embankment with their Plymouth wrapped around a hundred-year-old maple and the engine in their laps."

A. J. shook his head slowly. "If you don't wanna talk about it," he said, "I understand, it being Christmas Eve and all."

"No," Jerry answered, "it's okay. I haven't thought about it for a long time, but maybe I ought to. The police investigator told me they died instantly, but I always wondered what crossed their minds in those last few seconds as they went down the embankment. I wonder if they thought about me.

"Did I mention that I'm an only child?" Jerry continued. "Mom wanted to adopt when she found out she couldn't have any more kids, but for some reason Dad was against it. Growing up, I had mixed feelings about the question. I wouldn't have minded having a younger brother to pick on, but I also enjoyed getting all the attention. After my parents died, though, I figured it was probably best they hadn't adopted. Why put another child through all the grief and guilt?"

"Guilt?" A. J. asked.

"Yeah," Jerry explained, "I didn't spend much time with them after I left home. Always regretted it."

"Must've been tough," A. J. suggested.

"Yeah, but life goes on, as they say." Jerry stopped and leaned back in his chair. He stared at the ceiling for a moment in silence. He knew what was coming next and wasn't sure he wanted to talk about it. But the memories were flowing like spring sap now, and he figured it would be easier to talk about it than to get flooded with the feelings. He sighed and shrugged. "The next winter," he told A. J., "this willowy strawberry blond named Brenda McDonald landed a job as a sales assistant at Lumenescent. She'd just graduated from the U. Came originally from Nebraska, but decided she'd stick around and find a job in Salt Lake rather than move back to the farm. She wasn't a head-turner after the order of, say, Cindy Crawford or Julia Roberts, but I soon noticed something. At first I thought it was just me, but after a while it was obvious that nobody could take their eyes off Brenda. I finally decided it was her smile. It was beautiful and just a tad mischievous, but it didn't start with her lips, if you catch my drift. It was in her eyes. You could fall into those eyes and vanish, body and soul. At least I did. Just thinking about them was enough to make me forget where I was. Sometimes it was enough to make me forget *who* I was."

"Sounds like quite a gal," A. J. commented, taking a big bite of fruitcake. "Wish I'd met one like that when I was younger. 'Course, that kind of gal never gave me the time of day."

"Well, I'd never been so smitten," Jerry said, "but Brenda didn't know I existed. To her I was just one of the salesmen. There were ten of us, and she had to keep up with all our orders."

"So what did you do?"

"I started finding excuses to hang around her desk whenever I was in the office, and I spent evenings dreaming up interesting assignments I could give her. The idea was to make her feel her job was more exciting when I was around, but I also did it because she would have to report back to me. I paid close attention to everything Brenda said about herself to anyone, and I never forgot a single word of it. After a while I felt I knew her just about as well as I knew anyone. I knew what she liked, what she disliked, the kinds of jokes she laughed at, the kinds of food she craved—Italian and Korean—the foods she detested—anything with coconut—the kinds of movies she liked—romantic comedies—her interests, hobbies, family, friends, her one incurable TV habit—reruns of *The Dick Van Dyke Show*—her favorite color—forest green—everything. I even remembered a concept I picked up once in a sociology class, 'the principle of least interest.' Basically, it says that any relationship is controlled by the partner with the least interest, so I forced myself to exercise almost perfect patience and restraint. Without letting on to any romantic intentions, I just quietly became part of her life. By the time I asked her out, she wondered why I hadn't done it months before. Of course she accepted."

"Sounds like the perfect conquest," A. J. remarked with a grin.

"Maybe," Jerry shrugged, "but for some reason I always felt like I was the one who got conquered. Dating her wasn't like any experience I'd ever had. It was like finding a missing part of myself. She was absolutely delightful, especially her cockeyed sense of humor. I never knew what was going to come out of her mouth next, but I didn't ever have to pretend anything with her. I just enjoyed her company more than anything I could imagine. I liked the way I felt when I was with her. I liked who I was when we were together. And after the second date, I was sure she felt the same. Our relationship had this natural, unforced quality to it. It simply blossomed and grew without any effort or complications."

Jerry knew he was starting to ramble, but he didn't care. In a way that surprised him. It was liberating to talk about Brenda, to reach out and embrace all the feelings he'd been running from for so long. And A. J. was a good listener. He seemed genuinely interested.

"We started dating in the spring, and by June we were spending nearly every evening and weekend together—bike rides, picnics, movies, long walks. We'd find any excuse to be together, and when we weren't together, we were either talking on the phone or thinking about each other. I used to play guitar a little," Jerry confessed, "and sometimes I'd take it along, and we'd just sit in the park and sing. We knew all the same songs. I used to have a decent voice. Brenda's was a bit breathy, kind of like someone had a stranglehold on one of her vocal cords, but she wasn't unpleasant to listen to, and when we sang together our voices blended well, at least to my unbiased ear."

A. J. laughed at this. "You'll have to sing me a Christmas carol when you're through with your story." He got up and walked to the refrigerator to pour himself another glass of eggnog.

"I don't think so," Jerry said, shaking his head. "I think I lost my voice somewhere on my 'personal trek.'"

"So why didn't you marry this Brenda?" A. J. asked. "Or did you?"

Jerry's face clouded over. "No. Things didn't work out," he answered lamely.

He stared off into space for a while. He didn't tell A. J. what happened, and he didn't intend to. This part of the story was just too painful . . .

* * *

"Tell me about your dreams," Brenda said one day. They were lying on their backs on the grass at Liberty Park, taking turns identifying shapes in the passing clouds. "By the way, that one's an eggbeater," she added, pointing skyward.

"An eggbeater?" Jerry looked at her to see if she was serious. Her nose wrinkled in concentration at the cluttered sky, then she turned her head and winked.

"Just seeing if you're paying attention," she said.

"You know I don't dream," he exclaimed. "I've told you that before."

"Everybody dreams, silly," she teased. "You just don't remember yours. But that's not what I meant. I was talking about the other kind of dreams, like what do you want from life? Or what do you want to give to life? What do you see yourself doing twenty years from now?"

"Looking at you," he answered. In all the time they'd spent together, they had somehow avoided confronting the notion of marriage head-on, although it hovered in the air around them whenever they were together. This was as close as he'd ever come to actually broaching the subject.

"No," she said, apparently annoyed at his attempt to be romantic when she was clearly in a philosophical mood. "I mean, what're you going to be doing with your life twenty years from now?"

"Don't know if I've ever thought about it that way," he answered. "I just try to enjoy one day at a time. I never had any big plans to conquer the world or make a million bucks or run for president or anything."

"I said dreams, not nightmares," she replied.

"So what are *your* dreams?" he asked.

"I want to help people," she said.

"Help people?" A hint of disbelief crept into his voice. "Most people are beyond help."

"Oh, don't be so skeptimistic," she shot back.

He cast her a bewildered look, she shrugged, and they both laughed at the word she'd accidentally concocted.

"No, I'm serious," she said after a moment. "I want to make a difference somehow, make the world better for people."

"That's very idealistic," he said with a hint of sarcasm. "What are you going to do, join the peace corps? Start a religion?"

"Both," she said. "Either would be better than selling light fixtures."

"What's wrong with light fixtures?" Jerry asked. He was getting exasperated. "People need lights, you know."

"Yeah, but *anybody* can sell lights."

"So *that's* it," he said. "You don't want to be just *anybody*. You want to be special. More special than *I* am?"

"This isn't about you, Jerry. It's not even about me." She frowned at him. "Maybe that's a new idea to you."

"What do you mean by that?" Something in her words stung him deep inside, but he wasn't sure why.

"Oh, you wouldn't understand," she said in a frustrated tone, then looked away.

He knew she was trying to tell him something important, but apparently he didn't realize just how important it was. He felt he knew her as well as he knew himself, but he was mistaken. He knew her likes and dislikes. But he didn't know her hopes and dreams. And this blindness had spoiled the only chance she would ever give him to find out what they were. It was a kind of Catch-22. After that day, things were never the same.

Looking back now through the long lens of trying to forget about himself and everything else for three years, Jerry could easily see he had been about as self-centered as a one-year-old with a dirty diaper. His universe had been full of one idea: Jerry Carlson's happiness. And he had viewed Brenda as little more than the key to that happiness. What he hadn't considered was *her* happiness. He just assumed she was already happy.

After the picnic at Liberty Park, their time together started filling up with long stretches of silence, as if Brenda wasn't quite sure what to talk about. And Jerry began to feel uncomfortable. He knew something was wrong, but he didn't know quite how to confront her about it. Finally, one evening she suggested to him that they start seeing other people.

"What other people?" he asked incredulously. Since he'd first laid eyes on her, he had been unable to even think about anyone else.

"Well, Josh, for starters," she answered coolly. "He's been asking me out for weeks now. I'm tired of telling him no."

Jerry was devastated. Josh was the spoiled son of Lumenescent owner Randy Monk, a rich kid with a Corvette, an MBA from Harvard, slick black hair, a haughty smirk, and a hundred and one ideas on how he was going to remake his dad's business in his own image after the old man retired in two or three years. Josh could put on a sincere facade, and he had a vocabulary that never ended, but Jerry saw right through him. And what he saw he couldn't stand. One thing Josh wanted to do was put all the salespeople on straight commission. Brenda's intentions now gave Jerry one more reason to despise the heir apparent.

"That's not much of a reason to go out with a slimy snake," Jerry objected.

"I happen to think he's a nice snake," she said with a flicker in her eyes. "Besides, he's going somewhere. Unlike some people I know, he's got big plans. Someday he'll make a bunch of money, and he wants to do all sorts of things with it to help the community."

"What community?" Jerry asked sarcastically. "The only community he cares about is his own little community of one."

Brenda didn't even respond. She just turned and walked away.

"One date with Slick," he told himself, "and she'll come running back to me." But she didn't. In fact, as time passed, Jerry found it increasingly difficult, and then impossible, to get a date with her. She was too busy—always with Josh in his 'Vette or at his posh pad in the Avenues. And one day, Jerry finally figured out it was over. Just like that. The door had slammed in his face, and he hadn't even known it. He didn't even understand what he'd done wrong. Everything had been so right, then suddenly it was all wrong.

* * *

"So why didn't it work out?" asked A. J., breaking into Jerry's reverie.

"She found somebody else," he answered.

"Doesn't seem fair, does it?" A. J. observed. "So when she dumped you, is that when you took off?"

"Yeah, more or less."

"So where did you go?"

"Not very far," Jerry answered. "I was here in Salt Lake—on the street."

"Homeless?"

"Yeah."

Jerry watched A. J.'s face. A puzzled look finally gave way to resignation.

"You sure you want me running your storage units here?" Jerry asked.

"Why not?" A. J. answered. "I need the help. You need the job."

"Thanks," Jerry said. "I do need the job."

"You need a friend too," A. J. stated. "I can tell there's a whole lot more you're not telling me, but I won't prod. If you ever want to talk, you know where to find me."

"Thanks, A. J.," Jerry said. "Maybe sometime."

It was true, though, that there was a lot he wasn't telling. The rest of the story was now staring Jerry in the face, but he wasn't ready to share it. Not now. Perhaps not ever . . .

* * *

After Brenda had turned him loose, his life hit the spin cycle. His motivation at work drifted away like cheap perfume on a stiff breeze. The lighting business, Jerry learned, wasn't similar to, say, selling meat to restaurants. There were no steady accounts with consistent, repeat orders. It was all new business, the bigger the better—show homes and commercial construction were a salesman's best friend. The aggressive could do very well. The unmotivated, well, they were liable to starve. Jerry had always been a good performer, but now his sales were both few and infrequent. After a couple of months, Randy called him in for a chat, and when Jerry walked out of the old man's office, he carried his final paycheck with him.

Jerry looked for work unenthusiastically, and in the few interviews he had, he came across as an emotional quadriplegic. As was so often the case, failure bred failure, and eventually he found he couldn't even get an interview. Soon he stopped trying. His money ran out fast. Most of it went to car payments. Somewhere in the process of losing Brenda to Josh, Jerry had bought a Ford Explorer. He couldn't get approved for a loan on a Corvette or a Beamer, but he figured a flashy SUV might turn her head back in his direction. All it did was turn him into a financial black hole.

Jerry had never been one to save much. His parents had left him little—he'd sold their house to pay for the paramedics, the funeral, and the down payment on a condo—and he hadn't built up much equity. He had always been free with his money, a true child of the early eighties, and after he was fired his habits didn't change. If anything, they got worse. He didn't feel like cooking, so he ate at restaurants three meals a day. When his bank balance crossed the equator, he started using the Visa and Discover cards. Cash advances bought him some time, but by Christmas he knew he was in big trouble. It was only a matter of time before the bank came to take away the Explorer and the condo, and he didn't want to be there when it happened.

So one day after dinner at Harrington's, a high-priced eatery on south State Street, he just didn't go home. He knew it would be easier that way. He had stuffed a few clothes into a backpack and thrown his sleeping bag and an extra blanket into the back of the Explorer. Fetching them after dinner, he left the vehicle in the restaurant parking lot with the keys locked inside and started walking, heading nowhere in particular. And somewhere in the night he crossed the border between despondency and despair. His only regret had been leaving his guitar and a box of photos he'd found in his parents' house when he cleaned it out, but he'd left both in the condo on purpose. He wanted to sever all ties to the past, and anyway, how could he take care of either a box of old photos or a guitar on the streets?

* * *

Jerry sat at the table now in silence and smiled a grim smile. Actually, he now realized, it hadn't been as painful to dredge up all these memories as he had feared, partly because telling A. J. about his past had made it seem just that—the past, but partly because this wasn't really such unfamiliar territory he was traversing. Although he'd consciously avoided thinking about the disintegration of his life and the heartbreak of losing Brenda, it had always been there with him, just below the surface, haunting his every footstep, peering at him from the shadows of consciousness. Now that he had finally confronted these ghosts, he found them not at all as fearful as he'd imagined.

Yes, he'd made mistakes. Yes, he would probably do things differently if he could do it over again. But he realized he couldn't change the past. All he could do was live with it and try to make the best of the present. In his three years on the street, perhaps his mind had atrophied, but one thing had become clear—he finally understood what Brenda had been trying to tell him that day at Liberty Park when she had asked about his dreams. She had wanted to help people, she said, and make a difference for good in the world. He had been unable to comprehend her desires, partly because he had never really needed the kind of help she was talking about. Some people— perhaps Brenda was one of them—were born with a healthy dose of empathy. Others had to learn it the hard way, by suffering. Jerry was one of the latter group, and in his prestreet life he had never suffered. Oh, he had grieved and mourned and felt a terrible ache inside when his parents had died, but that was a suffering no one else could cure. That sort of suffering you simply had to endure, and time either brought healing or it didn't. But the other sort of suffering he had never known, the sort someone could completely obliterate with empathy, understanding, and a little effort. Three years on the street had made Jerry an expert on this kind of suffering. He knew, for instance, that you could take away hunger and cold and even restore self-respect with something as simple as money or work.

Yes, he decided, Brenda had been right. But it wasn't his fault he hadn't known these things. He wished she had given him a chance to learn them before she'd given up on him, but even her rejection had taught him things he couldn't have learned any other way. He wasn't bitter toward her, he discovered now, and in a way that was a relief. Part of him had feared that if he thought about her, he would hate her because of what she had done to him. But there was no hate in him. In fact, he no longer blamed her for his personal collapse. He now saw that he had fallen into a ditch of his own digging. If anything, he simply hoped never to see Brenda again, not because he didn't still love her in some deep corner of his heart, but because he was embarrassed, and he was afraid she would remember the last time they met.

This was another incident he would never share with A. J., perhaps not with anyone. It occurred quite by accident about a year after he'd dropped off the map. One day during the Christmas season, he'd planted himself outside the east door to the Crossroads Plaza with his cup and sign. He'd been there about three hours and was staring off into space with $1.75 in his cup when his eyes focused on a woman crossing the street half a block to the north, heading toward him. She looked like Brenda, and when she came closer he was sure it was her. What could he do? He certainly looked different with his worn clothes, shaggy beard, and weather-beaten face. But what if she recognized him and saw what he had become? Part of him wanted to run from her, but another part of him wanted to stay, wanted her to look at him, recognize him, realize just what she'd done to him, maybe even pity him. Pity was at least an emotion, and the pitiable part of him coveted it.

But now he noticed she was indeed looking at him, bearing down on him, coming straight for the door where he sat. *Oh no,* he thought. *What do I do?* Now that it was happening, he couldn't bear to face her, so he looked down at his cup. And at that moment several things happened. A hand reached toward the cup and dropped in a twenty-dollar bill. Jerry was so astonished he looked up to see who had been so generous, but the man was already past him, pushing through the door with other shoppers. Then Brenda's voice called out from fifty feet up the sidewalk. "Jerry!" she yelled, and his blood froze. "No," he said to himself. "Please, no." He looked up at her, and she seemed to be staring right at him, hurrying toward him, but when she reached the Plaza entrance, she rushed right past him, craning her neck to see over the crowd into the mall ahead of her. "Some other Jerry, I guess," he told himself with a measure of both relief and sadness. But when he looked back down at his cup, the twenty was no longer there. It had vanished into thin air, or perhaps into somebody's pocket. He took his cup and sign and wandered slowly away from the door. At least he was no longer torn over his one big question. He knew he didn't ever want Brenda to see him again.

And even now, now that his life had somehow been given back to him by a stranger named Max, Jerry was still in no condition to face

Brenda again. The memory of their last encounter was too vivid, too painful. But it was a comfort to know he didn't hate her. That had been his greatest fear.

"So, Jerry," A. J. said, bringing him back to the present, "you got any plans tomorrow?"

"Me?" Jerry chuckled, then heaved a big sigh. "You've got to be kidding. After spending the last three Christmases on the street, it'll be nice to just sit here in the warm apartment, maybe watch a little TV or find a good book to read. Don't worry about me. I've got a piece to go before I'll feel like I'm back to normal, but I'm okay."

"You sure?"

Jerry sensed genuine concern in A. J.'s voice. He nodded, then stood up and yawned.

It was getting late, and A. J. took this as his cue to excuse himself. "Well, have a nice Christmas, Jerry. You deserve it."

"I don't know about that," Jerry answered, "but thanks anyway. And thanks for the eggnog and fruitcake. Never could stand the stuff when I was younger, but it tasted real good tonight."

After A. J. had closed the door and driven off, Jerry wandered back into the bedroom, turned out the light, and closed his eyes. Somewhere in the darkness he drifted off to sleep, and somewhere in his sleep he had a dream. In it he was talking to Max, but Max stood behind him where Jerry couldn't see his face. He knew it was Max by the voice, the same voice he'd heard on the phone, but he also knew because you just know some things in dreams, things you wouldn't know awake. And in his dream Jerry realized this, and he knew that *because* he knew this he had indeed dreamed before. Often. Brenda had been right after all. Suddenly it occurred to Jerry that this dream was almost too lucid to be a dream.

"Jerry," said Max's voice from behind him, "look over there."

Jerry looked, and there on an endless field of grass was an airplane, a small, old-time biplane. Jerry was no expert on planes, but somehow he knew this one was a Sopwith Camel. He also knew this was a tiny model plane, not the real item.

"Why don't you fly it?" Max suggested.

"Funny, Max," Jerry deadpanned. "It's just a model plane."

"So what? Why don't you fly it?"

"I can't fly, Max. I've never flown before."

"So? There's always a first time."

"But I don't know how to fly."

"This is a dream, Jerry. You can do anything in your dreams."

The next thing Jerry knew, either he had shrunk or the plane had grown, and he was climbing onto the lower wing and into the cockpit. The engine seemed to start on its own, and suddenly Jerry found himself bouncing across the field, faster and faster, and then he was airborne.

"I don't know how to fly this plane, Max," he heard himself saying, but the wind blew the words back into his mouth.

"Don't worry, Jerry," Max's voice came from behind him. "You're doing just fine."

"I don't know how to land it," he yelled, but somehow he already knew the answer.

"This dream isn't about landing, Jerry. It's about flying. Aim for the sky."

Suddenly the voice changed, and he recognized it immediately. It was Brenda. "You're doing fine, Jerry—for a rookie."

He tried to turn and look at her, but as is often the case in dreams, his muscles wouldn't cooperate. He could only look straight ahead. Slowly the plane nosed upward all by itself and flew straight toward the morning sun, and Jerry woke up. And he remembered the dream.

* * *

On Christmas morning Jerry slept late since the facility was closed for the holiday. But about nine o'clock he was hungry and headed out to the kitchen for a bite to eat. He put a piece of bread in the toaster and peeled one of the oranges A. J. had left for him, then sat down at the table. There in front of him was a small, rectangular box wrapped in green paper with gold angels and stars, and a gold bow.

"That was nice of him," Jerry said aloud, assuming A. J. had come back and left it while he was sleeping.

He shook it gently, and it rattled. Something with lots of small pieces. He tore the paper away and found himself staring at a box with a picture of a Sopwith Camel on the front. It was a model airplane. A folded note was taped to the box. He removed and unfolded it. *Aim for the sky, Jerry,* it said. *Merry Christmas. Max.*

* * *

Pit Bull

The week after Christmas was busy as small business owners came to their storage units to count year-end inventory and others showed up to take care of matters they had pushed aside until after the holidays. Most of this activity took place in the daylight hours, so it was rare for Jerry to find anyone when he made his rounds before closing up for the night. But on Thursday, as he walked along the back row of units, he noticed a low-slung El Camino parked in front of one of the units and light peeking out from beneath the door. As he approached the unit, he could hear the dull echoes of objects being moved inside.

Just as he was about to rap on the door with his knuckles and yell out that it was closing time, the door rolled upward, and he found himself face to face with the young man he had seen the day he first arrived at the storage units. The light was above and behind the young man, and it gleamed off his shaved head. The diamond ear studs glittered, and the rings protruding from his substantial neck gave him an oddly unnatural appearance, like something from an android catalog. In spite of the cold night air, he wore a tank top, and in the shadows Jerry could not make out the tattoo on his arm, but knew it was there and knew what it said.

"Closing time," he said weakly.

The young man was caught totally off guard. For a moment he stood still as stone, then he dropped the box he was holding, whipped a handgun from his belt, and pointed it straight at Jerry's face.

"Timing's a bit off, it seems," Pit Bull growled.

Jerry backed away from the gun, but Pit Bull advanced toward him and Jerry retreated slowly. Suddenly, however, the young man stopped and seemed to stare at something straight behind Jerry. The intake of his breath was like the hiss of a snake. Jerry didn't dare turn around to look, but he could see the young man was scared, even more scared than Jerry was.

"What the—" Pit Bull started to say, then suddenly he turned and ran for his car. He didn't quite make it, though. He hit a patch of ice, slipped awkwardly, and fell headfirst into the bumper. A dull groan escaped his lips, then he lay still. Jerry stood frozen in place for a few seconds, then turned slowly to see what had frightened his assailant, but nothing was there.

Just then, Jerry heard a roar down at the end of the row of units and saw A. J.'s van careening around the corner. It screeched to a stop right in front of Jerry, and A. J. jumped out.

"What's going on here?" he yelled. "I got a call from somebody. They said you were in trouble."

Jerry took a deep breath, and suddenly the paralysis left him and he shook all over. "This young guy was about to make you find a new manager," he said, his voice quavering. "I was just making the rounds when he opened the door here. I guess he didn't want me to know what he was up to. But he got scared over something and ran. Slipped on the ice and cracked his head on the bumper."

A. J. walked over and felt for a pulse in Pit Bull's neck, then he turned toward the open storage unit. "Let's see what made the kid so antsy." He walked into the open unit, rummaged around for a minute or two, then sighed.

"Meth lab gear," he declared. "Seen it once before when the police came and cleaned one out. Never caught the owner. They'll get this one, though. Guess we better tie him up and call the cops."

"But who called *you?*" Jerry asked.

"Didn't say," A. J. replied. "Just said you were in trouble. Maybe somebody else was here, peeking around the corner, and didn't want to get shot. Could have called me on a cell phone."

"How would he know your number?" Jerry asked.

"Good question. I suppose they'd call 911 first, huh? Oh, well, somebody knew, and they called me. That's all I know."

* * *

Later that night, after the police had listened to Jerry's story, gone over the evidence, locked up the storage unit, draped it with yellow tape, and hauled a very groggy Pit Bull off to jail, Jerry found his old pack and pulled a slip of paper from it. On the office phone, he dialed the number Max had made him write down. Three rings, then a familiar voice came on the line.

"Hello, Jerry."

"Max," he said, "how'd you know?"

"Know what, Jerry?" Max asked.

"You called A. J., didn't you—told him I was in trouble and where to find me?"

"Were you in trouble, Jerry?" There was something odd in the way Max asked this.

"Max, what did Pit Bull see that scared him so bad?"

"Who?"

"The kid who was going to give me an early send-off tonight, Max. What did he see?"

"You think I can read people's minds, Jerry?"

"Who are you, Max? What's going on?"

"I'm just who I told you I am," said Max. "And you've got important things to do in your life, Jerry. But don't call again unless it's an emergency. You've only got two more calls. Happy New Year." The line went dead.

second christmas

....

Vacation

The next year was a good year but a difficult one for Jerry. For three months he went through the motions of living, enjoying the simplest of comforts—a hot shower every morning, a warm bed to sleep in, enough food to eat, the nightly news to keep him connected with the world around him. He was starting to feel almost human again. But after three months, he started to go stir-crazy. He could imagine what being in prison was like. He felt cooped up. In the back of his mind, he even wondered if the freedom of life on the street wasn't actually preferable to a job that in many ways was like incarceration, maybe even solitary confinement.

A. J. treated him well, but he came around too infrequently. When he did drop in, he usually apologized for making himself so scarce, but explained that Jerry was running the units so well he didn't need to worry about them. He had become a good friend, though, and Jerry looked forward to chatting with his employer. After their conversation the previous Christmas Eve, A. J. was particularly sensitive to Jerry's emotional well-being.

"You sure you don't need a couple of days off?" he'd ask, but Jerry would politely decline.

"I don't really have anywhere to go or anybody to see," he'd explain.

After six months on the job, Jerry needed to get out, even if he didn't have anywhere to go or anyone to visit, so he asked A. J. if he could take a couple of his vacation days.

"Sure," A. J. said. "I can cover for you. Where you plannin' on goin'?"

"I'm not sure," Jerry told him, even though he had a pretty good idea where he would end up.

"You want the truck?" A. J. offered.

Jerry considered this for a moment, then declined. "I don't really need it," he said.

When he finally walked out the door that clear June morning, he stood for a moment on the sidewalk looking this way and that. He glanced back at the office door and took a half-step back in that direction, then turned toward the street and walked off hesitantly toward the bus stop. He caught the bus on the corner and headed for downtown Salt Lake, a place he hadn't visited since Max's call took him away. Stepping out on the corner of West Temple and South Temple, he walked east, past Temple Square—now boasting beds of flowers and tall trees laden with green leaves—and on toward the crosswalk and his old place on the planter box.

It was a prime location, so he wasn't surprised to find another homeless man sitting there with a cup and a sign. Jerry walked over and sat down next to him. The man shot him a surprised glance.

"What's your name?" Jerry asked.

"Ron," he said, then turned away. Dressed in dirty, rumpled clothing, the homeless fellow was still stiff and suspicious, not used to having people stop and chat. Jerry understood.

"How long you been on the street, Ron?" Jerry asked.

"Too long."

"What kind of work did you do?"

"Used to own a restaurant." He looked back at Jerry and studied him now for a moment.

"Tough business," Jerry commented.

"Yeah. My partner walked off with all my money."

"Sorry to hear about it."

Ron turned his head again. The light had changed to red, and people were coming across the street toward him. Jerry understood. If someone stops to talk, no one puts coins in your cup. Jerry stood up.

"See you again, Ron," he said and dropped a ten spot in the cup.

"Thanks, man," he said. "What'd you say your name was?"

"Jerry."

"See ya, Jerry."

Jerry wandered away, not quite knowing where to go. He circled the block a few times, wandered through the ZCMI Center mall, then headed northeast. Half an hour later, he was out of the city and hiking up an all-too-familiar trail. The June grass was just beginning to dry out, and the scrub oak was putting on thousands of tiny acorns. A magpie flew past, landed on a branch high in an old maple, and cawed at Jerry, eyeing him suspiciously. Turning from the trail, Jerry pushed his way through a thicket and found the little clearing. No one had disturbed it. He pulled some old branches out of the way and uncovered a folded tarp. Unfolding it, he found inside two dark blankets, a couple of ragged shirts, and a pair of threadbare jeans. The smell of them was enough to make him wrinkle his nose. He supposed he'd smelled that way—like dirty gym socks—for most of his time on the street, but it was hard to remember now. The whole three years were slowly fading into a welcome haze.

He stood and stared at the tarp and its contents for some time, a confused look etched into his face. At length, he picked up one of the blankets, spread it out, lay down on it, and stared up at the blue sky. Coming here, he'd had half a mind to leave his new job behind and return to the simple life of camping and begging, but now a new thought took shape. "I'm crazy," he said to the sky. He looked around at the clearing and scratched his chin. "So what do I do now?" he asked. "Max said I had important things to do, but managing a bunch of storage units doesn't seem like one of them. Where do I go now?"

He wanted to call Max, but he was quite certain the answer would be "Jerry, you've just wasted your second call." He was anxious for Christmas to come. He was anxious to escape from the storage units. But he also knew when the time came, he would feel guilty about leaving A. J. to find another manager to replace him. He sighed and got up.

Folding the old shirts and jeans into the tarp, he covered it with the dry branches. The two blankets he put under his arm. Without a backward glance, he forced his way through the oak brush, marched down the path, and headed straight for a laundromat. He spent an hour getting the blankets clean, then wandered back over to the

ZCMI Center. Ron was still sitting on the planter box across the street. Jerry crossed, plopped down next to him on the granite ledge, and handed him the blankets.

"If you don't catch a break before fall," Jerry said, "these'll come in handy."

Ron gave him a half-suspicious look, but took the blankets with a nod of his head.

"Don't mention it," said Jerry.

Nothing about his life on the street held any sway over him now, so after grabbing a bite at the food court for old time's sake, he caught a bus and headed south. At Forty-eighth South and State Street, he pulled the cord to signal the driver and got out at the next stop. Eight blocks east of State and a couple of blocks south of Forty-eighth he found Garfield Avenue, and there on the corner was a familiar grove of aging condos. They had been fairly nice when Jerry first moved there, but now they were looking sunbleached and a bit ratty.

He walked around to the back of the complex and stared up at number 855. A flood of memories came back, mainly of the hours he and Brenda had spent there. They'd had some long talks, seen a handful of good videos, and experimented with exotic dishes there—Thai, Korean, Mexican, and Indian. He remembered the time they had tried a recipe Brenda unearthed in the newspaper, a concoction called "enchilada squares." The dish turned out looking like something from an airsick bag and had the texture of month-old pumpkin pie. They took one bite each, then threw it away and sent out for pizza. Now he smiled at the memory.

Several nights they had also played two-handed cutthroat Rook until the wee hours of the morning, battling against each other and two dummy hands they dubbed Fred and Wilma. Wilma had a penchant for trumping Jerry's best cards. Brenda claimed it was a "woman thing."

After a few moments he shook his head to clear out the memories, turned, and walked away. On the way there, he had half-considered going to the office to ask what had become of his possessions, but he thought better of it now. Best to leave the past behind.

But before the day was over, Jerry had one final visit he wanted to make. Walking back to State Street, he caught another bus south and got out in Sandy. On the way to his destination, he passed an old elementary school. He stopped, grasped the chain-link fence, and stared at the playground. School had let out an hour or so earlier, but in his mind's eye he could see a swarm of kids playing dodgeball. He could see Beckie Selander with her pug nose and pigtails and a little boy who threw the ball at her but missed on purpose. He heard echoes from long-vanished classrooms: nouns and verbs and long division and Mikey Microbe. He also saw a skinny little third-grader being stuffed into a garbage can by the school bully, Chase Madsen, a sixth-grader who in later years graduated from reform school just in time to enroll at the state penitentiary with a major in armed robbery and a minor in car theft.

Jerry finally sighed, turned away, and walked on. Eventually he came to a familiar house and was pleased to see that the current owners had kept the place up nicely. They had painted the siding recently, the lawn was neatly trimmed, and the flower beds were in full bloom. He stood on the sidewalk for some time, remembering all the years he'd spent there. His room had been in the front left corner of the house, and he could see it through the window. A boy about ten years old came into the room and walked to the closet. Jerry remembered how he used to wake up on summer mornings when he was about that age and listen to the birds outside his window. In his mind he could almost smell bacon cooking and hear his mother call out that breakfast was ready. Suddenly the front door opened, and the boy he'd seen in the bedroom ran down the steps. He stopped for a moment when he saw Jerry staring at the house and considered him with obvious curiosity.

"Why you cryin', Mister?" he asked.

It was only then Jerry realized streams of tears were coursing down his cheeks.

"I used to live here," he said. "Grew up in this house."

"Really?" the kid sounded genuinely interested. "How long ago?"

"I'm almost thirty now," Jerry told him. "Is that your bedroom there on the left?"

"Yup."

"That was my room too."

"Wow, that's cool. You wanna come in and see it? I've got a new Michael Jordan poster."

"Thanks, but no." Jerry smiled. "But tell your folks thanks for taking such good care of the place."

"I will. See ya, Mister."

"What was your name?" Jerry asked as the boy headed off down the street.

"Steve."

"See ya, Steve."

Jerry could picture his dad in the yard, trimming the hedge, mowing the lawn. He could see his mom planting petunias or Sweet William or four o'clocks. He missed his parents, he realized, more than he'd ever admitted to himself. What would they think of him now? He shook his head and tried not to imagine. The past three years would have devastated his father, a practical man who never showed much emotion but was a kind and responsible father. Jerry took one last long look and walked away.

When he showed up at the storage units before suppertime, A. J. was surprised.

"Jerry, I thought you were gonna take a couple days off."

"I was," he said, "but I really don't have anywhere to go. I've lost track of all my old friends. Been away too long, I guess. It's no fun to wander around alone."

"You know what you need, Jerry?" A. J. said.

"What?"

"A wife."

Jerry tried to suppress a wistful grin. "Not many prospects here at A. J.'s social club."

"Hey, I could line you up with somebody," A. J. offered. "I've seen a couple of cute receptionists at the dental clinic."

"Nah. Not yet." Jerry wondered if the day would ever come when he would be completely over Brenda.

* * *

Calvin

For almost a year, Jerry had kept Max's cell phone on the nightstand next to the model Sopwith Camel. He picked it up on December 17, charged the two batteries, and carried it with him night and day. Max had said to turn it on a week before Christmas, and no way was Jerry going to miss the call. He had hundreds of questions, but now the anticipation made him nervous. What if Max asked him to do something ridiculous or embarrassing or dangerous? What if he didn't call at all? Finally, just after lunch on the twenty-second, the phone rang. Jerry fumbled with it and almost dropped it, but hit the button after the third ring.

"Hello?"

"Hi, Jerry. How are you?"

"Fine, Max."

"No, Jerry, tell me the truth. How are you?"

"Torn in two," Jerry admitted.

"I figured you would be."

"I appreciate the job, Max," Jerry said, "but I'm going nuts here by myself. I'm ready to rejoin the human race, I guess, but I feel bad about leaving A. J. high and dry."

"Don't worry about A. J.," Max said. "He knows you're a temp. All his managers are temps. He'll find somebody else."

"Are you saying it's okay to leave?"

"You think it's your destiny to manage storage units for forty years?" A heavy dose of good-natured sarcasm flavored his voice.

"Well, not exactly."

"Good. Glad to see you're coming to your senses."

"Am I supposed to look for another job?" Jerry asked.

"You've been reading the classifieds, haven't you?"

"Yeah," he confessed. "But I kinda felt guilty about it."

"You even called on a couple of them, right?"

"Yeah, but they just didn't feel right."

"Good for you, Jerry."

"So what am I supposed to do, Max? You apparently have some sort of plan for me. What's next?"

"This afternoon an older gentleman will drop in to pay his rent. He'll walk with a stiff sort of limp and have trouble writing the check. Ask him about his arthritis."

"That's it?"

"Yup. That's it."

"How do you know he'll show up, Max? How do you know these things? Are you sending him here?"

"Don't you trust me, Jerry?"

"Sure," he said, but he knew he didn't sound convincing. "Anyway, what choice do I have?" he added.

"None." Max chuckled to himself. "Just talk to him, Jerry, and have a Merry—"

"Max," Jerry blurted out.

"What, Jerry?"

"Don't hang up yet."

"Okay, but my timer's ticking."

"Max, why're you doing this?"

"Doing what?"

"Helping me out."

"You needed help, didn't you?"

"Yeah, but why me? Why not somebody else?"

"Who says I'm not helping somebody else?"

"Sorry, didn't think about that. But what's in this for you?"

"Oh, satisfaction, I suppose."

"But there's got to be a catch somewhere in all this. You're not just doing all this for nothing."

"You're right. Don't worry, Jerry. I'll get plenty out of this someday, I hope."

"I knew it." Jerry almost didn't want to know. "So what's the catch?"

"Well, I don't know about a 'catch,'" Max told him, "but one of the rules I forgot to mention last year is that whatever you get because of my calls you'll eventually have to give back."

Jerry was silent for a moment, trying to figure out exactly what this meant.

"So am I better off hanging up right now and going back onto the street?"

"What do you think?"

"I don't think you would have called in the first place if you didn't want me off the street."

"I think you're starting to trust me, Jerry."

"How did you know about my dream, Max?"

"What dream would that be?"

"The one about the Sopwith Camel."

"A dream about a Sopwith Camel?" said Max innocently.

"Yeah, the night before I got your gift. You had to know."

"Not really," Max suggested. "Maybe your mind knew what the gift would be. In the subconscious, time sometimes does funny things. Sometimes, I hear, it even runs backward. Haven't you ever heard about people dreaming things that haven't happened yet?"

"Yeah," Jerry admitted.

"Well, don't underestimate yourself."

"Max?"

"Yes, Jerry."

"Why was Brenda in my dream?"

"Was she now?"

"Yes."

"Well, if I had to guess, I'd say it was probably rather important if it was in your dream. Dreams have meanings on several levels."

"How good are you at interpreting dreams, Max?"

"Nice talking with you again, Jerry. Let's do this again next year. Merry Christmas."

"No, Max, don't hang up," Jerry yelled, but the line was already dead.

"Merry Christmas, Max," he said softly.

* * *

Later that afternoon, the office door opened and a man who appeared to be about sixty stepped gingerly into the office. He limped stiffly over to the counter and said hi to Jerry. Jerry had seen him before, but had never paid much attention to the obvious symptoms of arthritis the man showed. He struggled a bit to pull a checkbook and pen out of his coat pocket, then wrote out the check slowly and with great care. Still the letters were shaky, all hard angles.

"Which unit?" Jerry asked.

"G-11."

Jerry looked up at his face. He had a full head of striking silver hair, brilliant blue eyes with deep crow's feet at the corners, an Adam's apple that looked like a golf ball stuck in his throat, and a scar just below his lower lip. The only odd thing about the face was his eyebrows, which were still jet-black, in stark contrast with his hair.

"Arthritis bothering you today, sir?" Jerry asked, his heart almost in his throat.

"No more than usual. It's a danged nuisance most days."

"I'm sure it is."

The man handed Jerry the check. It was from the Wood Nook. The signature was shaky but legible: *Calvin Thomsen.*

"What kind of business is the Wood Nook?" Jerry asked.

"Custom furniture," Calvin answered. "We do everything from simple student desks to fancy dining room tables, even a grandfather clock or two."

"Sounds like interesting work. Bet your arthritis makes it difficult."

"Well, I don't do much of the actual production anymore. Fingers just won't perform like they used to, you know. But I've got about ten employees, most of 'em better than I ever was anyway," he added with a twinkle in his eye. "I just take the orders, visit with the customers, and make sure the work gets done on time."

"Hmm," Jerry observed, pausing to see if the man would keep talking.

"I've been thinking, though," Calvin continued right on cue, "I'd like a little more free time. Been thinking about getting somebody to manage the place for me. Thelma's been telling me she'd like to travel a bit before my arthritis gets too bad. We've got enough money, and the business pretty well takes care of itself. New customers all the time. We do good work, and people tell their friends."

"What kind of person you looking for?" Jerry asked.

"You know somebody who might be interested?" Calvin responded.

"Maybe," said Jerry, wondering again how Max could have known.

"That wouldn't be you, now, would it?" Calvin asked.

"It might be." Jerry grinned.

"Why don't you come by and visit me at the shop? We can talk about it."

"Well," Jerry hesitated, "it'd have to be late in the evening or on Sunday. I'm pretty much tied here." He knew he could use a vacation day, but he preferred not to have to do any explaining to A. J. If this worked out, better to break the news all at once.

"Listen, come by my house some evening when you close up here. Here's my address." Calvin pulled a business card from his pocket and wrote slowly on the back of it.

"How about the day after Christmas?" Jerry asked. "About 10:15? That's not too late, is it?"

"Sounds fine. I don't sleep very well anyway. Tend to just stay up late rather than lie awake in bed."

"Thanks, Calvin," Jerry said, glancing at the business card.

"Just call me Cal," he answered. "And you're . . ."

"Jerry. Jerry Carlson."

"Good, Jerry. I'll see you in a few days."

He turned and walked stiffly toward the door.

* * *

Christmas Eve was again one of the busiest days of the year. When closing time rolled around, Jerry was tired and not much in the mood to watch TV, so he curled up in bed with a book and promptly fell asleep. In the night he found himself flying again, which he hadn't done for some time now, but this time he was going in circles. Suddenly a voice spoke from behind him. He tried to turn, but once again his muscles refused to respond.

"Where we going, Jerry?" the familiar voice said.

Suddenly Jerry knew where he was trying to fly and why he was going in circles. "I'm trying to get back to where I came from," he explained.

"Don't you know, Jerry," said Max, "you can't ever go back. You can only go again." A laugh erupted from the seat behind him.

"Go where again?" Jerry asked.

"Straighten her out," Max replied, "and head for the horizon. We'll get there eventually."

When Jerry woke up, the sun was shining and he felt oddly at peace with himself. He walked out to the kitchen, and there on the table was a wrapped gift reminiscent of the one he had found the previous year, except this one boasted plain red paper with a pure white ribbon and bow. Jerry considered the gift for a moment, then tore away the paper. Inside was a brand-new Bible with a black leather cover, his name embossed in gold on the front. He turned it over in his hands a few times, gently opened it, and inside the front cover he found a card.

Merry Christmas, Jerry, it read. It was signed by Max.

He began leafing through the pages, and when he came to the book of Jeremiah in the Old Testament, he found part of a verse underlined in red pencil. "Before I formed thee in the belly I knew thee," it read.

He thumbed through more pages, and in the New Testament he found another underlined verse: "I came forth from the Father, and am come into the world: again, I leave the world, and go to the Father."

He wondered why Max had underlined these verses. As a boy, Jerry had gone to Sunday school now and then. His parents had insisted. But it had been so many years now, and a good deal of what he had once learned was now lost somewhere in the once familiar but now deserted back country of his mind. He decided maybe it was time to refresh his memory, and he figured Christmas Day was probably a good day to do it, so he spent the better part of the morning reading in the Bible. His study was somewhat random, but what he read was familiar, and the passages left him with an ache inside, a feeling somewhat similar to those he felt whenever he thought about his parents.

* * *

The day after Christmas was a slow day at the storage units, especially after dark. Most people were worn out from getting up early the day before and from overeating. Jerry made his rounds earlier than usual, put on a new pair of Dockers and a button-down shirt he'd bought himself for Christmas, and warmed up A. J.'s old truck. He wanted to arrive a few minutes early.

Cal lived in a nice neighborhood in South Jordan, a community a few miles south of A. J.'s storage units. Jerry had noticed from the address on the business card that the Wood Nook was only a few blocks away from the units. He figured Cal used G-11 for his business, probably to store items that wouldn't fit in the shop. Lots of businesses used storage units that way, Jerry had discovered. As they grew they tended to overflow their square footage, and it was cheaper to rent space than to expand or relocate—at least in the short term.

Cal's house was an attractive, two-story brick and stucco affair with a zillion Christmas lights hanging from the eaves and from several large trees in the yard. It looked like an extension of Temple Square in downtown Salt Lake where the Mormons put on a yuletide light show to rival the aurora borealis. One of the few highlights of his homeless days was wandering with the Christmas throngs through the glittering wonderland of Temple Square every December. Cal's yard brought back that memory, and a sudden warm glow filled Jerry's heart. He parked the old truck in the street and sauntered up to the door.

"Hi, Jerry," said Cal as he opened the door. "You're early."

"Slow day at the storage units," he responded.

Cal invited him in and introduced him to Thelma, who came out of the kitchen wiping her hands on a towel. "You want some pumpkin pie?" she asked. "We've got a little left over from Christmas dinner."

"No thanks, ma'am," Jerry answered.

Cal led Jerry into the family room, where flames licked artificial logs in the gas fireplace. He motioned for Jerry to take a seat in an over-stuffed chair next to the fire. Cal sat across the room on the sofa. The room itself might have come from a Courier and Ives museum. Thelma was evidently into holiday decor just an iota less than Martha Stewart.

"So tell me about yourself, Jerry," Cal began.

Jerry spent the next ten minutes giving Cal a brief history of his life, putting as positive a spin on things as he could. He'd printed up a resumé on the computer at work, but kept it in a folder he set on the floor next to the chair. He would give it to Cal only if he asked for it.

"So you worked at this lighting business till when?"

"About four years ago," Jerry answered. He knew what was coming next. He figured he could try to talk his way around the truth, but he also knew he didn't want to. He'd made mistakes. He figured it would be best to own up to them. He also figured this might be a good chance to put Max's magic touch to the test. He'd either get the job or he wouldn't, but he didn't want to hide anything.

"Why did you quit working there?"

"I didn't quit," Jerry answered. "I got fired."

He looked Cal in the eyes to gauge his reaction. Nothing.

"Why?"

"It was commission work, and I quit selling."

Cal just looked at him nonjudgmentally and left the words hanging in the air between them.

"My life kind of fell apart," Jerry explained. "I just couldn't sell lights anymore."

"Girl dump you?" Cal asked.

"How'd you know?" Jerry couldn't suppress a grin.

"Been there, done that," Cal laughed. "Didn't get canned over it, but I should have. Fortunately for me, and unfortunately for him, my dad was my boss." He laughed even harder.

Jerry chuckled with him, then said softly, "My dad was dead by then."

"I'm sorry, son." Cal looked at him sympathetically. "Life's full of hard knocks. So you started working for A. J. when?"

"A year ago last week."

"What about the years between getting fired and hooking up with A. J.?"

"I was on the street."

"Homeless?"

"Yeah."

Cal scratched his chin and closed his eyes. "Must have been hard," he said finally.

"It was almost like not being alive at all," Jerry answered.

"You alive again now?" His eyes popped open, and he cast Jerry a long, shrewd look.

"That's the reason I'm here tonight."

"Gets kind of lonely at the storage units, I bet."

"Very. It was exactly what I needed to get my feet under me again, but I'm ready to move on."

"And you figure managing my shop is a step up?"

"It feels right," Jerry said. And it did, for the simple reason that Max had opened the door for him and pointed the way.

"You think you can handle it?"

"Sure."

"Good enough for me," said Cal. "And just leave that resumé in the folder, Jerry. I don't hire people based on how well they write creative fiction. I read their faces. Yours tells a whole lot more than your words do. I would have hired you the other day at A. J.'s, but I wanted to talk to you first."

"Thanks, Cal," Jerry said. "For looking past my past, you might say."

"Don't mention it. It's just who I am. When can you start?"

"I've got to give A. J. enough time to find a replacement. That may take a while, but maybe I can help him."

"Whenever you're ready, give me a call," said Cal. "And if you get a few free minutes during the day sometime, drop by and meet the gang."

"Sure."

Jerry was walking on clouds as he made his way back to the truck. On the way home he stopped at Arctic Circle and bought himself their biggest banana split. He felt like celebrating. He sat in the back all by himself until midnight and couldn't help grinning. He hadn't felt this good since, well, since just before Brenda found that eggbeater in the sky and started asking him questions he couldn't answer.

When he finally returned to his little apartment at the storage units, there on the kitchen table was a card. He opened it, knowing already what it said.

Congratulations, Jerry, he read. *Get ready to fly. Max.*

* * *

Julie

Jerry called A. J. the next day and broke the bad news to him.

"Well, I figured you wouldn't last too long," A. J. told him. "You were too on the ball. But, hey, don't worry about it. I'll find somebody else."

"Maybe I can help you," Jerry suggested.

"How so?" asked A. J.

"Can you cover for me tomorrow for a few hours?"

"Sure."

An idea had been hatching in the back of Jerry's mind. He thought it just might be the answer to A. J.'s dilemma. So the next morning he took the bus downtown and marched on over to his old bench. Just as he had suspected, there sat Ron with his cup and sign.

"How's it goin', Ron?" Jerry asked, sitting down next to him.

"Same as ever." Ron turned his head and looked suspiciously at Jerry. Then a hint of recognition dawned in his eyes. "You the guy with the blankets?"

"Same one."

"Hey, thanks. I been lots warmer this winter."

"How long you been on the street, Ron?"

"Couple years."

"How long you been out of work?"

"'Bout three."

"Tried to find a job?"

"Tried for a long time, but it's hard to find a job when you ain't got an address."

"I know," said Jerry.

"How would you know?"

"This used to be my spot."

Ron looked at Jerry with squinted eyes, studying him up and down.

"I remember you," he said finally. "You had a beard and long hair. Always wanted your spot, but you always got here too early."

Jerry laughed. "Ron," he said, "how would you like an address?"

"You serious?"

"Sure, but there's one catch."

"What's that?" Ron's face was puzzled.

"You have to take the job that goes with it."

"You serious?"

"I already answered that question."

"What job?"

"Mine."

"Yours?"

"Yeah, I got a new one. Need to find a replacement."

"What kinda job?"

"If you've had your own restaurant, you can handle it easy," Jerry answered, divining Ron's uncertainty. "Come on. I'll tell you about it on the bus. By the way, what's your last name, Ron?"

"Southwick."

"Great, but you know what? Before we go meet your new boss, let's get you a haircut and a shave and a shower, and maybe a set of new clothes. You want to make a good impression, don't you?"

"I guess."

Ron looked completely baffled. Jerry laughed. He remembered how he had felt the year before when Max had called. At least Ron could see his benefactor.

* * *

Midafternoon, Jerry and Ron walked through the door of A. J.'s Storage. A. J., true to form, was busy recaulking the bathroom. The man was a whirlwind of energy, a nonstop do-it-yourselfer.

"A. J.," said Jerry, poking his head around the door, "I'd like you to meet my replacement. This is Ron Southwick."

A. J. looked Ron up and down, and all he saw was a nicely dressed, clean-cut man with an impish grin and startled eyes. "Where'd you find him?" he asked.

"Oh, just picked him up off the street," Jerry answered with a laugh.

"Oh, another drifter like you?" A. J. said, and Jerry laughed. Ron just looked puzzled.

"Just like me," Jerry said. "Listen, A. J., Ron's been a bit down on his luck lately, but he used to own a restaurant here in town. The storage units will be a cinch."

"Whatever you say, Jerry."

"I'll stay around for a week and train him," Jerry offered. "Besides, I need a few days to find me a new apartment."

* * *

A week later, Ron was up to speed on the new job, and Jerry had found a nice little apartment not far from the Wood Nook. He felt he was ready to take another leap into the unknown. He had stopped in a few days before to say hello to his new coworkers—a handful of serious craftsmen, a delivery driver, a materials buyer, a bookkeeper, and Cal—and had taken away a good first impression. It was a busy shop, always more work to do than time to do it in, or so Julie Linquist, the bookkeeper, had told him. But that was the way they liked it. Cal paid his craftsmen well, plus time and a half for overtime, which they could log pretty much any day they wanted to. Cal did absolutely no advertising, according to Julie. All his customers were either repeat business or referrals from friends who were pleased with the furniture they'd ordered. His prices were on the high side, but he could get away with it because the quality of the workmanship was unrivaled. This enabled him to be generous with his employees, which in turn motivated them to do their finest work for him. It was a true win-win arrangement.

When Jerry showed up for work a couple of days after New Year's, Cal took him under his wing immediately and taught him everything he did. It took a good month, but by the beginning of February, Jerry felt he knew not only everything Cal did, but also Cal's approach to business, which Jerry suspected lay at the root of the older man's success. Cal treated everyone as a friend. Employees, customers, vendors—everyone got the same treatment. Implicit trust with an expectation of excellence. Only the best would do for Cal's friends. He gave his workers full freedom to choose their hours and to try any new methods that might improve a product or save time producing it. He also let them experiment on their own time with designs of their own. Use of the machines was free, and they could each display one piece at a time in the small showroom. If a piece sold, all Cal asked was enough to cover the cost of materials plus ten percent of the profit for overhead.

Needless to say, everybody loved Cal. He had three children, all grown, and even though they had all worked in the shop earlier to put themselves through school, none of them wanted to inherit the business. One was an optometrist, one was a fire fighter, and the youngest had already made millions when she sold her upstart software business to a major player in the high-stakes, high-tech world.

When Cal felt Jerry was ready, he started staying away two days a week, then three, and finally he would only drop in sporadically to check on things. During the spring and summer, he vanished for a month at a time, showing up again unexpectedly with trinkets and souvenirs for his employees from the Oregon coast, Mount Rushmore, or the Grand Canyon.

Once he got used to his new situation, Jerry felt he had the best of both worlds. He had constant demand for a high-quality product.

He had motivated workers, and he was able to pay them generously. They realized Cal deserved a break, and even though they missed him, they wanted him to enjoy life a bit before his health deteriorated to the point that he couldn't. They also seemed to like Jerry. He was on the quiet side, but he exuded an air of confidence. This came partly from Cal's open trust in him, but partly from something inside that none of them could quite put a finger on. In short, Jerry could be the good guy with the customers and the other workers, but he didn't have the stress that turning a profit infuses into most business situations. All he had to do was keep everybody happy. It was all about relationships, he discovered, and to his surprise he found he thoroughly enjoyed this aspect of the work. He also found himself becoming increasingly interested in the technical aspects of designing and building furniture. Every moment he could spare he would watch the craftsmen at work and ask them questions about what they were doing or why they were doing it in a particular way. This, of course, pleased the workers to no end. His interest in their craft was genuine, so they were both flattered and eager to teach him all they could.

Jerry lived a simple existence. His tastes were modest, even meager. On the street he had discovered he could live with few comforts and almost no conveniences. And at A. J.'s, because he had precious little time to go shopping, he discovered he could spend far less than he earned. He brought this habit with him to the Wood Nook, and after a few months he realized Cal was paying him much more than he needed. So the next time Cal came in, he confronted him with an idea. Would it be okay, Jerry wondered, if he gave up part of his salary and used it as a bonus to be split among Julie, Mark, and Kevin? Mark was the delivery driver, and Kevin was the materials buyer. They were the only employees who didn't have much chance to earn overtime or pick up a little extra cash from selling their own creations. Cal told him it was his decision.

So Jerry spent his days busy and happy, but in the back of his mind something was nagging at him. He knew what it was, and he also knew it wouldn't go away. It was Brenda. In a quiet corner of his heart, he was lonely. After Cal turned things over to him, it became increasingly evident to Jerry that Julie, the bookkeeper and all-around office assistant, had an enormous crush on him. He knew the shop workers teased her about it when he wasn't around. And when he was there, he'd catch them aiming knowing looks in Julie's direction, and he'd see how her neck flamed red as she tried hard not to blush. When they were alone in the office, going over invoices or payables, he could tell she was nervous. She couldn't keep her hands still, and her eyes shifted away from his whenever he looked her direction, as if she didn't want him to know she'd been staring at him. It was flattering in a way because Julie was an attractive woman, but Jerry's heart was torn. He knew if he handled this poorly, work relations might suffer, and he didn't want to risk upsetting the easy equilibrium that prevailed at the Wood Nook.

Finally, about two months after Cal had turned the reins over to him, Jerry threw caution to the wind and asked Julie out to dinner and a movie. She was so excited she almost couldn't contain it, but said yes and then made an excuse to hurry out into the shop. He could hear laughter and a chorus of congratulations coming from that direction moments later. He smiled to himself and wandered out into the parking lot so she wouldn't be embarrassed when she came back.

Jerry hoped he'd done the right thing. He couldn't just go on pretending to ignore Julie's obvious feelings. And he also wanted to know if that empty place in his heart could be filled by someone other than Brenda. He had to find out, and he really hadn't met any other women yet who were at all interesting to him. He thought about fishing out the cell phone, but he knew what Max would tell him. So he bit the bullet and planned a date.

* * *

By this time, Jerry was the owner of an old maroon Corolla, and when he picked Julie up for the date, they were both nervous—Julie because she was a bit on the insecure side anyway and she really liked him, and Jerry because he hadn't been on a date for more than four years—the last time he and Brenda had gone out.

They went to the movie first. Jerry figured it would be easier to spend time together being distracted by the show, getting used to each other's company, and then talk over dinner. The show was mediocre, a comedy whose writers apparently didn't possess a funny bone in their bodies, but his plan worked. When they came out of the theater, they both felt more at ease. They drove to Chin Po's in Sandy for dinner, and though the exterior didn't look very authentic, the restaurant made the best Chinese food in the valley.

"So, Julie," said Jerry after the waiter had taken their order, "tell me about yourself." He knew it was a lame request, but he couldn't think of a better way to break the ice.

"I grew up in Ogden," she told him. Ogden was an anomaly in Utah, Jerry knew, a government town whose major industries had been Hill Air Force Base, the IRS service center, and the Defense Depot till the latter was shut down during the military cutbacks of the post-Reagan years. When the high-tech boom transformed much of the state, Ogden had gone from Utah's second-largest city to an also-ran in the population race. Lots of people grew up there and left. Julie was one of them. "I moved to Salt Lake when I was seventeen," she added.

"With your family?"

"No, I left home."

"Why so young?"

"To get away from my dad. Mom was just an alcoholic, but Dad beat me."

Jerry hadn't expected this kind of openness and wondered if Julie expected the same in return. He certainly wasn't ready to ante up. "Oh," was all he could manage.

"I moved in with my cousin who was going to the U," she explained. "I finished high school here, then enrolled at Salt Lake Community College."

This told Jerry something. Her grades weren't good enough to get her a scholarship at the University of Utah. No wonder, considering what her home life must have been like. Without a scholarship, she couldn't have afforded the U anyway.

"What did you study?" he asked.

"Accounting," she said, and then added self-consciously, "I wasn't very good at it."

"Did you get your degree?" he asked.

"No," she said, and looked down at her hands on the table. They were small, delicate hands. All her features, in fact, were delicate. She was about 5'2" and so slender he couldn't help but wonder about eating disorders.

"I didn't have enough money," she explained. "Had to get a job."

"Is that when you went to work for Cal?"

"No. I spent a year as a temp, mostly receptionist-type work, then Cal hired me."

"Well, your accounting seems fine to me," Jerry told her. "Not that I'm an expert or anything," he ended lamely.

"Oh, I'm not doing much more than bookkeeping," she admitted, "and Cal taught me most of what I know. I couldn't follow those accounting textbooks with all their dry explanations, and I didn't have a clue about the problems."

"How long have you worked for Cal?" Jerry asked.

"Oh, five or six years," she said.

Jerry was trying to work out how old she was. He'd never asked, assuming it was one of those things you just didn't ask a woman: age, weight, true hair color. He figured if she had lasted a couple of years at the community college, she'd be maybe twenty-six or -seven by now. Just a bit younger than Brenda.

"What about you?" Julie asked.

"What about me?" Jerry replied. He wasn't sure he wanted her to know anything about his past. He hadn't hidden it from Cal, but this was different. He needed the employees to have confidence in him.

"You must have lived an interesting life," she said, eyes beaming.

"What makes you say that?"

"Well," she stammered, "it's just written all over you. There's something about you that's, well, just different."

"I really haven't done anything very exciting," Jerry confessed.

"Where did you grow up?"

"Right here in Sandy."

"Really?" She sounded genuinely surprised. "I thought you were from somewhere far away. Does your family still live here?"

"No," he said quietly. "My parents died when I was in college. Car crash."

"I'm sorry," she said. "Brothers and sisters?"

"No, I'm an only child."

"I've got four brothers and one sister," Julie revealed. "I'm third in line. We're not very close, though. We all just wanted to get away from home, and seeing each other just brings back painful memories."

"That's too bad."

"It's worst during the holidays," she told him. "Everybody at the shop has family get-togethers. Cal found out about my dysfunctional family a couple of years ago, and he invites me over on Christmas Eve to be with his family. He has all his kids and grandkids there. Thelma puts on a huge feast, but I kind of feel like an extra left shoe. Still, it's better than being alone."

Jerry thought about his own holidays. Since his parents died, he had spent Christmases alone. The year he and Brenda had been involved, things fell apart well before the holidays, and he had been on the street by Christmas. For the next three years, he'd spent Christmas day in the little clearing up the canyon. It wasn't worth the effort to walk all the way down to the city. Downtown Salt Lake was like a ghost town on Christmas.

"What's wrong?" Julie asked.

Suddenly Jerry realized his mind had wandered down painful paths, and his face must have shown it.

"Nothing," he said. "It's just that Christmas hasn't been so great since my parents died." That was certainly true.

"I'm sorry," she said. "I shouldn't have brought it up. Tell me about your parents, though. What were they like?"

Now that he had to think about it, Jerry didn't know what to say. "I don't know," he said finally. "They were just regular people. My dad was a bit paunchy and bald when he died, but Mom said he used to look a lot like me."

"So are you going to get paunchy and bald when you get older?"

"I hope not," he laughed. He closed his eyes for a minute, trying to see his parents' faces. He was sorry he hadn't kept the box of old photos.

"Do you have any pictures of them?" Julie asked as if on cue.

"I lost them a few years ago," he answered.

"I'm sorry," she said. "That's too bad."

There was an awkward silence, then Julie spoke again.

"So, where did you work before you managed the storage units?" Cal had told them all where he'd found Jerry the day he came by for introductions.

"Well," Jerry hedged, "I was a salesman for a few years. Lighting fixtures. I told you my life's been kind of boring. Tell me about the guys in the shop," he said, intentionally steering the conversation away from his past.

For the next twenty minutes, while they ate, Julie talked about the other employees at the Wood Nook. Jerry was genuinely interested and picked up many useful pieces of information that he filed away until later, when they might come in handy in dealing with situations at work. When she ran out of things to say, a brief and awkward silence followed.

Suddenly Julie said, "You know, Jerry, you and I have a lot in common."

"Do we?" he asked, surprised at her boldness.

"Don't you think so?" she asked with an eagerness in her eyes he wished he could return.

"I suppose so," he said as lightly as he could.

They chatted about nothing in particular for the rest of the meal, then Jerry took her home. When he got in bed that night, he found he couldn't sleep. Every word, every thought, every feeling from the date came back to him. He realized he was overanalyzing everything, but he couldn't help it. He wanted to know one thing, and at about two in the morning, just before his brain finally shut down from exhaustion, he came to a conclusion: maybe he wasn't such damaged goods after all. He had enjoyed the time together with Julie. Yes, he'd been cautious, perhaps overly so, but he felt good. It meant a great deal to know someone could be attracted to him. He decided he'd ask her out again, but he'd also have to be careful, knowing that workplace romances could blow up in your face.

* * *

When Cal caught wind of the "JJ Affair," as the other workers dubbed it, he came directly to Jerry and asked him to go for a ride with him.

"You drive," Cal said, and tossed him the keys. "I've got too much to say, and I'm afraid I might drive off the road." He grinned to let Jerry know it was his arthritis and not the meeting that concerned him. "I don't care where, just drive."

"Well," he said, as they pulled out of the parking lot, "I hear you and Julie are an item."

"We've been out three or four times," Jerry replied.

"You like her?"

"Sure. She's a nice person."

"Of course she is. I hired her, didn't I?"

Jerry laughed at Cal's perception of his own impeccable taste. "But you hired me too," he countered.

"Well, every man's entitled to a mistake now and then."

"I think I've used up my allotment already," Jerry suggested.

"Then you can't make one in this case, can you?"

"What are you getting at, Cal?" The older man's tone worried him.

"Like you said, she's a nice gal."

"So?"

"She's also pretty fragile. Kind of like a five-thousand-year-old vase—looks fine if you don't touch it, but if you're not careful, it falls apart."

"I know. Maybe she's not the only one." And this was true. Even though Jerry had recovered in many ways from his years on the street, some places in his heart were still painful to the touch. One place in particular, he knew, couldn't take another rejection like Brenda's. He was vulnerable, and he knew it. Because of this he knew it would be difficult to give his heart freely, as he had to Brenda.

"Maybe not," Cal countered, "but you two aren't the same, you know."

"How so?"

"I don't know if Julie's looking for the same thing you are."

"Well, I'm not even sure what I'm looking for. What's *she* looking for?"

"The dad she never had. I've tried to play that part to a degree, but I'm pretty safe. I'm old enough to *be* her dad. But it can get confusing if you try to mix romance and surrogate parenting."

"I'm not trying to be a father figure, Cal."

"But you might be one anyway."

Jerry pursed his lips and thought about Cal's words.

"Just don't hurt her," Cal added. "Be careful you don't write checks with your tongue that your heart can't cash."

"Are you trying to scare me off?" Jerry wondered aloud.

"No. Just trying to make sure you know what you're doing."

For all Jerry knew, he was in over his head already. Anyway, when it came to romance, was there a man alive who knew what he was doing? Men were supposed to be clueless, weren't they? But he saw Cal's point.

After that day, Jerry tried his best to go slow, to be extra cautious and not let things get out of control with Julie, but it was like trying to rein in a wild stallion. She wanted commitment, and he wasn't so sure he didn't want it too. He enjoyed being with her, enjoyed the way she looked at him, talked to him, held his hand when they walked together, and their first kiss had been a long-overdue and memorable experience. But somewhere in the back of his mind, something still nagged at him. Finally he realized what it was. The principle of least interest. He was on the "less interested" end now, and he knew it. It wasn't that he wasn't interested at all. It was just that no one could conceivably be as interested in Julie as she was in him. He knew he could never match her intensity, and yet he wondered if it really mattered.

He thought about breaking things off somehow, but he didn't know how to accomplish it without hurting her. So out of sincere concern for her fragile feelings, he kept taking her out. At work they couldn't avoid each other, of course, and by now the other employees were teasing them openly. One of the guys in the shop, Marty, was particularly fond of it. Every time he'd see them together, he'd ask Julie to show him her hand. Seeing her ring finger still empty, he'd look at Jerry and say, "Hey, boss, you're not keeping your employees happy."

Jerry would laugh uneasily, Julie would turn three shades of red, and Marty would shake his head in disbelief. This same ritual was replayed perhaps three or four times a day. Finally Jerry had to speak with Marty about it. He found him working at the lathe one day and sat down to watch. Jerry started asking questions, as he often did around the shop. Why that tool? What grade of sandpaper do you use on different kinds of wood? How do you get all the legs to look identical? And so on. When Marty had finished the part he had been turning and was inspecting his work, Jerry said quietly, "Marty, ease up on me and Julie, okay?"

Marty looked up, surprised. "I thought you two were an item," he said.

"We like each other," Jerry told him, "but I don't know if it'll ever become more than that. I just don't want her to get hurt."

"Well, boss, you're the one who controls that, not me."

"I suppose so," Jerry admitted, "but go easy on her. She gets embarrassed easily."

"I noticed," Marty chuckled. "It's good for her."

Jerry left it at that, but during the next few days, Marty stopped his hand inspections.

* * *

"Jerry," Julie said over dinner the next week, "can we talk about us?"

"Us?" He almost choked on a clam from his chowder. "I thought that's all we ever talked about."

"No," she said, clearly exasperated at his deflection, "I mean *us!*"

"Oh, *that* us."

He had thought a great deal about *them*, but he was reluctant to talk about the subject because he knew exactly where the talk would lead. He had analyzed their relationship from every angle. He knew he liked her. He knew she was crazy about him. He also knew he could make her happy with very little effort. And most of all, he knew she was dying to marry him. He'd been in her shoes before, and he suffered with her. And he knew in his heart he just didn't have it in him to turn her away. So instead he had tried to delay the inevitable. The inevitable, however, had finally arrived.

"Yes," she said, "*that* us."

"You go first," he suggested.

"I think you know what I'm going to say," she answered. "You know how I feel about you. I think I know how you feel about me."

Jerry wanted to say, "Then tell me, because I'd certainly like to know too." Instead he just nodded.

"Don't you think it's time we started to think about the future?" she continued.

"I think about it all the time," he answered.

"So, am I in it?" she asked bluntly.

"I suppose you are," he admitted, and it was a revelation to himself. He had indeed thought about the future. He had imagined what being married to Julie would be like. In a practical, objective sort of way, he knew life would be good. But always, somewhere in the back of his mind, came totally uninvited thoughts of Brenda. Usually he pushed them aside as irrational intrusions, but now and then he let his mind wander, and he imagined what life would be like if they had gotten married. He knew this was utter silliness. In fact, he figured she was married and had two or three kids by now. He'd looked for her once or twice in the phone book, but her name was no longer listed. He assumed that meant she'd changed it. And now, suddenly, she was there in his mind again, silently intruding while Julie was trying to wring a commitment out of him. It was disconcerting.

"When?" Julie asked.

"When what?" Jerry answered, coming out of his momentary reverie.

"When's the future going to happen?" she asked.

"In the future?" Jerry guessed.

Julie laughed. "You're impossible, Jerry Carlson," she scolded.

"I told you I'm a basket case," he said. "Give me some time, Julie. I'll figure things out eventually."

* * *

Two Down

The last day of June, A. J. called. Jerry hadn't heard from him for a couple of months.

"Jerry," he said, "sorry to give you bad news."

"What happened?" Jerry asked. He wondered if one of A. J.'s brothers had died or if the storage units had burned to the ground.

"I had to let Ron go."

This news was sobering to Jerry. He felt instantly responsible. "What for?"

"I guess he couldn't kick the booze. I really thought he'd work out, but he was spending all his money on whiskey and was hung over too many mornings."

"I'm sorry, A. J.," Jerry told him.

"I am too, Jerry. Thanks for trying. You don't want to come back, do you?"

"Don't think I can, A. J."

"I knew you couldn't, but I figured I'd ask."

"Have you found anybody else?"

"No, but I will."

When he hung up, Jerry sat quite still for a long time. The next day he told Julie he had to run an errand in Salt Lake. "I'll be back before noon," he assured her.

He found Ron just where he guessed he would: on the planter across from the ZCMI Center. He was there with his sign and cup, looking like an unfortunate part of the scenery.

"You can take people out of the street," Jerry concluded, "but you can't take the street out of some people." He almost went over to talk to Ron, but thought better of it. "What good can I do anyway?" he said to himself. "I tried, but it wasn't enough."

It was an education of sorts for Jerry. He had naively assumed that by opening a door for somebody, the other person was obligated to walk through it. Now he knew better.

* * *

By the Fourth of July, Jerry knew he had to do something about Julie. He was inching closer to proposing, but something kept holding him back. Part of him wanted the stability he felt would come into his life from marriage, but part of him resisted the commitment. He assumed it was just fear—fear of giving his heart completely to someone. He seriously doubted Julie would ever reject him as Brenda had done, but still he hesitated. For some reason he just couldn't bring himself to take the plunge.

Things were getting uncomfortable at the Wood Nook too. Everyone seemed to be waiting for him to make some move, Julie most of all. She had stopped asking about the future, but she hinted often enough. Finally, Jay, one of the craftsmen, approached him at lunch.

"Jerry," he said. "You can't wait forever."

"I know," Jerry answered. "But it isn't as simple as it seems."

"Nothing ever is," said Jay. "But Julie's a good girl. And she needs somebody like you."

"I know." And he did know. Julie needed nothing more than a good husband. So many things in her life that had gone wrong could be made right by a husband who loved her and treated her like a queen. But was he that man? That was the question.

"Well," Jay told him, "don't string her along forever. We're all getting a bit impatient."

Finally Jerry made a difficult decision, one he hoped he wouldn't regret. After dark he grabbed his old backpack, headed out the door, and walked for ten or fifteen minutes. When he reached the local junior high school, he turned into the parking lot, then walked around to the back of the school and out onto the baseball field. Home plate was at the far end of the field, and behind the backstop was an old apple orchard that would soon blossom into a fine crop of new houses. Climbing the bleachers, he looked around to see if anyone was in sight. As far as he could see, he was alone. The sky above was sprinkled with stars, and the moon was just a sliver on the western horizon. He sat down on the top row of bleachers, leaned back against the aluminum railing, and stared up at the soft summer stars. Closing his eyes, he took a deep breath, as if he were about to jump into deep, cold water.

After a long time, he exhaled slowly, pulled the cell phone out of his backpack, and punched the buttons slowly. He waited a moment, took another deep breath, then hit send. There were two rings, then a familiar voice.

"Hi, Jerry. You're out late tonight. What can I do for you?"

"Wanna guess?" he asked wryly. The fact that Max knew he was "out" was both disconcerting and comforting.

"Sure," said Max. "I'm good at guessing games. Let's see—you've been spending a fair piece of your time with a certain Julie who works at the Wood Nook, and you're wondering whether or not you ought to marry her."

"You're a mind reader, Max."

"One of my lesser talents, Jerry."

"Do you have someone watching me all the time, Max, or do you just know?"

"Yes."

"Thanks for the info."

"No problem, Jerry. But that's not why you called, is it?"

"Of course not."

"So you want me to tell you whether you ought to marry her or not?"

"No," said Jerry. "Fooled you for once, Max. I just want to know if it's important who I marry. Does it matter? I mean, if we get along and she's a good person, does it matter who she is?"

"That's a philosophical question, Jerry. My, you've changed in a year and a half. You're asking if there's a one and only for everybody, and if you don't find that one and only, will it upset some grand eternal plan."

"Am I?" Jerry was surprised. "I thought I was just asking if there's a person I'm supposed to marry or if any good person will do?"

"Well," said Max slowly, "if there's just one person you're supposed to marry, there's also just one person everybody else is suppose to marry, right?"

"I guess so."

"So, what happens if the person you're supposed to marry doesn't choose to marry you? What if she falls off a cliff or gets hit by a drunk driver or runs off with Josh?"

"Josh? How'd you know about him?"

"Who? Oh, I was just pulling a name out of a hat," Max explained. "But answer the question, Jerry."

"Well," he said, "God would have to prevent all that, I suppose."

"But God's not a deterministic God. Sometimes He intervenes, keeps us from taking a wrong step, but mostly He lets us choose. And our choices affect other people. Sometimes their choices affect us. Sometimes their choices change our entire life, right?"

"Right," Jerry answered. "So you're saying it's my choice?"

"Of course."

"So I should marry Julie?"

"I didn't say that!" Max scolded him.

"I thought you said it doesn't matter who I marry."

"I didn't say that, either."

"Then what did you say?"

"That there's not just one person on earth who's meant for you. That doesn't mean there aren't millions of women who would be wrong for you."

"So is Julie wrong?"

"Let me ask you one question, Jerry. How do you feel when you're with Julie?"

"I feel good. I feel needed."

"And how did you feel when you were with Brenda?"

"Giddy," Jerry answered somberly. "Like I was in heaven. Like I wanted the feeling to last forever. Like I couldn't stand to be away from her."

"I think you get my point," Max suggested.

"But Brenda's not the only one who can make me feel that way?"

"You're a quick study, Jerry."

"But what about Julie? I happen to know she feels that way about me."

"Love's a two-way street, as you ought to know."

"The principle of least interest?"

"You really did pay attention in school, Jerry. I'm impressed." Max paused. "Now, I'm not an expert on this, but I think it's safe to say if there's not balance in a relationship, love on one side or the other generally turns into something that looks like love but isn't. Sometimes it even turns into something very opposite from love."

"So I should stop seeing Julie?"

"I don't think I said that either. My, you're not listening very well today, Jerry."

"But when will I meet somebody like Brenda?"

"That's a good question, Jerry. In fact, you're asking better questions all the time. I'll think about that one. Maybe you should too. By the way, thanks for the call. Two down, one to go."

Click.

Jerry sat and stared at the phone. Then he looked up at the night sky and shook his head. This wasn't going to be easy.

* * *

He kept on dating Julie for a couple of months, but he let her know immediately he wasn't ready for any long-term commitment. He suggested they start seeing other people, although he hadn't really met anyone who was all that interesting to him. More to make his words honest than because he wanted to, he started dating a woman he'd met at his apartment complex in the laundry room one day. She was a divorcée with a three-year-old daughter, and she talked a blue streak. He could tell she was on the prowl for anyone who could take over the responsibilities her husband had abandoned when he had opted for a life of increased solitude. The first time she and Jerry went out, she spent half the date castigating the no-good bum for a million things he had done and another million he hadn't. Jerry figured no man alive could live up to the expectations she had acquired, but he was glad to go out with someone who could carry on a whole conversation by herself and who would be rather easy to let go after a date or two.

Things were a little off-kilter at work for a week or so after Jerry had given Julie the bad news, but he still asked her out now and then, and soon things were pretty much back to normal, except that the teasing stopped. The shop workers were sensitive about the situation. They all liked both Jerry and Julie too much to make either feel uncomfortable, and more than anything they wanted the atmosphere at work to be what it had always been, so they just let it go without so much as a backward glance.

When Cal found out, he had Jerry take him for another ride. All he said was, "I figured you two weren't right for each other. I want Julie to be happy, but knowing both of you the way I do, I figured you weren't the one to make it happen. I've watched you two together, and I wasn't seeing the look in your eye I was seeing in Julie's. Or in Thelma's," he added with a wink.

Jerry wondered if this was some sort of indictment, but Cal didn't seem at all upset with him, so he figured the old man was just a shrewd judge of character. Still, in a corner of his heart, Jerry was saddened by this turn of events. He was more lonely now than ever. He pondered his last question to Max continually, but came up empty. Jerry had never been a social animal, and after his years on the street, he was even less so now. He just didn't frequent the places where an eligible bachelor like himself might meet the kind of woman he really needed and wanted. At college he'd found dates in his classes or study groups. At Lumenescent he had found Brenda. But the only woman at the Wood Nook was Julie, and the customers were largely wealthy, married women looking for a new piece of custom furniture to spruce up rooms they'd grown bored with. By December, Jerry was ready to throw in the towel and declare himself ineligible.

Through these discouraging times, Jerry found himself alone at his apartment many evenings, and often he would pull out the Bible Max had given him and read. He didn't read sequentially, but hunted around in the book until a chapter caught his interest. He found some comfort in the Bible, and he also found some surprises. Every now and then he would thumb through the book, looking for something to lift his spirits, and he would happen upon another underlined passage. He was almost certain these verses had not been underlined before, but after this happened twice, he went through the entire book, one page at a time, and counted only ten underlined passages.

The next night, however, as he searched for something to read, he found a verse that definitely hadn't been underlined the night before. It was in Paul's first epistle to the Corinthians, the eleventh verse of the eleventh chapter: "Nevertheless neither is the man without the woman, neither the woman without the man, in the Lord." Jerry read this twice, closed his eyes, and took a deep breath. Rather than feeling inspired, he felt more discouraged than ever. He closed the book, put on his coat, and went for a long walk. Winter had come early this year, and it was a bitterly cold night, but he was numb before he ever went out. When he returned home an hour and a half later, he found the kitchen light on. He was sure he had turned it off when he left, and when he found the Bible open on the table, he knew someone had been there.

He picked up the book, and a new verse had been underlined: "For we are saved by hope: but hope that is seen is not hope."

third christmas

....

The Address

About mid-December, Jerry started having odd dreams. Perhaps they were odd because he was having them at all, or at least remembering them. Until now, Jerry had had only two dreams that stayed with him when he awoke: the dreams about flying the Sopwith Camel.

Now, however, he awoke every morning with memories of new and bizarre flights. Sometimes he was in the plane with Max, and Max would talk to him about altitude and airspeed and keeping the nose up and the wings level with the horizon. Sometimes he flew over salt flats, which stretched out like a white tablecloth in all directions. Sometimes he soared over rough mountains and fields of sagebrush, sometimes over forests and meadows, sometimes over red sandstone formations only a God with a sense of humor would have created. Sometimes the horizon looked like the horizon in Utah, but it would change color from dream to dream as he neared it. One night it would be deep green, the next it would be bright orange, then the faintest purple. And then some nights he knew he wasn't in Utah at all. In fact, sometimes, he knew he wasn't even on earth. He was cruising above oceans of methane gas or over craters on the moon or seas of ice or rivers of molten lava. Occasionally in all these journeys he was alone in the sky but was flying straight toward the sun, and the sky turned all yellow and warm and brittle, and he was frightened about what lay on the other side of the yellow. And one night he awoke in a cold sweat and knew Brenda had been in the plane with him. He hadn't been able to see her face, but he knew from the feeling in his heart that she was there with him.

The next morning he turned on the cell phone and carried it with him to work and set it next to his pillow when he slept. That night he dreamed again, but this dream was more bizarre than ever. He was flying the plane, but the wings were gone. And the next night he was flying, but without any plane at all. All he had to do was lift his arms like Superman, and the next thing he knew, he was soaring through the air like a bird. It was the most liberating feeling he had ever known, and when he woke up, he lay in bed feeling incredibly heavy, aching all over from the unyielding force of gravity pinning him to the sheets and keeping him from floating up to the ceiling.

The next night he flew again without the plane, and this time he found himself gliding low over a forest of evergreens. Snow lay heavy on the ground, and as the sun went down, the trees were dark shadows against the brilliant snow. Then, off in the distance, he saw a faint light. As he drew closer he could see it was a tree, taller than all the rest, infinitely tall it seemed, and it glowed as if light was welling up within it and streaming out of each twig tip. To his astonishment, he found himself heading straight for the tree, and he could neither swerve to the side nor pull up into the clear night sky. He was heading straight for the light. Just before he crashed into it, though, he awoke, breathless, with eyes wide open.

* * *

The days leading up to Christmas were very busy at the Wood Nook. Many of the custom pieces had to be finished by the twenty-fourth, in time for harried husbands or wives to pick them up and hide them from their unsuspecting spouses for a few hours until they could be unveiled triumphantly on Christmas morning. Cal said he traditionally did a quarter of his business in December, and Jerry believed him.

Julie had decorated the office for the season, and this reminded Jerry that his own apartment was far from festive, so on the twentieth he went out and bought a tree, a few ornaments, and a couple of strings of lights. He hadn't had a Christmas tree since his parents died, so this was a novel experience for him. He figured it might lift his spirits. But he had no idea how to decorate a tree. First off, he was what Brenda had called "interior design impaired." Second, his mother had always been the one to decorate the tree when he was young, and she had wanted no help from a bungling youngster whose room decor leaned toward sports posters and whatever he had picked up on the way home from school—snail shells, rusty bike wheels, and oddly shaped pieces of wood. Her tree had to be "just so." The final challenge was that Jerry's first tree was a bit on the skeletal side. The big, bushy ones were long gone from the lot by the time he went hunting. So he did his best, and when he finished and stood back to look at his work, it reminded him more of a Charlie Brown tree than anything his mother had ever produced.

"Oh well," he said to the tree. "It's not like anybody but me's going to see you." He'd planned on asking Julie out before Christmas, but he doubted he'd bring her to his apartment. After looking at the tree, any remaining doubt turned to certainty.

He was putting the empty boxes in the closet when his cell phone rang. He'd left it on the kitchen table while he decorated because when it was on his belt, the strand of lights kept getting caught on it as he wound them round the tree. Now he stumbled into the kitchen, grabbed the phone, and pushed the button.

"Max?" he blurted out.

"Merry Christmas, Jerry," said the familiar voice. "Got your lights strung?"

"You're either a Peeping Tom or the devil himself," said Jerry, feeling a bit testy.

"Guilty as charged," Max laughed. "But even the devil could find a better tree than that."

"I happen to like it," Jerry replied. "It was homeless."

"Good for you, Jerry."

"Thanks for the Bible, Max."

"Don't mention it."

"And for marking those verses."

"What verses would those be, Jerry?"

"Oh, forget it. You're hopeless."

"I trust you're not, though," Max said.

"Close," Jerry answered, and his voice sank a little. "So, what's it going to be this year, Max? Another new job? I'm kind of liking the current one."

"No, not unless you get canned. Something easier this year."

"What? Is it time to give back everything you've given me?"

"Not yet," Max replied. "You haven't got anything worth giving yet, Jerry." He laughed long and merrily.

"A regular Santa Claus in reverse you are," Jerry suggested.

"I've got to play by the rules too, Jerry."

"What rules?"

"I'll tell you someday, maybe. But for now, here's what I want you to do." Max paused.

"I'm listening," said Jerry.

"I want you to look up an address for me," Max continued.

"That's it?"

"Yeah, that's it. You have to go tomorrow night, though, and you have to knock on the front door before eight o'clock."

"Can I knock and run?" Jerry asked, only half in jest.

"No, Jerry." Max sounded a bit exasperated.

"Okay," Jerry said, and suddenly he grew suspicious. "Who lives there?"

"It's a secret."

"Is this your house, Max?" Jerry asked. "Do I get to meet you?"

"Not yet. No, this isn't my house. My house is just a bit bigger than this one." He laughed again, obviously enjoying the consternation in Jerry's voice.

"Well, give me the address," Jerry insisted.

"1418 East 8950 South."

"That's in Sandy."

"Don't be late."

"What do I say when they answer the door?"

"Oh, you'll think of something."

"Max?"

"Yes, Jerry."

"Who are you?"

"I told you."

"You said your name is Max, but who *are* you?"

"That's not an easy question. Let me turn it around. Who are *you*, Jerry, aside from your name and where you work?"

Jerry was suddenly speechless. He didn't know how to answer.

"See, Jerry. It's not such an easy question, is it? Let's just say I'm your friend."

"Then why can't we meet?"

"Maybe we will someday. Merry Christmas, Jerry. Pleasant dreams tonight."

The line went dead.

* * *

That night Jerry dreamed again. He knew he had dreamed, and when he woke up in the morning he had a strange feeling what he had dreamed was very important. But for some reason he couldn't remember a thing about it. It was the same feeling he got when he couldn't remember somebody's name. Try as he might, it was just beyond reach of memory. He could feel all around it but couldn't touch it.

That day at work he was busier than ever. All day the phone rang until Jerry was sure the circuits would burn up. People were asking if their furniture was going to be finished by the twenty-fourth. He and the craftsmen had worked out a schedule to accommodate all the last-minute orders. It would be tight, but they figured they could make it if they all worked lots of overtime until Christmas Eve. In spite of the hectic pace, Jerry was on pins and needles all day. He'd been a bit somber of late, singing his own arrangement of the pre-Christmas blues, but that day was different. He wasn't sure what Max had in store for him, but at least it wasn't another evening of staring at the walls, watching a stupid sitcom on TV, or taking Julie out on what he knew was a pointless date.

He left work at 6:30 and went home to clean up and grab a bite to eat, but he found he was too nervous to be hungry. He wandered around the apartment for a few minutes, looked at his pathetic little Christmas tree, and glanced at his watch every ten seconds. Finally, just before 7:15, he walked out the door. He didn't want to be late.

Driving slowly so that no cop would have the slightest reason to pull him over, he made his way south and east to Sandy. The traffic was heavy, but he still arrived fifteen minutes early. He found the street easily and drove past the house. It was a modest little brick home with lights strung along the porch and a tree in the front window. The numbers 1, 4, 1, and 8 ran down the brick next to the door. An old Subaru, older than his Corolla, was parked under a small car port to the side of the house. A light was on in the back right corner room, he noticed as he drove by. He pulled down the street a half block or so, parked in front of a darkened church building, and sat for ten minutes. His palms were sweating even though it was twenty degrees outside and the car heater was on its last leg. He sat there trying to imagine what would happen when he rang the bell. He practiced what he might say. "Hi, you don't know me, but my friend Max, who I've never met, sent me here tonight." "Hi, my name's Jerry Carlson, and Max says hi." "Hi, you're probably wondering what I'm doing here, and so am I."

Finally he turned the car around, drove back to the house, and parked in front. Slowly, he stepped out onto the sidewalk and closed the door as quietly as he could. Taking a deep breath, he marched up the walk, up the steps, and stood on the porch. The doorbell was broken, and a little sign next to it instructed him to knock loudly. He held his hand up to the door, paused a moment, took another deep breath, then rapped on the door with his knuckles. A moment later he heard footsteps, and the door opened a crack. Then it opened wider, and he found himself staring into a face that scared him to death.

It was Brenda. She looked just as she had the last time he'd seen her, except her hair was cut shorter. He didn't know what to say. His first instinct was to run, but his feet felt as if they were encased in concrete. He knew the look on his face ranked somewhere between sheer idiocy and utter confusion. But then he looked at her and realized her expression was a mirror image of his own.

"Jerry?" she finally stammered. "Jerry?"

"Yes," he whispered. His vocal chords were as paralyzed as the rest of him.

"Jerry," she said a bit louder, "please come in."

Finally his feet obeyed his brain, and he stepped past her into the house. The exterior may have been quite ordinary, but now he could see that the inside was vintage Brenda. Interior design impaired she was not. The house looked like a Christmas village inside, and it smelled of pine, cinnamon, and nutmeg. The tree was spangled with bows, tiny brass horns, hanging angels, and twinkling white lights. A star perched on top. Jerry's head was spinning. He felt like a wanderer who, lost in the woods, knocked at a cottage door only to find himself invited inside by a beautiful princess. He scanned the walls for photos of a husband and children, but found none. A good sign, he hoped.

"Let me take your coat," she said. "Have a seat." She motioned toward the sofa.

He took his coat off without saying a word and handed it to her. She draped it across an overstuffed chair next to the door, then sat on the other end of the sofa, half turned so she was facing him. An awkward silence followed, neither of them apparently knowing where to begin. Finally Brenda spoke.

"Jerry, where have you been? I looked for you, but no one knew where you'd gone."

"I went away," was all he could bring himself to say. "But I'm back, I guess." Then he paused. "You looked for me?" he asked.

"Yes," she said, and looked down at her feet.

When she looked up, a gentleness glowed in her eyes.

"You've grown a mustache," she observed, as if she didn't know quite what to say. "I like it."

"You've cut your hair," he stammered. "It's nice."

They stared at each other for an awkward moment. Jerry could feel a great divide between them, like a sheet of ice, tall and wide and formidable, but brittle, as if the merest touch would shatter it. Both of them seemed hesitant to reach out and probe its thickness and strength. Finally, Brenda spoke softly.

"I know I hurt you, Jerry. I'm so sorry." She looked away and brushed a tear from her eye. "Was it because of me you went away?"

"No," he said, and he knew it wasn't a lie. "It was because of me."

"Jerry," she said, staring at him again, "there's something different about you, isn't there?"

"I suppose so," he said. "Life doesn't let you stay the same forever."

"No, it doesn't," she said softly, almost to herself.

"Your place looks great." He spoke clumsily, trying to change the subject before it got so heavy it ran aground. "You own the house?"

"No, I'm just renting."

"Oh," he said ponderously, as if she had made some profound remark.

"Can I get you something to eat?" she asked. "Have you had dinner?"

"Actually, I haven't," he confessed, suddenly realizing he was hungry.

"Come in the kitchen," she said, reaching out and taking his hand, "and I'll fix us something."

The touch of her fingers sent a thrill through his whole body, a feeling, he suddenly realized, he had never experienced with Julie. She pulled him up from the sofa and toward the kitchen and held on just a little longer than she needed to. Jerry's head was spinning. Of all the things he had imagined after Max's phone call, this certainly wasn't one of them. He almost felt he was having an out-of-body experience. He wanted to pinch himself to see if it was real. And all the while his heart was pounding like a drum. He was afraid Brenda might hear it—it was so loud in his own ears.

She led him to the kitchen table, a small rectangle too small for more than two, and busied herself with a tossed salad and a few apple slices while they both gathered their wits. Finally, she brought the salad and apple slices to the table, set a plastic container of dipping caramel between them, and sat down facing him.

"Hope you weren't expecting steak and baked potatoes on such short notice." She grinned.

"Frankly," he said, "I wasn't expecting anything. I didn't even know you lived here."

She stared at him in amazement. "You didn't know? Then what are you doing here?"

"It's a long story," he answered, shrugging his shoulders. "When I . . . came back, I looked for you in the phone book, but I didn't see a listing."

"I've got the number listed under 'L. McDonald.' That's my middle initial. No address. It's not safe for a single woman to put too much info in the phone book," she explained.

"Well," he went on, "when I didn't see your name there, I just figured you'd married Josh and his Corvette or moved back to Nebraska."

"No on both counts," she said with a grim laugh. "Josh was the second biggest mistake of my life. He talked a good show, but when I started digging behind the facade a bit, I found there wasn't much there except a whole load of ego."

"So what was your biggest mistake," he asked hesitantly, "if Josh only comes in second?"

"Breaking up with you."

They gazed at each other for a long, searching moment. Brenda seemed on the verge of tears, and Jerry could feel a lump in his throat the size of a grapefruit. Could this be real? he wondered. Was this really happening?

"Anyway," he said, lowering his eyes and scooping some caramel with an apple slice, "for the past two years I've been working out in West Valley. I've got this friend who—how shall I describe it?—who kind of looks out for me. He called last night and said he wanted me to come to this address before eight o'clock tonight. I had no idea who lived here."

"Is he some kind of private eye or something?"

"To tell you the truth, I have no idea," Jerry laughed. "Why?"

"Well, I just got home at 7:30, and I was going to leave again at 8:30."

"I'm sorry. I didn't know," Jerry faltered. "If you have to go . . ."

"No," she assured him. "It was nothing. I was just going to run over to my boss's for an hour or so. His wife invited me to their family Christmas party. I can call and tell them I've got company. It's no big deal. I think they're worried about me or something."

"Why?"

"Because I don't have any family here in Salt Lake. And I haven't really been dating much lately," she added with a blush.

"You haven't?" he asked incredulously. "I thought you'd have guys following you around all day long just begging to take you out."

"I had a boyfriend last summer," she admitted sheepishly. "Fortunately, he wasn't like Josh, but . . . well, he wasn't like you either. We got along okay, but he wanted to get married. I wanted him to also—just not to me."

Jerry grinned but didn't know what to say. "Maybe I'm not like me anymore either," he finally suggested. "You said there was something different about me."

"Not different in a bad way," she replied. "I just meant there's something in your eyes that wasn't there before. You look, well, more aware somehow, like some part of you woke up or something, if that makes any sense."

"It's just age," he quipped.

"No, it's more than that."

"So I take it you don't work at the light store anymore," he said, trying to steer the conversation away from his recent past.

"No. After I dumped Josh, things were a little tense there. Besides, Randy retired early—he wasn't feeling well—and turned the place over to his scheming son. The consensus among the employees was that Josh would run it into the ground within two years. I figured I'd better get out before things got really ugly. And they did. I talked with Stan—you remember, he used to work in shipping—anyway, he told me things were falling apart fast. Then, about a year ago, Randy died. I saw his obituary in the paper. I haven't checked, but I'm pretty sure Josh has gone out of business. As for me, I've been working at a credit union for a few years and volunteering a couple of evenings a week at the homeless shelter downtown."

This hit Jerry in the solar plexus, and for a moment he thought he was going to have a heart attack. Several times he'd almost been hungry enough to go wait in line for dinner at the shelter. But he hadn't had the patience. Now he was glad he'd gone hungry. Or at least part of him was. But in a corner of his heart he felt a stabbing pain. If he'd known she was there, he could have seen her, at least from afar, and known she was fine. But, of course, she would have probably seen him too, and he didn't want to think about that.

"Did I say something wrong, Jerry?" she asked.

He realized his feelings were written all over his face. "No, Brenda," he said. "I'm just sorry I didn't know where to find you sooner."

"So am I, Jerry."

They ate in silence for a few minutes, then Brenda suddenly looked at the clock on the microwave. "I'd better call Sylvia," she said, "to tell her I'm not coming."

"I don't want to keep you from your party," Jerry said, more out of politeness than because he really felt that way.

"I'd rather stay home," she told him, "unless you have to go."

"No, I can stay until you kick me out," he assured her.

"What if I don't?" she grinned.

"Then I'll be forced to do the gentlemanly thing and leave on my own at a decent hour," he said. "I'd hate for you to get the wrong impression about me."

"Me get the wrong impression of Jerry Carlson?" she asked with an impish grin. "I don't ever make the same mistake twice."

He looked at her and smiled, took a bite of salad, and figured he'd wake up soon and realize this had been nothing more than a wonderful dream. She got up, went to the phone, and called Sylvia. "Sorry I can't make it tonight," she said. "I've had company drop in. Thanks so much for the invitation, though." When she came back to the table, she was smiling.

"Where are you working, Jerry?" she asked. "My, we've got some catching up to do, don't we?"

"I manage a custom furniture shop," he said. "Before that I was managing some storage units. That's why I didn't have a phone number in the book. I lived at the facility and used the office phone for any personal calls. I didn't get my own phone until just after the most recent phone book came out."

"Furniture?" she asked.

"It's a wood shop."

"Sounds fun. How'd you get into that?"

"It's a long story, Brenda, but for now let's just say the owner was one of my customers at the storage units." He'd had a few minutes to sort things out now, and he wasn't so sure he was ready to tell Brenda anything else about Max. In fact, he wasn't sure he would ever tell her, or anyone else. The whole story belonged somewhere on the scale between unbelievable and outrageous.

"I still want to know how your friend found me, and how he knew I'd be here at eight," she said, almost reading his mind. When they were dating, they had often been on the same wavelength, so much so that they'd often started to say the exact same thing, only to stop short and laugh. Then Brenda would always say, "Great minds think alike . . . and so do ours." Jerry thought of that now and smiled.

"So do I," he told her. "So do I."

After the salad and apples, Brenda pulled a carton out of the freezer.

"Care for some ice cream?" she asked.

"Sure," he said. "Why not?"

She dished up a couple of generous bowls of something called "Outrageously Chocolate," and they went back into the living room. This time she sat close to him on the sofa.

"I should ask, I guess," she said coyly, "if you're unattached—or are you seeing somebody?"

"I was," he answered, "but, well, she wasn't like you."

"She must be extremely good-looking and intelligent, then," Brenda said with a grin.

"Something like that," Jerry replied.

An awkward silence followed. Jerry wasn't sure if he'd said the right thing. He wanted to tell her how beautiful she was, how much he'd longed to see her, how afraid he'd been that he'd never find anyone like her, but he knew he'd probably stumble over his words and make a mess of things.

"Can I see you again?" he said finally.

"Sure," she said, and then with a glint in her eye, she added, "I have an idea."

* * *

Christmas Eve

The next day Jerry was all nerves. He couldn't concentrate on work, and he couldn't sit still for ten seconds. Finally the workday ended, and Jerry drove nervously into Salt Lake City. He met Brenda in front of the Downtown Mission. She was waiting for him and reached up and gave him a quick hug when he arrived.

"Thanks for coming," she said.

A line of hungry, ragged men, women, and children flowed out the Mission's door and snaked down the street. It was the week of Christmas, and these people had nowhere to go—no warm home to return to, no friends to invite them in, no money to buy food with. On the drive into the city, Jerry had plenty of time to prepare himself for what he knew would be a difficult experience, but now that he saw them, he realized no amount of remembering could have prepared him for the desperation, despair, and emptiness he saw in these haggard faces. He knew the vacant look in many of the eyes, and he remembered the sense of being displaced from time and space, existing in a dimension where nothing changed, where hope was a stranger and the future was just a monotonous rerun of the past.

When they had parted the night before and Brenda had asked him if he would come to the shelter and help out, he had almost said no. But his desire to see her again outweighed his fear of the memories that might surface. He also knew, without question, that he couldn't afford to say no. How else would Brenda interpret his reluctance except as an unwillingness to serve the needy? He certainly couldn't tell her about the years he'd spent on the street. Not yet. Perhaps not ever. Without knowing it, she had him over the proverbial barrel, and now that he was here, the memories did indeed come flooding back—the bitter despair, the numbness of body and mind, the minute and temporary kindnesses of total strangers, the inability to think about anything but the next meal and the next night of dreamless sleep in the clearing up the canyon. That he had lived this way for three years was now a wonder to him. But he realized many of the people he was now staring at had lived like this far longer than three years.

Brenda looked up at him and studied his face. "What are you thinking, Jerry?" she asked.

"I'm thinking how hopeless these people must feel," he answered with difficulty.

"I think that every day," she replied. "It's what keeps me coming back. And I can't help but think there's got to be a better way to help them. Handouts just perpetuate the vicious cycle they're trapped in."

Jerry didn't know what to say. Of course there was a way out, he knew. But not everyone had a Max. And not everyone, Ron had taught him, wanted a Max.

The shelter's kitchen was in the basement, a large room with white walls, cafeteria tables, a stainless steel counter where volunteers disbursed food, and another where the patrons returned their dirty plates. Reverend Del Greco was behind the counter, getting ready to serve tonight's meal—beef stew with a roll and canned beans on the side, and pudding for dessert. Not fancy fare, but heavy and hot and loaded with calories. Del Greco greeted Brenda with a huge smile and a hug. She introduced Jerry, who received a hearty handshake and a pat on the shoulder.

"Thanks for coming to help," the reverend boomed. "We've got a big line tonight. Cold weather brings 'em out in droves." He sent Brenda off to help in the kitchen. He kept Jerry by his side at the serving counter.

"Till you've had more experience," he explained, "we'll keep you out of the kitchen. You'd probably just get in the way. That's why I stay out here." He laughed merrily. He was a heavy man, round and jolly like Santa Claus, but with wispy, dark hair and a heavy, black beard.

At the appointed hour, Del Greco opened the door, and the stream of hungry and homeless flooded in. Soon all the tables were full, and many sat on the floor against the walls. A few even took their trays outside into the cold. Jerry was sobered by the number of women and children who came through the line. He made sure the children walked away with an extra large portion of pudding.

"It's hardest the week of Christmas," Del Greco told him at one point. "Lots of these kids don't have anywhere to go. None of them are getting much from Santa. Most of them figure Santa can't find them if they don't have an address or a chimney. Kids are generally born with a healthy share of hope. They're terribly resilient, but it's hard to see how fast that hope gets depleted when their moms don't have any."

"I can imagine," said Jerry. He knew a little about living without hope.

"Jerry," said Del Greco, studying his face with a wrinkled brow, "do I know you from somewhere? Have you volunteered here before?"

"No, I've probably just got one of those faces," he answered, but he also figured the reverend had probably seen him a few times sitting on the planter box at the ZCMI crosswalk.

"Oh well," said Del Greco, shaking his head, "for a minute there I was sure I'd seen you somewhere, but I can't remember. I see so many faces every day, my brain's like a blender."

When the last of the evening's clientele had gone through the line, Brenda came out from the kitchen wiping her hands on an old apron. Her eyes glowed, and Jerry knew it wasn't because he was there. He was quite sure this look came from the difference she was making. She walked up to him and took his hand.

"Where did you two meet?" Del Greco asked.

"It's a long story," Brenda told him. "To make it short, we worked together about five years ago."

"I had a feeling the two of you didn't meet just yesterday," he said. "If you don't mind my being forward, you look like you belong together."

Brenda blushed, and Jerry grinned awkwardly. Then Del Greco leaned over and whispered in Jerry's ear. "Don't let go of her," he said. "She's as good as gold."

"Don't worry," Jerry told him. "I'm not that stupid."

Brenda wanted to know what the reverend had said, but Jerry made a motion like he was zipping his lips. Del Greco shrugged his shoulders and walked away.

"Ooh, men," Brenda exclaimed. "They're all the same."

"That's not what you were telling me last night," Jerry said.

Brenda laughed and pulled Jerry toward the counter. "Grab a plate, stranger," she said. "It's customary for the volunteers to eat with the patrons."

They took their trays to a table where two places had been vacated and sat next to a young mother and her two small children.

"Hi, Debbie," said Brenda. "How are you tonight?"

"I'm fine, Brenda," the woman answered. "I had a job interview yesterday."

"Great. Where?"

"Oh, just a warehouse out in Murray. They need people to do inventory."

"Temporary?"

"Yeah." She sounded both disappointed and hopeful.

"Well, go for it. It's a little cash, and it might open a door." She looked down at the oldest of the two children, a girl about five years old. "How's Lucy, Amanda?"

Amanda held up a ragged doll. "She's not feeling well today, Aunt Brenda," the little girl answered. "Her eye got tired and fell out."

"Oh, I'm sorry. Maybe Santa will bring you a new Lucy."

"I don't think so," Amanda answered. "Mommy says Santa isn't coming this year 'cause we're giving our toys to poor kids in Africa."

"That's a nice thing to do," said Brenda. "I'm sure Jesus would be proud of you."

"But Mommy says she might get a job. Then she might be able to get me a new dolly."

"And how's Jesse?" Brenda asked, leaning down so she was nose to nose with the younger child.

"Fine," he giggled.

"And how's Sport?"

"He bit me yesterday, on the finger." The little boy held up a stained, old brown puppy with stuffing leaking out of one leg.

"Well, Sport," said Brenda, "you'd better behave, because Jesse is one of my all-time favorite people. If you bite him again, we'll have you for dinner."

Jesse giggled and hugged the stuffed animal in a stranglehold. "No," he squealed. "You can't eat Sport. He wouldn't taste good."

"Would you like to meet my friend Jerry?" Brenda asked the kids.

"Sure," they said.

"Jerry Carlson," Brenda said, "this is Amanda Pochman and her brother, Jesse. And this is their mom, Debbie. Jesse and Amanda and Debbie, this is my friend Jerry."

"Hi," they said in unison.

Jerry just smiled in return and nodded his head. He didn't know what to say.

"Debbie's husband wasn't very nice to her, or to the kids," Brenda explained, "so they came here to live for a while until Debbie finds a job."

"I'm sorry," said Jerry. "I hope you find something soon."

"Thanks," said Debbie, "I'm sure I will." But Jerry thought the hope he could see in her eyes looked very fragile.

* * *

When they finished eating, they helped clean up in the kitchen, then walked out into the frigid night. Their breath hung in the air like little grey clouds.

"Let me guess," Jerry said. "Santa's going to bring Amanda Pochman a new dolly this year."

Brenda laughed. "Am I that transparent?" she asked.

"Only to those who have met you at least once," Jerry replied. She looked up at him warmly, and he put his arm around her waist.

Brenda had taken the bus to work and then to the shelter so Jerry could give her a ride home. When they got in the car, Jerry reached with his key for the ignition, but Brenda caught his hand and held it in hers.

"Not yet," she said. "Let's talk a minute before you get distracted with driving."

"Sure," he said.

"I didn't tell you last night, but I saw you once—I think it was four years ago—at Christmastime."

Suddenly Jerry's mouth went dry. He remembered the day as if it were yesterday, but he had been sure she hadn't noticed him. Now he would have to explain everything. He wasn't sure he was up to it, especially after the evening he'd just spent serving meals to people who looked all too familiar and whose expressions he'd seen before—in the mirror.

"It was Christmastime, maybe four years ago," she repeated, "and I saw you over by Crossroads Plaza."

Jerry just nodded. He couldn't think of anything to say.

"I was just crossing the street," she continued, "when I saw you by the door. I hurried to catch you. I could see you quite plainly. You put a bill in a beggar's cup, then you disappeared into the mall. I tried to catch you, but you were gone. I even yelled your name, but I couldn't see you in the crowd. I looked everywhere in the mall for you, but I couldn't find you."

Jerry was stunned. He'd assumed she was yelling after some other Jerry. He was flattered to think it was him she was thinking of, but she'd obviously been mistaken. "You're sure it was me?" he said finally, his voice barely a whisper.

"Oh, it was you," she answered. "You even had the mustache."

"I'm sorry," he stammered. "I don't remember."

"I thought you had gone away for a couple of years."

"I had," he said. "Maybe you're mistaken."

"It sure looked like you," she assured him.

He shook his head. How could he ever tell her the truth—that he was the beggar and not the generous donor?

"Oh well," she said, "at least I know this is you." She leaned over and gave him a kiss on the cheek.

He turned to look at her and found that she hadn't moved away. Her eyes met his, and the next thing he knew, their lips met, and they kissed for what seemed an eternity.

* * *

When they reached her house, she invited him in for some hot cocoa and Christmas cookies a neighbor had brought over. The cookies were a bit dry, but they dipped them in the cocoa and gazed at each other and were content.

"How's your family?" Jerry asked her.

"Same as ever. My dad's still making ends meet on the farm, working himself to death. Mom's gotten involved in all sorts of community things. And my little brother's almost ready to graduate from college. Can you believe it? He wants to go on to grad school, but Dad wants him to come back and take over the farm eventually. I don't think it'll ever happen."

"You see them often?"

"No," she said, and her eyes grew sad and distant. "About twice a year. I generally go back in the summer for a few days, and they come out to visit once in the winter, after all the farm work is pretty much done for the year. They don't like to travel."

"You miss them, don't you?"

"Of course I do," she said, "but Dad'll never leave the farm—I think they'll bury him out in the cornfield—and there's nothing for me there. I certainly don't want to take over the farm when Dad can't manage it anymore, and I wouldn't make much of a farmer's wife."

"Oh," he said, "what kind of a wife do you think you'd make then?"

"A socialite," she said, and grinned mischievously. "Or at least a social *climber*."

"Working at a credit union and volunteering at the homeless shelter—I'd say you're not going about this the right way."

"Hey, I always figured I'd find a toad somewhere and kiss him and turn him into a prince."

"You kissed one earlier tonight, and I don't think he's turned into anything but a rather boring furniture shop manager."

"I must be out of practice." She closed her eyes and puckered her lips for dramatic effect.

Jerry laughed, broke off a piece of dry cookie, and pressed it to her lips. "Yuck!" she exclaimed.

"I don't think this is a situation where practice will make perfect," Jerry suggested.

"Felt pretty perfect to me earlier," she said.

"Well, if you want to kiss the toad again, the toad's willing, but I don't think he'll ever turn into a handsome prince."

"Let's see," she said, leaning out over the small table.

Jerry met her halfway, and when they eventually parted, Brenda scrutinized him carefully.

"I think it's working," she pronounced. "You're looking better all the time."

When they finished their cocoa, Jerry pushed his chair back from the table.

"As much as I'd like to stay," he said, "I've got a couple of very busy days before Christmas, and I'm afraid I didn't get much sleep last night."

"You too, huh?" she said. "I suppose you're right, but can we do this again sometime—like maybe tomorrow?" She got his coat and walked with him to the door.

"What, the homeless shelter or the hot cocoa?" he asked.

"The kissing, you fool. If I'm going to turn you into a prince, I've got a lot of work ahead of me."

"Sure," he said. "Are you volunteering at the shelter tomorrow?"

"No. I'll be there the next day, Christmas Eve."

"Then let me take you to dinner tomorrow. And we can play Santa the next night."

"Sure," she said. "No argument from me."

"Where do you want to go?"

"Surprise me."

"I've never been able to surprise you," he protested.

"You certainly did last night when you showed up on the doorstep."

"I think I surprised me even more," he answered.

"Sometime you've got to tell me more about this friend of yours," she said. "What was his name?"

"Max."

"Max what?" she asked.

Suddenly Jerry realized he'd never asked.

"You know," he stammered, "I don't even know." His face must have been a study in perplexity because Brenda laughed and gave him a big hug.

"What kind of friend is this, anyway? He sends you back to me, and you don't even know his last name."

"I've never asked," Jerry confessed sheepishly. "We've always had, well, other things to talk about."

"What does he look like?"

Jerry looked at her and started chuckling to himself. "You won't believe this," he said.

"Let me guess," Brenda interrupted. "You've never met him."

Jerry shrugged sheepishly.

"Jerry," she said, a pensive look in her eyes, "is this perhaps an imaginary friend? Does your therapist know about this Max?"

"No," Jerry laughed, "but maybe she should."

"She?"

"Yeah, her name's Maxine, and I don't know what she looks like either. She doesn't come into the room until I'm lying on the couch. Then she sits behind my head and listens quietly and says 'Umm' fifty or sixty times a minute."

"Oh, you're hopeless," Brenda said, pushing him toward the door.

He put his hand on the knob, then turned and reached out with his other hand and pulled Brenda close. They kissed again, and then he opened the door and walked out into the cold.

"Jerry," she said when he was halfway to his car. He turned and looked up at her. "Whoever this Max is, tell him I'm grateful. I haven't been so happy in my entire life."

"I'll tell him," Jerry answered, then turned and walked away. After he heard the door close, he said softly to himself, "Maybe next year."

* * *

Later that night he lay in bed and stared at the ceiling. In spite of how exhausted he was, sleep was nowhere in sight. Still, he couldn't help wondering when he was going to wake up. His body tingled all over. It seemed impossible, but he had just spent two straight evenings with Brenda. Her face filled his mind, and he could still feel the touch of her hand on his fingers, her kiss on his lips, and her voice in his ears. How had Max known? He wanted to call, to use up the last of his three contacts. He had to know. But he knew Max wouldn't tell him, and he also knew when he used the last call, Max would be gone forever. He certainly didn't want that to happen now. So far Max had given him more than he'd believed possible. He didn't want that to end.

And then it hit him. Suddenly he felt sick inside. Yes, Max had given him so much, but Max would also ask him at some point to give it all back. Tears started in his eyes, and he cried out to the ceiling, "No! No! No! You can't do this to me, Max! No! Please, no!" He rolled over and buried his face in his pillow, and violent sobs shook his entire body. The pain was almost more than he could bear.

Finally, he regained control of himself, and for the first time he seriously believed Max wasn't just some rich guy who had ways of knowing where Jerry was and what he was doing. "Oh, you're cruel, Max," he said to the walls. "Too cruel. Maybe you *are* the devil. So what am I doing? Selling my soul for the things you're giving me?" But Jerry didn't want to believe that. Maybe Max wasn't the devil. Maybe he was some kind of angel. Jerry didn't consider himself a very religious person, but he had listened well enough in Sunday school when he was young to know how God often operated. He gave people things only to ask that they give them back—to prove their love for Him or to show they were worthy to live with Him someday.

Jerry thought things out carefully and decided that if this was true, he had two options. He could run away again, leave Brenda to avoid the awful pain that was sure to come later, or he could enjoy the time they had together and hope the memory of it would make the pain more bearable. He finally concluded he was no different from a husband whose wife had been diagnosed with terminal cancer. In such circumstances, there was no question what true love would do. So he would play the grieving husband. But there was one difference.

Brenda didn't know the diagnosis, and there was no way she would find out from him. He would enjoy every minute with her, never letting on to the terrible secret he held in his heart. It was a grim fate, but the alternative was to fade away in despair, to shrink from life rather than embrace it. He was sure this was not what Max intended.

Now more than ever he wanted to call his secret benefactor. He wanted to know who Max was, wanted to find out how Max had known where to find Brenda, wanted to know when and how, and most of all why he had to give her up. But he already knew Max's answers. He also considered calling just to get Max out of his life forever. He knew now he would receive a gift every Christmas, a gift he would find diffi- cult to part with but one he would eventually have to give back. Even though Max had not said so, he was fairly sure the point where he would have to give it all back was the third phone call. Max had told him he would be out of his life after the third call. Implied in this somewhere, Jerry felt, was Max's timetable for Jerry to pay up.

Life was not easy, Jerry concluded. But he also decided he would make the best of it. And somewhere in the darkness, sleep found him, and he flew again without wings. Brenda was with him, and this time he could see her there by his side, shining in the night sky like a comet.

* * *

The next morning Jerry awoke early and staggered out to the kitchen. He grabbed a container of yogurt from the fridge, a spoon from the dishwasher, and sat down at the table. There in front of him was his Bible, opened up to the Gospel of St. Luke, and underlined were the words "For unto whomsoever much is given, of him shall be much required." Suddenly, Jerry lost his appetite.

In spite of the lack of sleep and the sobering realization that had fallen on him the night before, Jerry was still as excited as he'd been in years. When he got to work that morning, he felt as if someone had slipped him an overdose of caffeine. He was animated and energetic and couldn't sit still for ten seconds. At about eleven o'clock, Cal dropped in to see how the Christmas crunch was going, and after a couple of minutes, he pulled Jerry aside and said, "Who put a quarter in you, son? Are you in love or something?"

Jerry laughed and said, "How'd you guess?"

"It wasn't hard." Cal seemed both pleased and perplexed. "You were a bit down last time I saw you. I take it, then, it isn't Julie?"

"No." Jerry looked down at the floor, then back up at Cal and gave him a look that said, "I hope I haven't messed things up too much."

"Does she know?" Cal asked.

"Not yet. It's only been a couple of days."

"Love at first sight?"

"Well, yes and no," Jerry answered. "It was love at first sight, but that was more than five years ago."

"Five years ago?" Cal mused, scratching his head. "If I remember your story, it was about five years ago your life went in the tank over some gal. This wouldn't be the same one, would it?"

"Same one."

"And you still want her after what she did to you?"

"No hard feelings," Jerry said with a shrug. "She feels bad about it."

"And she wants you?"

"Yes, I think she does." Something about telling Cal, hearing himself say it out loud, made the whole head-spinning experience of the past two days suddenly very real. Yes, Jerry told himself, Brenda really did want him. It made his heart almost burst just thinking about it. A grin broke out on his face. He just couldn't keep it in.

"I'm happy for you, Jerry." Cal put a hand on his arm. "Let me tell Julie about it, okay?"

"You don't think I should?"

"No, I know her better than you do. I'll tell her, though, that you wanted to."

"Fine with me."

* * *

Julie apparently took it well, at least publicly. Jerry never found out what Cal said, but things were just fine at work. He was sure Julie was disappointed, but she didn't let it show. And Cal must have said something to the other employees because they stopped commenting, and one or two of them even asked Jerry on the sly who his new flame was. They seemed genuinely interested. He figured he'd leave them in the dark for a while. Besides, it wouldn't be wise to bring Brenda by the shop for introductions just yet, not so soon after Julie found out about her. Maybe sometime in January.

Jerry and the rest of the crew worked late the evening of December 23. When he finally left, he drove straight to Brenda's. She was waiting for him, and he took her to his favorite Mexican restaurant. When they got back to her place, she went into the bedroom and came out with a couple of large sacks.

"Guess what we're doing tomorrow?" she said.

"Serving food?" he hazarded a guess.

"Yeah, but what else?"

"If I remember right, you said you needed practice kissing toads," Jerry told her.

"Before that."

"Playing Santa with a little girl and her brother?"

"What a memory!"

She reached into one of the bags, pulled out a pair of triple-x green sweatpants and a bright red sweatshirt that was roughly the same size, and handed them to Jerry.

"Who are these for?" he asked. "Andre the Giant?"

"You," she said with an impish grin. "You and several pillows."

"Oh," he said slowly as the light went on in his head.

She then pulled out another set of oversized sweats, these with red pants and a green shirt.

"For *moi*," she said.

She reached into the other bag and extracted a Santa hat with flowing white hair and a curly, white beard attached.

"For you."

Next came another hat and beard.

"We can't play Santa without costumes," she said.

"You think we'll fool anyone with neon sweats and dime-store beards?" he said.

"We're not trying to fool them," she said. "We're trying to make them smile. I figure this ought to do it. Besides, do you know how much a real Santa suit costs, even to rent?"

She made him put on the giant sweats, then stuffed a couple of pillows inside, put on the cheap hat and beard, and looked at him. All of a sudden, she started to giggle and couldn't stop. Jerry felt absolutely silly. Finally, when she gained enough control to speak, she dragged him into the bedroom and stood him in front of the mirror.

"What do you think?" she asked.

Now he was the one who couldn't stop laughing. He looked like a bright red and green basketball with a hat and beard.

"We'll just tell the kids we're Santa's helpers," she said.

Jerry made her put on her outfit. Then they stood in the living room and stared at each other and laughed until their sides hurt. Finally they reached for each other and embraced, and that made them laugh even harder, because they couldn't get close enough to kiss without losing balance and almost tipping over—and anyway, the beards got in the way.

When they finally took off the costumes and collapsed exhausted on the sofa, Jerry was as happy as he had ever been. He'd forgotten how funny and spontaneous Brenda could be. With her, there was always something new.

* * *

The next night, Christmas Eve, they met again at the Downtown Mission. Jerry had left his car at work and taken the bus downtown this time. Brenda brought the costumes, and they found an empty room upstairs where they put them on. When they walked down into the kitchen, Reverend Del Greco took one look at them and let out a howl.

"Look what the dogs dragged in," he said. "It's my cousin Constantine and his wife, Sofie."

He walked up to Brenda, pulled her beard down, and gave her a big kiss on the cheek. "Well, if it isn't our little Brenda. Put on a little weight, have you? No dessert for you tonight. And who's your twin brother?" He pulled down Jerry's beard and gave a hearty laugh. "We fed you too much last time, too. You're starting to look like me."

Del Greco put both Brenda and Jerry at the serving counter this time, and he went back to help in the kitchen. When the doors finally opened and the stream of the hungry and homeless poured in, Jerry was amazed at the many grins they coaxed out of weathered and weary faces. When Debbie and her two kids came through the line,

Amanda took one look at Brenda and said, "You're not Santa Claus. Neither of you. You're Aunt Brenda and her friend Harry." She nodded with a knowing look.

Brenda laughed and said, "We're just Santa's helpers tonight, honey. He's too busy to serve food, so we're helping out."

When all were served, Brenda slipped off to the room upstairs and came back with a plastic shopping bag. She and Jerry approached the table where Debbie and the kids sat and knelt down next to Amanda.

"Hey, Mandy," Brenda said, "guess who I saw today?"

"Harry," Amanda declared, "and he's right there."

"I suppose he is kind of hairy," Brenda laughed. "But guess who else I saw?"

"Who?"

"Santa Claus."

"Really?"

"Would Aunt Brenda tell you a lie?"

Jerry looked and saw Brenda's fingers crossed behind her back. He reached over and tried to untwist them, but she clenched her fist and went on.

"Santa said he might not know where to find you later tonight, because he's really busy and you just moved and all, but he gave me something for you."

She pulled a box out of the plastic bag. It was wrapped in Santa paper and decked with ribbons and bows. She handed it to Amanda.

The little girl tore the paper off in a flash, opened the box, and there staring up at her was a doll, just like the old Lucy, but brand-new. Amanda pulled the doll out of the box carefully, held it to her neck, and hugged it so hard Jerry thought its eyes would pop out too.

"Thanks, Santa," the little girl whispered.

"I'll tell him, sweetie," Brenda assured her.

Jerry looked at Jesse, whose face was lost somewhere between anticipation and fear.

"Santa didn't forget you either, Jesse," Brenda told him.

She reached into the bag and produced another wrapped box. Jesse tore it apart and discovered a stuffed bear.

"Santa thought Sport could use some company," Brenda told him.

He hugged the bear, a look of total ecstacy in his eyes.

"What do you say, Jess?" Debbie prompted him.

"Thanks, Bwenda," he said.

With tears starting in her eyes, Debbie looked at her friend. No words would come out, so she just reached out and squeezed Brenda's hand.

"Things'll get better, Debbie," Brenda told her. "Just give it some time."

Debbie nodded, then hugged her two little ones. Brenda took Jerry's hand and pulled him away. "Let's leave them by themselves," she said. "Besides, I've got to change into my toad-kissing outfit. Can't do it with all this stuff on."

Jerry laughed, and they headed up to the empty room where they had put on the Santa costumes. When the sweats and pillows and beards and hats were all stowed away in the garbage sack Brenda had brought them in, she reached for Jerry's neck and hugged him tight.

"Best Christmas Eve I've had in years," she whispered.

She reached out with one hand and flipped the light switch. Suddenly the room was dark, except for the soft glow coming through the window. The moon was nearly full and riding high in the sky. Jerry put his arms around Brenda's waist, pulled her close, and kissed her.

"It's working," she said. "You're looking better all the time."

"The lights are off," Jerry reminded her.

"I see better in the dark," she replied, then reached up and kissed him again.

Suddenly Jerry knew something in his heart. It started quietly, then grew until it almost overwhelmed him. His whole body tingled. It was as if he could see the future, or at least part of it. He was standing before an open door. On the other side was a brilliant light and an incredible warmth. Behind him was total darkness and cold loneliness. He knew he had to step through or he would fall back into the pit from which he'd been pulled.

"Brenda," he said, and his own voice surprised him, "will you marry me?"

She pulled away slightly and looked at him with surprising intensity. Her face was smiling, but a tear slipped from her eye and coursed slowly down her cheek.

"I don't deserve you," she said, "not after all the pain I caused you, but yes, I will, if you really want me. And I promise I'll spend the rest of my life trying to make you happy."

He hugged her tight. "Let's forget the past," he said. "I wasn't worth marrying before anyway. Don't know that I am now, either, but it sure feels right."

"It does," she agreed.

They stood for a long time in the moonlight, holding each other, and Jerry knew deep inside that this moment could never have meant so much or been so right if he hadn't been through the difficult years on the street. And somehow it seemed appropriate to be holding onto the brilliant hope of a new life just a few feet above the heads of those whose pain and hopelessness were a poignant reminder of what his own life had been just a short time before. Suddenly he felt Brenda's dream from so long ago reach out and envelop him. The pain was gone, and in its place was a new feeling. It was not pity, but compassion, and he knew somehow that his life would never be the same.

Finally Brenda pushed away from his embrace and looked him in the eye. "I don't know about you," she said in typical Brenda fashion, "but I can't stand it any longer. I've got to tell somebody."

"Who?"

"How about Reverend D?"

"Okay," he said.

"In fact," Brenda added, "let's ask him to marry us."

"Okay," Jerry agreed. He hadn't had time to work out any of the details yet. "When?"

"When what?"

"When shall we get married?"

"Can you think of any reason to wait?" she asked him.

"Not unless you want a big fancy reception or something," he answered.

"You know me better than that," she told him. "I just need enough time to fly my parents and my brother out. How about New Year's Eve?"

"Works for me," he said.

"Jerry, do you have any family you want to invite? Cousins, aunts, uncles?"

"None I'm close to," he answered. "My grandparents are gone. My mom was an only child, but my dad had a brother who lived somewhere in New England. I can't even remember where. I only met him a couple of times, and that was when I was still in elementary school. My dad and his brother were opposites in many ways and were never close. I don't even know if Uncle Bob ever married or had any kids. But there are a couple of people I'd like to invite. I'd like my old boss at the storage units to be my best man, and I'd like Cal, the owner of the furniture shop, to be there too."

"I'm sorry your parents can't be here," Brenda said. "I hope they would have approved."

"I can't imagine they wouldn't have," Jerry exclaimed. "They'd want me to be happy, and I am."

* * *

The good reverend was so excited at the news he stood on a chair and banged a serving spoon on the bottom of an empty pan to get everyone's attention, then announced their engagement to all the patrons who were still there. He was also extremely pleased to perform the marriage. They decided the best time would be just before dinner on the thirty-first, when all the patrons were there, waiting for their meals. Brenda told Del Greco that it would ensure a short and to-the-point ceremony. He laughed merrily and agreed. His reputation for long-winded sermons was surpassed only by his generosity.

After they made a few arrangements with the reverend, Brenda drove Jerry home. On the way he asked her if they could drop by the furniture shop first. He'd been planning a little surprise all day, even before he'd decided to pop the question.

"I forgot something I have to take care of," he told her. When they arrived, he offered to show her around. "May as well see where your future husband spends his days," Jerry explained.

He took her into the office, which, on the heels of the busy Christmas season, was snowed under by a paper blizzard, and then led her back into the shop. He took his time explaining each machine and what it did. Then he took her into the small showroom and let her walk around admiring the various pieces. She stopped especially long in front of a curio cabinet, and he could see the wheels turning.

"You like this?" he said.

"Oh," she answered lightly, "just letting my imagination run away with me. You know me and decor."

"It's yours," he said.

"Oh, no," she shook her head pensively. "I'm sure I can't afford it."

"I didn't say you had to buy it."

She gave him a curious look, as if she hadn't heard him right.

"Merry Christmas," he said. "It's your gift."

"Oh, Jerry," she exclaimed, "I can't. It's too expensive. I'm sure you've got better things to do with your money—like buy me a ring."

They both laughed, but Jerry was adamant. "I've got enough money for a ring and this cabinet and a few other things. Besides," he added, "I don't have to pay the price on the sticker."

She looked at him, then back at the curio cabinet, then back at him. "Are you sure?"

"Sure I'm sure," he said. "I've got quite a bit saved up. I was just waiting for the right investment, and I won't find a better one than this."

"You could get a newer car," she teased.

"It's yours," he repeated.

"You're serious, aren't you?"

"Repeat after me," he responded. "Thank you, Jerry, for the nice Christmas gift."

Instead, she hugged him so tight he empathized with Amanda's new doll.

"I can have it delivered anytime," he said.

"Where to, though?" she asked. "My place or yours?"

"Yours," he said with a wry smile. "I don't think you'll like my place very well."

She looked at him obliquely. "That bad, huh?"

"Remember, I'm interior design impaired."

"How could I forget?" She thought for a minute. "But that makes your commute a lot longer. What if we look for a new place? A new start for both of us."

"Maybe we should," he said. "Maybe we should."

* * *

When they finally arrived at his apartment, he was a little reluctant for her to see it.

"It's quite late," he said. "You probably need to be getting home, don't you?"

"You afraid I might scare Santa Claus away or something?" she said sarcastically. "Come on, Jerry, it can't be that bad."

He gave her an "I surrender" look and led her to the door. He unlocked it, opened it, flipped on the lights, and cringed.

"I was right," Brenda informed him. "It's not that bad. It's worse!"

Suddenly Jerry saw his little cave through her eyes. It wasn't just a "guy's apartment." It had "former homeless person" written all over it in bold letters. At least it wasn't messy, perhaps because there was so little to make a mess with. The tree, of course, looked pathetic, but the lack of everything else glared accusingly at him. The furniture was spare, the walls were bare, and the place had absolutely no personality—not even a refrigerator magnet to liven up the kitchen.

"Are you sure somebody lives here?" Brenda asked.

"Just us escaped inmates," Jerry answered.

"So that's where you 'went away' to."

"Well, it had to come out sometime."

"So I'm rescuing you from this halfway house? At least I believe you now about being able to afford the curio cabinet," she said, and started giggling. "Jerry, you really do need a woman in your life. Maybe three or four."

"Wasn't polygamy banned in Utah a hundred years or so ago?"

"In your case, I think they just might make an exception," she suggested. "Don't tell me you've only got one shirt and one pair of jeans."

"Two," he said, and she looked at him like maybe he was serious, then they both started laughing. "Old habits are hard to break," he said at length.

* * *

Later that night, awake in bed again and unable to sleep, Jerry marveled at the turn his life had taken in just three days. It seemed impossible, he thought, but in a mere week he would be married to someone he had given up hope of ever seeing again, someone he had been *afraid* of seeing. But now she was marrying him. Was this possible? Of course it was, he told himself. Because of Max. And someday, some undisclosed day in the future—maybe next month or next year or twenty years from now—he would have to give Brenda back. The pain of this thought stabbed at his heart like an icy knife, but he seemed impervious to it now, and he wondered at this. And suddenly it occurred to him his love for Brenda was different now than it had been those five and a half long years ago. Because he knew she was a gift and because he knew that gift would someday be taken back, his love was completely void of the possessiveness, the self-centeredness that had dominated his heart before. If Brenda would have him, he would enjoy every day, every minute of their life together, but he would not seek to possess her. He just wished to be with her, to make her happy, to give her joy—until the day he would have to give her up. And suddenly he realized what a liberating, healing, all-consuming love this really was.

With that peace in his heart, Jerry finally drifted off to sleep, and once again he dreamed. He dreamed of the brightly lit tree out in the forest, and underneath it was a package. It had his name on it, but when he tried to open it, he found he couldn't. Then an all-too-familiar voice spoke from behind him. "It's not yours to open, Jerry. It's yours to give." And in the morning when he woke up and stumbled into the kitchen for a glass of juice, there on his tiny table was that same gift with his name on it. He tried to open it again, and this time the wrapping paper tore away easily. He lifted the lid, and inside was a card and a smaller box. The card said, *Congratulations, Jerry,* and the box contained a diamond ring, his mother's wedding ring. He recognized it immediately, and he also was certain his mother had been buried with it on her finger.

fourth christmas

··

The Envelope and the Key

Brenda quit her job at the credit union in November because Jerry was making plenty of money, and besides, she wanted time to get both herself and the nursery ready before the baby arrived in mid-January. They didn't know whether it was going to be a boy or a girl. Brenda had an ultrasound in September, but they decided to have the technician just write down the gender and seal it up in an envelope. If for any reason they needed to know, they could always look, but they both kind of wanted to be surprised with their first child. Not knowing did present a few problems, though, such as in buying baby clothes and in trying to figure out a name, but they covered their bases as well as they could. They bought a few either-or outfits— yellows and greens—as well as a pink one and a blue one. They could either return the unneeded outfit or give it away as a baby gift—or maybe even save it till next time, assuming they had the opposite sex on the second go-around. And they decided on two names they liked. If it was a boy, Brenda joked that they should call him Max, after Jerry's mysterious friend, and if it was a girl, Maxine, after his therapist. In the end, they agreed on Jeffrey and Megan.

They had found a nice little rambler about halfway between the Wood Nook and the credit union and had moved in on New Year's day. Mostly it was Brenda's things they had moved, as Jerry had few possessions, but what mattered most to them was that they were together. Brenda's family had stayed for a day or two after the wedding, just long enough to get to know Jerry a bit. Brenda's father was a practical man of the earth and immediately took a liking to his new son-in-law, but they had to get back to the farm, they said, and left long before they wore out their welcome. The newlyweds then took a couple of days off work and went on a short honeymoon to Park City. When they got back, they were busy with their jobs and with the more important task of making each other happy.

When Jerry first learned they were expecting, it gave him something new to think about—not only the major increase in responsibility raising a child would entail, but also the sobering thought that this was one more thing Max would eventually ask him to give up. And that point shed a whole new light on parenthood. This new child, he realized, was not really his. He or she was simply on loan for a while, and Jerry and Brenda would be expected to do their best to raise him or her before yielding up that responsibility.

December rolled around, and with it came the busy season at the Wood Nook. Jerry was so absorbed with work and so involved in preparing to become a father he almost forgot to turn on his cell phone. Brenda had asked him a few times during the year about his mysterious friend, but he had always talked around the subject without saying much. When she joked again on December 21 about naming their baby Max, Jerry nearly jumped out of his skin. He'd let three whole days go by without turning on the phone.

"Max!" he screamed. "I forgot."

He jumped up from the table where they'd been peacefully eating dinner, ran into the bedroom, rummaged through his sock drawer, and came running out with the phone. He turned it on, then groaned. The battery was dead. So was the spare. All this time Brenda was laughing so hard she almost went into labor.

"Jerry Carlson," she said at last, "what on earth are you doing?"

"I was expecting a call," he explained sheepishly.

"We have a phone there on the wall," she reminded him.

"It's Max," Jerry told her. "He always calls me before Christmas on the cell phone."

"Aha, finally zum information about dee myzterious Max," she said with a bad Eastern European accent. "And vy duss he only call on dee zell phone?"

"He just does."

Jerry retreated to the bedroom again, found the battery charger, and plugged it in.

"Why don't you just call him?" Brenda suggested.

Jerry didn't know quite how to explain this one, so he shrugged and said, "He doesn't want me to."

Brenda just shook her head. It was obvious she had a thing or two she wanted to say to Max if she ever got to meet him. But since Jerry had never met him either, she didn't press it.

* * *

The next morning, Jerry put the phone on his belt and went off to work. The Wood Nook was swamped with rush orders again this Christmas, and Jerry was so busy he almost didn't hear the phone when it rang. After three rings he realized it was the Max phone, as he'd come to call it, and he snatched it up and pushed a button.

"Hi, Max," he said, and a giant knot formed in his stomach. He hadn't had time to think about what Max might ask of him this year, but now that the call had come, he was suddenly nervous.

"Quite a year you've had, Jerry," said the familiar voice.

"Why don't you come over for Christmas dinner?" Jerry offered. He figured it didn't hurt to try.

"Sorry, already got plans," Max answered.

"Somehow I knew you would."

"You aren't offended, are you?"

"Me?"

"Although I suppose Brenda would like to know a bit more about me."

"It's crossed her mind."

"Well," said Max, "you know it's not good to have secrets in a marriage."

"So I've heard."

"Then why haven't you told Brenda everything about your past?"

"Well, it's kind of hard to believe."

"You're not a good liar, Jerry."

"Just good at changing the subject."

"Speaking of which," said Max, "how's business?"

"Absolutely nuts. We'll do better this year than last."

"Good, glad to hear it."

"I suppose you know we're expecting."

"So I heard. Boy or girl?"

"You tell me, Max."

"How would I know?"

"Same way you know everything else about me."

"You're not that hard to predict, Jerry."

"Thanks. Same to you."

Max paused. "Hmm. I hadn't ever thought of me that way."

"So what's the gig this year? You've got a big job trying to top last year's request. By the way, thanks. I'd ask how you knew, but I already know the answer."

"Well, I don't ever really try to 'top' anything."

"We're very happy," Jerry said. "I do appreciate it, Max. But I know someday you're going to ask me to give her up."

"Let's not dwell on the inevitable, okay, Jerry?"

"I try not to."

"It's all for the best, you know. But where were we? Oh, yes, this year's little favor."

"Favor?"

"Whatever. This year, Jerry, two things. First, I want you to tell Brenda about the time you were, well, 'away.'"

Jerry gulped. "Everything?"

"Everything, including me."

"Oh boy," Jerry muttered. "She really will think I need a shrink."

"Maxine?" A hearty laugh erupted from the cell phone. "She's doing well, thank you."

"You're impossible, Max. So what's part two?"

"You'll be getting an envelope one day soon. Just open it and follow the instructions."

"That's it?"

"That's it."

"What's in the envelope, Max?"

"Nice talking to you again, Jerry."

"Max!"

"Oh, and by the way, Jerry, I know Brenda was just teasing, and it really would mean a lot—kind of a token of appreciation, you know—if you were to name him after me. But don't do it, okay? It'd be bad form."

Jerry laughed as the line went dead. But that night when he got home, he hunted high and low for electronic surveillance devices.

"Jerry, what on earth?" Brenda asked, mildly amused.

"Bugs," he said. "That's the only way he can know all the things he knows."

"Who?"

"Max."

"Your imaginary friend?"

"Brenda," he said, "it's time we had a talk." He was standing on the kitchen table, looking at the light fixture.

"Finally," she sighed. "I was wondering when you'd come clean about all this strange behavior, but please get down off the table first. I'm afraid you're going to break your neck."

So they sat on the sofa, and Jerry told Brenda all about how his life had fallen apart after she'd left him.

"You remember I told you I went away?" he began. "Well, it was more emotional than physical."

He watched her eyes as the story unfolded, and when he got to the part about seeing her at the mall, she had a baffled look on her face.

"But I'm sure it was you," she protested.

"Oh, it was me all right," he assured her, "but I was the one with the shaggy beard and the cup and cardboard sign. I was scared to death you'd look at me and recognize me. I did get a twenty-dollar bill, though," he added, "right before you yelled my name. But when I looked up at you, someone must have taken it. It was gone from my cup."

She just shook her head and stared at him. "I don't know what to say, Jerry. I knew I'd hurt you, but I had no idea . . ."

"It's all in the past," he told her. "Not forgotten, but certainly forgiven. But the best part's still to come. You haven't heard about Max yet."

He then launched into an account of how he'd picked up the ringing cell phone in the bushes and all that had happened that first Christmas. When he finished, she just shook her head and laughed.

"I don't blame you for not telling me," she said. "If you weren't such a lousy liar, I wouldn't believe a word of it. So, what happened the next year?"

"I got a new job. And last year I got you."

"What about this year? You think he'll call?"

"He already did. Today."

A worried look came suddenly to her eyes. "And?"

"And I'm supposed to tell you all about my past and my good friend Max."

"That's it?"

"No. There's an envelope on its way."

"Uh-oh. What do you suppose . . ."

"Could be anything," said Jerry, "but there's a catch."

"What do you mean?"

Jerry took a deep breath. This wasn't going to be easy. "Max isn't just giving me all these things free of charge. There are certain conditions."

"Such as?"

"I can only call him three times."

"And you've already called him how many?"

"Twice."

"Oh. I see. Anything else?"

"Yeah. At some point I have to give back everything I get from his phone calls."

It took a minute for this to sink in. Then a tear sprang from her eye.

"Jerry," she said, "that would be pretty much everything. Your job, me, the baby."

"I know."

"That's hard."

"Well, I had to ask myself a tough question last Christmas," he said. "Do I turn you away and give up all the joy we might have together, or do I choose the joy for as long as we have together and then give it up? It really wasn't much of a decision."

"You know, you didn't even ask me about it. Did you consider I had a stake in this too?"

"Sure, but I didn't know quite how to tell you about it. You would have thought I was telling you a whopper. Besides, would your answer have been any different?"

What could she say? She put her head on his shoulder and didn't speak for a long while. At length she looked up at him and smiled. "You're a good man, Jerry Carlson."

"Oh, by the way," he said, "Max had one more request, more of an afterthought, but I think he was serious."

"What?"

"He said that in spite of your sincere desire, we shouldn't name the baby Max."

She laughed. "I like this Max. So modest. But it'll probably be a girl anyway."

"Don't be so sure," Jerry answered.

"Why?"

"Max called the baby a *him*. He said not to name *him* Max."

"You're sure he wasn't just referring to the baby generally as a male—you know, the way people do?"

"Max wouldn't make that kind of mistake."

"You're sure?"

"Well, we'll see. But if I had to bet . . ."

"Well, let's go buy some more blue outfits, then."

* * *

On Christmas Eve, a plain manila envelope addressed to Jerry arrived at the house. When Brenda checked for the mail midafternoon, there it was, and she was tempted to open it. She stared at it for several minutes, wishing she had x-ray vision, but eventually she propped it up against the napkin holder on the kitchen table. Jerry, she knew, would be a bit late that night—several last-minute orders to get out the door before Christmas—and they had plans for the evening. At Reverend Del Greco's request, they were playing Santa's helpers again, but this year Brenda wouldn't need a pillow to look the part. She had continued volunteering at the shelter even after quitting her job at the credit union, and Jerry joined her most evenings. They would have to take turns soon, she knew, once the baby came.

Jerry arrived even later than he'd hoped, and they had to hurry to get to the shelter before all the patrons were finished eating, so Brenda didn't mention the envelope. She knew Jerry would want some time and peace and quiet to open it. They hurriedly put on their ridiculous outfits, piled into the car, and drove like flying reindeer into downtown Salt Lake. Del Greco met them at the door and gave Brenda a big hug.

"We've got a huge crowd tonight," he said. "Word got around that Santa's helpers are making an appearance. I just hope his sack's full enough." He handed Jerry a large, bulging bag.

Brenda had helped Del Greco raise some money to buy gifts for all the kids who frequented the shelter with their parents, most of them single parents. Knowing she couldn't please everyone, she had finally decided on a stuffed animal for each child, then proceeded to buy about twenty percent more than she estimated were there on an average night. She hoped it would be enough.

Del Greco led them into the dining area, and a big cheer went up. The room was packed. "Santa's helpers have arrived," he yelled.

He led them to two chairs in the corner, then announced that they would be distributing gifts to the children, beginning with the youngest. That way none of the littlest children would go without. Jerry noticed that stacked behind the chairs was an enormous pile of quilts. He looked questioningly at Del Greco.

"I contacted LDS Humanitarian Services," he said with a shrug. "Asked them if they wanted to help out the homeless. They said they could donate a hundred hand-tied quilts. They also gave us a truckload of food."

So Brenda and Jerry sat together in their silly costumes and handed out stuffed animals to the kids and a quilt to each mother. Many of the women who came through the line hugged Brenda and whispered congratulations in her ear. After all the children and women had come through, the men who were alone and wanted a warm quilt came forward, somewhat embarrassed, to accept Santa's gift.

Debbie Pochman and her two children were long gone by now. The temporary job she'd interviewed for the year before had led to a permanent position, then a promotion. Brenda had kept in touch, and they had invited her and the kids over for dinner a couple of times during the year. Jerry had even tried lining her up with one of the woodworkers at the Nook, but she wasn't ready yet. She'd had enough of men for a while, perhaps for a lifetime, she said. There were other "special" cases Brenda would have liked to get involved in, but the prospects of impending motherhood kept her from overcommitting both her time and her emotional attachment.

By the time they were finished handing out gifts and visiting with many of the regular patrons, they were tired and just wanted to spend some quiet time together. But Brenda suspected their evening would not be quite as relaxing as they both hoped it would be.

"There's an envelope waiting for you at home," she said when they reached the car.

Jerry stopped and gave her a questioning look.

"So, what's in it?" he asked.

"How would I know? I only open your mail when it's bills."

He smiled at this.

"But it's got a key in it," she added with a mischievous grin.

"Shoulda known," he said.

"I couldn't help it," she protested weakly. "I felt the lump when I picked it up. It was pretty easy to tell what it was."

"Maybe it's a key to a new mansion up on the bench."

"Maybe you're dreaming," she replied.

"We'll soon find out," he said with a heavy sigh. He wasn't sure he wanted to know.

* * *

When they got home, Brenda picked up the envelope and handed it to him.

"You want to be alone?" she asked.

"No," he said. "No secrets between you and me, right?"

"Then let me open it," she coaxed.

He handed her the envelope with a shrug. She tore open the seal and pulled out a piece of paper with a key taped to the bottom of it. She stared at the paper for a minute and turned three shades of pale.

"You'd better sit down," she said, handing him the paper.

He took it and read the brief message: *Jerry, give Cal your two-week notice, then go to this address.*

"He wants you to quit your job?" Brenda asked, incredulous. "Of all the nerve! The baby's due in three weeks!"

Now Jerry did sit down. He stretched his feet out in front of him and tipped his head back and looked at the ceiling. "What on earth?" he asked himself.

"What if you don't do as he asks?" Brenda wanted to know.

"I'm not sure, but I think it means it's all over."

"What's all over?"

"My contact with Max," he said. "I assume it means everything goes back at that point."

"He's really got you between a rock and a hard place, doesn't he?" Jerry could tell his wife was none too pleased.

"Remember what happened last Christmas because I followed his instructions?" Jerry suggested.

"How can I forget?" she said, patting her stomach. Then she grinned. "Well, I guess we don't have a choice, do we?"

"We've always got a choice," Jerry answered. "But after last year and the two years before, I've got to trust him."

"Well, just warn me if Max asks you to jump off a tall building," she said. "But I'm going with you. The note didn't say you had to go alone. If there's some other woman from your past at this address, I want to be there. I mean, he gave you a key this time!"

"What other woman?" Jerry asked.

"Hey, I wasn't the one you kissed in high school," she reminded him. "And I wasn't one of the hundreds you chased in your college classes."

"Hundreds?" he laughed. "In my dreams."

"I thought you didn't dream back then," she teased. "Maybe we'd better have a talk about your past."

* * *

The day after Christmas, Jerry called Cal and asked if he could see him at home. Cal told him to come right over if he wanted, so Jerry did.

"I don't know how to explain this," he told the older man, "but I've got to quit."

"Better job come your way?" Cal asked.

"No," Jerry answered. "I can't think of a better job, other than maybe yours or Bill Gates's."

"Just got itchy feet?" Cal probed.

"No," Jerry said flatly. "Cal, I'd like to stay on, but I can't. I can't explain why, but I have to go."

"You rob a bank or something?"

"Wish I had," said Jerry. "Then at least I'd have an excuse—and enough money to live on for a while."

"Well, Jerry," he said, "I know you pretty well by now, and if you say you can't explain it, I'll believe you. But we'll all miss you."

"I'll stay for a couple of weeks to help you with the transition," Jerry offered.

"We'll survive," Cal assured him. "But don't make yourself scarce. Drop in when you get a chance."

"I will. And Cal, I can't tell you how much this job has meant to me. I owe you more than you'll ever know."

"Sure, sure," Cal scoffed. "It's not like I haven't enjoyed having some freedom. You've been worth every penny, Jerry, believe me."

* * *

The Wood Nook was open Saturdays until two. After Christmas, however, business slowed down substantially, so Jerry took off early that first Saturday. He and Brenda drove out to the address Max had sent, a location west of the Salt Lake downtown area, which told Jerry it was no mansion up in the foothills. After driving around for a few minutes, they finally decided the building they were looking for was an old warehouse, somewhat dilapidated; empty, but not yet vandalized. No gang graffiti or broken windows were visible from the street. There were no numbers on the warehouse, but this had to be the place. No other buildings nearby fit the address.

"Well," said Jerry, "all we can do is try the key."

They got out of the car and walked up to the main entrance, a dirty little glass-paneled protrusion cantilevered off the left side of the building. Jerry pulled the key out and tried it in the lock. It fit. He glanced over at Brenda. "Well, turn it," her look seemed to say, so he did. The lock clicked. He put his hand on the doorknob, turned it, and the door popped open as if the hinges were too tight. Jerry let go of the door, and it swung open by itself. They stepped inside and found themselves in a shabby, makeshift office. A couple of desks sat there, empty but for the dust, a computer, and an old IBM Selectric II. A grey file cabinet stood in the corner, also gathering dust.

Brenda closed the door behind them to keep the winter air outside, although it was almost as cold inside as out. They looked at the dusty room, looked at each other, and shrugged. A door on the opposite wall stood slightly ajar, so they walked toward it. It opened onto the main floor of the warehouse, which wasn't a warehouse at all, they discovered. At some point in the distant past, it had been converted into a production facility. Old machines stood like mechanical tombstones in a cement cemetery. Jerry wandered around, fascinated. Here was a lathe, a jigsaw, there a band saw, a drill press, a sander. He punched the "On" button on the sander. Nothing.

"I think the power's off," said Brenda.

They walked past other pieces of machinery, and in the far corner, away from the sander, was a station for painting and varnishing. The rear third of the building was still warehouse space. Steel shelves reached from floor to ceiling. Light filtered in through high windows on the north and south. One was broken, they now noticed.

"I wonder what business used to be here," Jerry said, "and why it went under."

In the northeast corner, a little room jutted out into the production floor. A sign on the door said *Manager.* Jerry turned the knob and pushed the door open. It banged into the inside wall. No doorstop. A desk butted up against the far wall in the left-hand corner. Another old computer sat there. A file cabinet, this one murky brown, stood in the far, right-hand corner. A small refrigerator and microwave sat forlornly on a card table. On the desk next to the computer, Brenda noticed an envelope, just like the one that had come in the mail on Christmas Eve. She picked it up, looked at it, and handed it to Jerry.

Jerry Carlson was penned across the front.

He undid the clasp, looked inside, and saw a small sheaf of papers. He pulled them out and set them on the desktop. The first one was a legal document, a deed. Jerry picked it up and scrutinized it, then handed it to Brenda.

"What is it?" she asked.

"The deed to this warehouse, I think," he said. "The address matches."

"But it's got your name on it," she exclaimed.

He laughed. "Here's your mansion," he told her. "Hope you like it."

"Beautiful," she replied. "When can we move in?"

"As soon as the power's on, I suppose. We can convert this office into a nursery, if you want."

"What do you think we could sell it for?" she asked, ignoring his joke.

"Maybe we could pay somebody to take it," Jerry suggested. "I don't know, but I have a hunch Max doesn't want us to sell it."

"I had a feeling you were going to say that," she deadpanned.

He picked up the next document and stared at it for a long while. A puzzled look came across his face, and he turned the page over, and then back again.

"What's wrong?" Brenda asked.

"Either nothing or everything," Jerry replied. "Here, look."

She took the document and studied it, then suddenly her mouth dropped open and she gasped. "Is this what I think it is?"

"I think so. It looks like a bank statement."

"With your name on it." She put the page down on the desk and stared at Jerry. "But it's got a balance of over a half million dollars. You didn't tell me you were this rich."

"I'm not," he said. "Or at least I wasn't until today." He pointed to a couple of lines on the statement. "Look at this. One check written from the account last month, for just over two hundred grand. I bet I know what that check was for."

"This warehouse?"

Jerry nodded. "And another dated a few days later for almost three hundred thousand. This account had a million dollars in it a month ago. What on earth is Max up to?"

Brenda picked up the next document in the stack and studied it. "I think I know," she said. "Here, look."

Jerry took the sheet from her. After a moment he laughed. "It's a schematic, a spec sheet. I see these all the time at work. But we don't do anything quite so, shall we say, rustic." He laughed again. It was a design for a birdhouse. And across the bottom of the page were the words, *Homeless Shelter—for the Birds.*

"You've got to admit," she said, "it's kind of cute."

Jerry picked up the next sheet. "Look at this," he laughed. It was another schematic. This one for a *Homeless Shelter—for the Dogs.*

"What is all this?" Brenda asked.

"I think I'm getting the picture," Jerry answered.

The next page in the stack was a business license for a firm called the Homeless Shelter. Then Jerry found photocopies of forms required by the state of Utah for creating a business partnership and a reply from the IRS granting a tax number. He studied these carefully and then sat down on the desk.

"It seems," Jerry said to Brenda, "that I'm the controlling partner in a new business called the Homeless Shelter. My signature's even on some of these documents, or at least a good forgery of it."

"You didn't sign them?" she asked.

"Not while I was awake," he said. "It looks like the business is set up so that the employees are partners with limited powers but are entitled to a share of the profits."

"What employees?" Brenda asked.

"All those people out there on the shop floor making birdhouses and doghouses," Jerry told her. "Didn't you see them?"

There were still a couple of pages on the desk Jerry hadn't looked at. Brenda picked one up.

"I think I've found your employees, Jerry," she said quietly, and handed him the paper. It was a deed for an apartment complex just down the street. Thirty units. "I think I also found where that other check went. If I had to guess, I'd say you're supposed to get some people off the street, Jerry. This Max, he's quite a guy. Where do you suppose he came up with the money?"

"Out of thin air, I suppose," Jerry answered. "And we're supposed to make birdhouses and doghouses? And sell them? This is so ridiculous I can't find words to describe it. Who would buy a birdhouse made by a bunch of unskilled homeless people?"

"I would," said Brenda. "I would because I would be moved by the idea that they were trying to earn their way out of the hole they've fallen in rather than just asking for a handout. Don't you see the appeal? You won't even need to advertise. You'll get free advertising from the media. It just might work."

"But do you realize how hard it's going to be just getting these people to be productive? Just getting them to show up two days in a row? Of course you do. You know as well as I do just how helpless and hopeless most of these people are. They've got drug and alcohol problems, some are mental cases, most of them are emotional wastelands walking around in deteriorating bodies—like I was. Do you know how hard this will be?" he pleaded.

"I do," she said. "But I can't think of a better thing you could do with half a million bucks, an old warehouse full of machinery, and an apartment building."

Jerry chewed on her words for a minute. She was right. What better thing could he do with half a million bucks and an old useless warehouse full of machinery that—thanks to Cal—he was now able to teach people how to operate? The products were simple, so simple even a derelict might be able to learn how to make them. And Brenda was right—they did have a certain appeal. It just might work. And if he was lucky, he could pull maybe forty people off the street. It would be like taking a cup of saltwater from the comprehensive ocean of human despair perhaps, but a cup was better than nothing. All he had to do was consider the change in his own life and multiply that by forty, and from that perspective a cup was immense, almost unfathomable.

"Okay," he said finally, "but will you be my vice president in charge of publicity and accounting?"

"I'd be honored," she said. "But I'll have to take a few accounting lessons from your old girlfriend."

There was one paper still lying on the desktop. Jerry picked it up. "Well, I'll be," he exclaimed.

It was a list of retailers, from Wal-Mart, the world's largest retailer, on down the line. Most of them were local, though, with the name and phone number of a buyer next to each company.

"You don't suppose?" he said.

"I'd bet a half million dollars on it," she replied.

"We've got lots to do," he said, feeling completely overwhelmed.

* * *

The Homeless Shelter

Jeffrey Harvey Carlson was born on January 11 without complications, and that was a blessing because Jerry had his hands full. He had gone to Del Greco and told him he was going to start hiring some of his clientele, and while the reverend was pleased with the gesture, he was by no means encouraging.

"You know what you're doing, Jerry?" he quizzed.

"Yes," Jerry answered, "I think I'm begging for ulcers. But I've got to do it." He knew he didn't sound altogether convincing.

"Whatever you say."

Del Greco offered him an upstairs room to interview in and let Jerry hand out fliers to everyone in the dinner line. After dinner Jerry sat at a table in the cafeteria and made appointments for interviews. The flier made it clear this was serious employment, not a one-day or even one-week job to give a person a little booze money. He listed the qualifications he wanted: homeless, willing to work, willing to abide by the rules. Then he listed the rules: no alcohol on the job, no drugs at all, must come to work sober, must be on time, and must be able to get along with others. No work skills required. He figured these people had faced enough rejection already. He didn't want to reject them again for insignificant reasons such as a lack of skills. He figured he would start with a workforce of about twenty, then expand to forty eventually, if the demand for birdhouses and doghouses warranted it. Of course, he might also have to reduce his workforce to zero if the demand simply didn't exist. Time would tell. Pay would be a free apartment, including utilities, a few dollars a week to buy essentials, and a share of any earnings at the end of every month, after holding out a reserve for future needs. He decided to make the hiring first come, first served. Those who were most eager or most desperate, he figured, would be first in line. And that first evening he set up thirty interviews.

The first interview was the next morning, and he couldn't have been more nervous if he were on the other side of the table. The applicant was a crusty, old gentleman with long, thinning, frizzy hair, a pair of cracked and scuffed glasses, and a red bandanna tied around his crown like a hat. He wore old clothes two sizes too large and smelled of cheap wine. Several teeth, mostly on the bottom row, were missing. His nose was swollen and red like an overripe apple, and he sported a straggly, reddish beard with streaks of grey. But he had a hopeful look in his bloodshot eyes and was definitely sober.

"What's your name?" Jerry asked.

"Nick," the man answered.

"Got a last name, Nick?"

"Allman."

"How old are you?"

"Isn't it illegal to ask that?" Nick suggested with a twinkle in his eye. His face was lined and scarred, and his skin had the texture of old leather.

"I'm looking for partners, not employees," Jerry responded.

Nick took this in, rolled it around in his head for a minute, then said, "Sixty."

Jerry wondered if he shouldn't rather be asking for mileage than for age.

"Got any identification? Driver's license, Social Security card, birth certificate?"

"Nope."

"Ever been arrested?"

Nick paused, and Jerry knew the answer. Many of his applicants would have criminal records, some gained in the name of a warm bed and a few hot meals.

"Never mind," Jerry said quickly. "It doesn't matter. Nick, tell me about your life. How'd you end up on the street?"

"I didn't end up there," Nick answered. "Always been there."

Jerry didn't say anything, so the man kept talking.

"I was an orphan. My parents died when I was four. Spent the next twelve years in an orphanage, but money ran out and they turned me loose when I was sixteen. They figured I could find a job. But I didn't have any skills, didn't have much education or any family or friends, so I wound up on the street. Been there ever since."

"Have you ever had a job?"

"Not a real one. Just day work here and there."

"You've been on the street your whole adult life?"

"Yup."

"Where do you stay at night?"

"Just here and there. Depends on the weather mostly. I've even built snow caves to keep warm."

"Really?" Jerry had never thought of this when he was freezing up in the thicket above the city.

"You do what you have to."

"What do you think you could do in this new business?"

"Anything. I can learn. I'm a survivor."

"Can you learn to bathe and wash your clothes?"

"I can, sir."

He looked Jerry in the eye, and something in the glance told him Nick was telling the truth. It made Jerry feel funny being called sir by a man twice his age, but it also felt good.

"Can you stay sober?"

"Don't know," Nick answered. "Never tried before, but I suppose it ain't that hard, not if you're warm at night."

"You'll have an apartment near the factory."

"What kind of factory?"

"A wood shop."

"What kinda stuff we gonna make?"

"Birdhouses and doghouses."

Nick looked at him askance, then shrugged. "Whatever you say, boss."

"One more question," said Jerry. "Why do you want to work now, after all these years?"

"Who says I didn't want to work before?" Nick answered. "I just gave up 'cause I knew what they'd tell me. I heard it all before."

"So why did you show up today?"

"I know you." He revealed a partially toothless grin. "You're Santy Claus. I figured you'd give me a chance."

Something in Jerry's heart went all soft and spongy, and he paused a moment before he could speak. "Be at this address next Monday at nine o'clock sharp," he said, and handed Nick a slip of paper. "I'll provide food the first week. And let me warn you, we won't be making anything for a few days. The factory needs a thorough cleaning and maybe a few repairs before we can get things up and running."

Nick took the slip of paper and stared at it like it was a handful of gold. "I won't let you down, sir," he said.

Jerry shook his hand and looked him in the eye. "Welcome to the Homeless Shelter," he added as the older man turned to leave.

Nick walked out a little taller and a little straighter than he'd come in.

The next interview was with Marci Martinez, a single mother chased out of her home by an abusive husband. Same story as Debbie Pochman's, except for a few inconsequential details.

"How old are your kids?" he asked.

"Four and two."

"Where will they stay while you're working?"

"I don't know," she said. "Haven't thought about that yet."

Neither had Jerry, so he spent a few moments on it now.

"What if we offered day care?" he said at length.

"Who would be with my kids?" she asked. "I don't trust them with just anybody, especially if you're hiring only homeless people."

"I'm not hiring anybody," Jerry answered. "I'm looking for partners. How would you like to be in charge of day care?" he asked.

"Me?"

"Sure, why not? You could help me screen applicants and pick two or three you could rotate with in taking care of the kids. We'd hold it at the apartments where you'll be staying."

"Sounds fair," she said, but with just a touch of skepticism. "Does this business have any chance of surviving?"

"That probably depends on you and the others I offer partnerships to."

He explained the way the partnership was organized, how profits would be distributed, living arrangements, the rules, and so on. When he finished, she asked the obvious question. "What are you getting out of this?"

"I don't know," he said. "I hadn't really thought of it that way. I saw it more as an opportunity to give, I suppose."

"You really are Santa Claus," she said, and rolled her eyes. "But I think you're a bit naive."

"How so?"

"You said our pay would be a portion of profits. But it takes time to build up a business and make it profitable. Most take about five years, I've heard."

"So have I," he said. "But I've got a little reserve to cover expenses in the short term, and I think we can turn a profit a lot quicker than five years." What he didn't say was that he was fortunate to have the two buildings paid for and a little reserve in the bank. He could keep expenses low and hope sales came sooner than later. "We'll see."

"I suppose we will," she answered. "What about security?"

"Security?"

"Listen," she said, "I haven't been on the street very long, but I do know a few of these guys you're hiring are going to bring some bad habits with them. I want my kids and me to be safe."

Jerry hadn't considered this. It now occurred to him he'd have to have an on-site apartment manager who could double as a security guard and peacekeeper. "I'll work that out," he assured her. "Don't worry about it."

When Marci finally left, Jerry was glad—glad he didn't have to answer any more of her difficult questions, but also glad she had asked them. She'd been on the receiving end of some bad breaks, he could tell, and was justifiably cautious. She wasn't about to be taken advantage of again.

The next interview was Lance Bodeen, a slight, shifty-eyed man with short, dark hair slicked back against the sides of his head. It didn't take Jerry long to figure out Lance was looking for a quick buck but wasn't willing to either play by the rules or commit to any long-term arrangement.

"Do I have to live at your apartments?" he asked.

"Yes," Jerry answered, making up a new rule on the spot. "At least at first, until we start making some money." He had several reasons for this. First and foremost was that a good portion of the pay would initially come in the form of free rent and utilities. He couldn't afford to pay much yet, not until they started selling some product.

"Well, I dunno," Lance said.

Jerry suspected Lance wasn't really a homeless person, but was one of those who masqueraded as one to get a free handout, then went home to a warm house at night, perhaps a brother's or an ex-wife's. "Maybe this isn't quite what you're looking for," Jerry suggested.

"Maybe not."

The next interview was one Del Greco had warned him about. Jerry had let the good reverend look at his list just to tell him anything he knew about the applicants. This one, Mike Gambol, was one of many who ended up on the street as a result of one mental illness or another. Mike had a particular brand of neurosis that made him think everybody was out to take advantage of him. He trusted no one. Everybody had ulterior motives. And on top of this he didn't see reality through quite the same window as the rest of humanity. He was constantly having run-ins with the other patrons, and when Del Greco would try to sort out what had happened, Mike's story was invariably at odds with everyone else's. You couldn't really say he was lying. He just perceived reality through some kind of mental filter that distorted everything to one degree or another.

Jerry felt sorry for Mike, but he knew his new little business was not the answer to Mike's problems. And taking him on would only create difficulties for everyone else. He told Mike this in so many words and felt awful afterward. But what could he do? He was no psychiatrist, and work was not therapy for some cases.

Jerry interviewed eight people the first day and thirty-five by the end of the week. All the interviews went pretty much as the first four had gone. He found a few individuals who were just down on their luck, a few who had been chased out onto the street by life's hard knocks and needed a way back, a few who were looking for a handout, and a few who were mentally ill. The challenge, of course, was distinguishing the last group from any of the other three. In the end, he picked eighteen of the thirty-five and told them to meet him on Monday morning at the factory.

By the time he went home late Friday afternoon, he was exhausted. Wading through the stories of all these broken and mangled lives had taken its toll. Not only did he have to sort fact from fiction, he had to evaluate personalities based on just a few minutes of conversation and then weed out those he felt might cause trouble. He found it difficult to say no, but deep inside he knew Max didn't expect him to save the whole world, just try to make a difference to a few. He hoped he had made good decisions.

When he walked through the door, he heaved a big sigh, tossed his coat onto the overstuffed chair Brenda had brought into the marriage, and plopped down on the sofa. Brenda came into the room carrying little Jeff and set him gently in Jerry's lap.

"Another big day, huh?" she asked.

"Yeah," he admitted. "I knew this would be hard. I just didn't know it would be so emotionally draining."

"Well, you can't do more than your best," she reasoned, sitting down next to him.

"I suppose you're right. It's just that I have no idea whether this is going to work, and I've been selling hopeless people hope all day long. It's tiring work."

"I made the calls you wanted me to make," she said. "Power's on, phones will be working Monday, and the heating guy checked everything out. Said the boiler's old, but still working fine. Your factory's ready to roll. All you need is a trained workforce."

"I just hope they're trainable," he said. "No telling how that will turn out."

"Time will tell."

"So," he said, holding Jeff up and bouncing him gently on his knee, "have you been a good eater today?"

Jeff gave him a blank stare, but Jerry felt very keenly at that moment what he had felt ever since Jeffrey was born—that there was a personality inside that little body, and whoever was in there was connected to Jerry by some secret link. Brenda had noticed it too. Jeff would get fussy and there was nothing she could do to calm him, but as soon as she handed him to Jerry, he would quiet right down and be as content as a dog getting scratched under his collar. There was definitely a bond that went far beyond words or explanation. And it was a two-way street. All Jerry had to do to rid himself of stress or worry was pick up his little son. As soon as he did, the whole world seemed to make sense. He knew his place in it, and he was at peace.

"So," Jerry repeated, tickling Jeff's belly, "you been a good eater?"

"I love to eat," Brenda answered for him, "but I haven't quite got this napping thing down yet. I like to cry when Mommy puts me in my crib."

"You'll learn to appreciate sleep when you get a little older," Jerry said with a yawn.

"I called Julie today," Brenda said.

"Oh?" Jerry would have paid money to listen in on that conversation.

"She was very nice. She offered to come out and help me get the accounting software loaded and give me a quick tutorial. She said we'll need to talk to a real accountant, or maybe even a lawyer, to get a handle on all the tax issues since this isn't, shall we say, a *normal* business."

"I suppose she's right. Did she sound jealous at all?"

"No, Mr. Ego, but she did ask about you and wanted me to tell you hi from all the old gang at the Wood Nook. She said your replacement is fine, but he's no Jerry Carlson."

"Hey, how could he be?" Jerry laughed.

"Lucky him," Brenda replied, and jabbed Jerry in the ribs with an elbow.

* * *

Monday morning Jerry found sixteen adults and a handful of small children waiting for him outside the Homeless Shelter factory. He unlocked the door, invited them all in, and had them sit on the factory floor. Within a couple of minutes, the other two showed up. *Eighteen out of eighteen,* he thought, *that's a good sign.* He could see them looking around at the equipment, questions on every face.

"Thanks for coming," he began. "Like I told most of you, before we can start producing anything, we've got to clean this place up, make sure all the machinery is working, and make some decisions about who will do what job. I'm as new at this as you are, so be patient with me. I *have* managed a custom furniture shop, so I'm not totally unacquainted with what we're trying to do, but there's plenty I'll have to learn as we go along, just like you."

Jerry had bought an old truck the previous week. He figured he'd need it for all sorts of reasons, and the first use he found for it was to haul cleaning supplies. He had a couple of his new partners help him bring the supplies in, and then he set them all to work cleaning the old warehouse. "Let's see if we can at least make this look like a place we wouldn't be ashamed to show to a stranger," he told them. "This is your business. Let's make it a place to be proud of."

It was a big job, but the sixteen he put to work went at it with gusto. Marci and Lana, another single mom, and all the kids went with him to the apartment building to get the day care going. They picked one of the apartments on the main floor and made this the day care center. He left Lana with the kids while he and Marci made a quick trip to buy toys and blankets and some food for the kids' lunches.

By the time Jerry got back to the factory, he was amazed at the transformation. The sixteen had worked hard and showed a sense of ownership that surprised Jerry. The place was already looking much better. He'd had the broken window replaced the previous week, and the air was warm and smelled of ammonia.

"Jerry," Nick called out when he saw him, "you know, if we had a little paint, we could make this place look real nice."

"What color?" Jerry asked.

"Orange Day-Glo," said Bart, who was standing next to Nick and leaning on a push broom.

A few of the others grumbled over this suggestion, but Jerry waved his arms to get their attention. "We'll let the women decide," he said. "At least they have a little taste."

As his new partners went off with new cleaning assignments, Jerry thought to himself, *This just might work. It just might.*

He wandered over to the manager's office and picked up the phone on the desk. It had a dial tone, so he called Brenda.

"How's the first day going?" she asked.

"Better than I'd hoped."

"I called the *Tribune* this morning," she said.

"Paper boy miss us again today?" he asked.

"No, I thought I might get us a bit of free advertising. I told them what you were doing. They said they'd send a reporter out in a week or so, after you've had a chance to get things up and running. Who knows? It's a good story. Maybe we'll get some sales from it."

"You're the marketing executive," he told her. "Whatever you say."

"I want to come with you tomorrow, see if I can help any."

"What about Jeff?"

"I've got Allie coming over to watch him for a few hours." Allison Marsh was a college student who lived down the street and always needed some cash.

"Sure, I could use somebody to clean the rest rooms," he told her.

"That's a man's job."

"I know, I know," he said. "You just want to come here and supervise me."

"How'd you guess?"

He said good-bye and walked back out into the shop. Bart and a couple of the women were going at it over color schemes. He suddenly realized Bart hadn't been joking.

"I still think orange Day-Glo's perfect for this place."

"Get serious, Jack," said Margo. She had biceps like a ranch hand and probably could have wrapped Bart around one of the steel girders that supported the roof. "This is a machine shop, not a Halloween party."

"No, it has to be orange Day-Glo," he replied. "Just a little trim here and there."

"You want this place to match your former wardrobe or something?" asked Laurie, one of the moms whose kids were over at day care. The others laughed. "I say green—forest green."

"Green," seconded Margo.

"Green," said Nick, who had just joined the group.

Bart stomped off in a huff, and Jerry realized this wasn't going to be quite like running the Wood Nook. All of his new partners had been living on the edge, some for many years, which had a way of making people both irritable and irrational in unpredictable ways, and it also made them a bit oversensitive. He figured he'd probably be playing referee more than he wanted to.

After Bart was out of earshot, Jerry whispered, "Green." The three remaining combatants all grinned. "But maybe we'll let Bart put a little orange Day-Glo at his workstation sometime."

"As long as you put his workstation out back behind the building," said Laurie.

* * *

The next morning Brenda drove over to the Homeless Shelter with Jerry. He gave her a brief tour of the budding operation, then took her over to the apartment building to show her the day care center.

"I'm glad you've got women running this," she said approvingly. "Maybe you ought to have women run the factory too. The place could use a little sprucing up, maybe a little orange paint here and there." He had told her about Bart.

They stayed and talked with Marci for a while, then ran to the store to pick up a few items Marci had thought of since they'd bought supplies the day before. When they got back to the factory to check on things there, Nick approached them.

"There was a guy here while you was gone," he told them. "Was askin' lots of questions."

"A reporter?" Brenda asked hopefully.

"Don't think so, ma'am," Nick replied and made a face. "Didn't seem too friendly. I think he was one of the neighbors. I sent him down to the day care center to find you. Just a few minutes ago."

"Must have passed him on the way," Jerry said. "Did he say what he wanted?"

"No, but he didn't seem too happy about what we're doing here."

"What, he'd rather have an old, run-down warehouse here?"

"Sounded like it."

Ten minutes later, Jerry and Brenda were in the office loading some software on the computer when Nick knocked on the door. "Guy's here again," he said. They followed Nick out onto the floor, and both of them stopped dead in their tracks when they saw who their visitor was. The visitor's mouth dropped open. He was obviously just as surprised as Jerry and Brenda were.

"Well," said Jerry finally, "if it isn't Josh Monk."

"It is," said Josh, recovering from his astonishment. His eyes were glued to Brenda. "What are you two doing here?"

Jerry wasn't sure whether he wanted to know what they were doing with the factory or why they were together again. "We're setting up a business," he said, opting for the safer answer.

"I can see that," Josh growled, sweeping the production area quickly with his eyes. His hair was still black and slick, and his mouth still had the old haughty slant to it, but something was definitely different about him. It may have been the clothes, but something else told Jerry times had been hard for Josh. The hard times, though, hadn't appeared to soften him. His eyes glinted with malice.

"So what are *you* doing here?" Jerry asked.

"I live down the street," Josh answered. "I have a certain interest in what kind of neighbors are moving in. These people tell me they're a bunch of homeless misfits you've pulled off the street."

"I doubt they put it quite that way," Brenda countered. Her voice was icy, almost angry.

"Well," Josh sneered, "the little woman speaks. Didn't think she'd ever say boo to me again. Is that a ring I see on your finger? You're not married to this loser, are you?"

"Who's the loser, Josh?" she asked. "He won my heart, and he's got the capital to start a business to help people. Not bad, I'd say. But I heard you killed your dad's business. Put a lot of people out of work. Rumors must have been true."

He was speechless for a moment, then changed the subject. "You know, I don't think the neighbors are going to take kindly to having this kind of riffraff on their street."

"They put up with you," Brenda shot back. "Why should they mind these good people?"

"Oh," Josh answered, "I'm sure they'll see lots of reasons." With that he turned and headed for the door.

When Josh was gone, Jerry put a finger on Brenda's forehead. "Tsssssss," he exclaimed, pulling his hand away as if it had been burned. "I didn't know you and Josh were such good buddies."

She glared at him for a couple of seconds, then cracked a smile and began to laugh. "Sorry," she said. "I couldn't help myself." Then she got serious again. "You know, I think when I finally saw through Josh, it was a revelation to him too. I think he finally saw himself for what he was. No more charades after that. He got all cold and hard on the outside and stopped even pretending that people were important to him."

"I have a feeling he's going to be trouble," said Jerry. "I wonder if Max knew he lived here in the neighborhood."

* * *

Later that night, just before he went to bed, Jerry picked up his Bible from the nightstand. He and Brenda had gotten in the habit of reading a few verses before they went to sleep. Now, however, he noticed a slip of paper poking out the top. He opened to that page, and a new passage was underlined: "Ye have heard that it hath been said, Thou shalt love thy neighbour, and hate thine enemy. But I say unto you, Love your enemies, bless them that curse you, do good to them that hate you, and pray for them which despitefully use you, and persecute you."

"He's got a lot of nerve, doesn't he?" Brenda suggested.

* * *

After a week, Jerry had most of the partners trained in the use of at least one of the machines or had them painting or varnishing. He put Bart in charge of shipping, partly because there was nothing yet to ship and partly because he didn't seem too eager to learn any of the production skills. On Wednesday they finished the first product and held a party to celebrate. The first birdhouse was nothing to shout about, but it was a start. A few more and they would probably get one good enough to show to local retailers.

On Thursday Josh dropped in again. He found Jerry in his office and marched right in without knocking.

"Carlson," he said, "the folks around here have signed a petition to get this pit and its lowlife workers out of the neighborhood. See you in court."

Jerry guessed he was on solid legal ground, but he used Josh's threat as an excuse to talk to his people about keeping their noses clean and being good neighbors.

* * *

Ever since the day they had first visited the old warehouse, Jerry had dreamed every night—or at least had remembered his dreams. In them he and Brenda weren't flying anymore. They were standing on the ground next to the glowing tree in the forest, and a large group of people was crowded around them. High up in the branches of the tree, they could see some kind of round, white fruit. He knew he should be able to fly up and pick it, but for some reason he couldn't get his feet off the ground. The first time he had this dream, Max's voice came from behind him telling him he and the others had to find a way to get the fruit without flying. And one person alone couldn't do it. The trunk was too broad and smooth to climb, and the nearest branches were a good twenty feet above their heads. At first, nobody would listen to Jerry's pleas to cooperate so they could eat, but as the nights wore on, Jerry began to get to know his fellows in the forest, and as he did, their faces came into focus. They were his partners at the Homeless Shelter, plus others he didn't know.

After a month or so, Jerry finally had convinced some of them to cooperate, and they had started to build a human pyramid. The problem was nobody wanted to be on the bottom. Each one wanted to be at the pinnacle where he or she could reach the fruit. Nobody trusted the others enough to believe they would pick the fruit and bring it down for the whole group to eat. Jerry tried and tried, but he couldn't figure out a way to convince them to trust each other. And in this dream, his head just didn't work as it normally did. He knew the answer was as plain as the nose on his face, but for some reason he just couldn't think of it.

"Max," he kept pleading. "Tell me the answer."

But no answer came. Max didn't seem to be in the dream anymore.

fifth christmas

....

Jeffrey

This was easily the hardest year of Jerry's life. The Homeless Shelter had sputtered into existence, and after several months of unexpected expenses and dashed hopes, enough orders finally started trickling in to keep them afloat. It had been a monumental task to keep the "partners" productive and happy enough to get the orders out the door on time. A few of the original eighteen had given up in the first month. Regular hours, sobriety, and working closely with the idiosyncracies of others were too much to ask of some, and they determined that their former struggles were easier than these newer ones. But Jerry recruited replacements, and this time he had a better feel for who would make it and who wouldn't. Still, he worked long hours and generally came home exhausted. He also didn't have the luxury of taking two-day weekends, holidays, or vacation time. There was always more to do than he had time for.

On top of these challenges, Josh finally made good on his offer to try to put them out of business, or at least out of the neighborhood. Jerry went to court three times to defend the Homeless Shelter before the judge finally threw the lawsuit out as frivolous and unfounded. The evidence weighing most heavily in their favor was the testimony of certain neighbors who had benefitted from service projects Jerry had organized among his partners. They had planted trees along the street where old ones had died and been torn out. They had also helped clean up the yards of several older couples who didn't have the time or energy to keep up with the demands of yard work. There had been no incidents where the formerly homeless had caused problems, and some neighbors were downright pleased to see the old, deserted warehouse being used productively again. Jerry put these people in the witness chair, and they made Josh look like a man with too many sour grapes to chew on.

The one bonus Jerry picked up from this little adventure was that Josh had questioned where the capital had come from. Jerry had the bank look into the initial deposit and discovered it had been made in cash, signed by himself. When asked by the judge to explain where a man with his background had come up with such a large amount of cash, Jerry replied truthfully that he had been given the money by an anonymous donor for the express purpose of helping the homeless. The fact that he had done just that rather than retiring to the Bahamas convinced the judge his story was on the up-and-up.

After being thoroughly thrashed in court, Josh never showed his face around the Homeless Shelter again, but every couple of weeks some sort of vandalism would occur. A window would encounter a large rock, a wall would collect some spray paint, or the parking area would sprout bouquets of roofing nails in strategic locations. Jerry knew exactly who was behind these acts, but he knew he couldn't prove it, so he just cleaned up and ignored it, hoping it would go away in time.

* * *

The only compensating joy in these first difficult months was the love Jerry found at home. Brenda treated him like a king, but it was Jeffrey who made the biggest difference. As he became more aware of his world, the personality Jerry had sensed in him blossomed. He had a zest for life that couldn't be contained. He squealed in delight over the smallest discoveries. One day while shopping with Brenda when he was about eight months old, Jeff received a shiny mylar balloon from a store clerk. When they got home, he crawled around the floor for hours, chasing the balloon and squealing like a greased pig. When he would catch the balloon every now and then, he would roll around on the floor with it until it got away, then he would start the game all over again. Brenda just watched and laughed. Eventually he wore himself out and fell asleep on the floor. When Jerry got home that evening, Jeff was at it again, and the two parents watched in wonder at the energy and joy this tiny body couldn't quite contain. He seemed to have an inexhaustible supply.

At almost a year, Jeff was still a daddy's boy. Jerry had bought Brenda a rocking chair from the Wood Nook as a gift for the new mom, but Jeff insisted his daddy rock him to bed every night. He would cry if Brenda tried to put him to bed—unless Jerry was working late—and then he somehow knew and would allow his mother to rock him. But on most nights Jerry sat in the rocker, held his son on his lap, and sang him all the old songs he used to sing when he was younger and still had his guitar. He'd considered buying a new one several times, but he just never found time, and he knew if he didn't have time to buy a guitar, he certainly wouldn't have time to play it. So he sat in the rocker with his son and sang to the accompaniment of the chair, which squeaked as it rocked back and forth. And Brenda would come into the nursery and look at the two of them and say, "I don't know if I've ever seen a love affair quite like this one." But she wasn't jealous. She knew how hard Jerry's life had been and how difficult it was now, and she was glad to see him so happy.

By December, Jeff was showing an unmistakable interest in walking. He would pull himself up to any nearby piece of furniture and then negotiate slow circles around it. On the fifteenth, at about ten in the morning, he decided he was tired of circumnavigating the overstuffed chair in the living room, and Brenda could see him eyeing the coffee table. "You can do it," she encouraged. He looked up at her as if he knew exactly what she had said, looked back at the coffee table, and then, with a grin a mile wide, attempted his first unassisted steps. To Brenda's delight, he took three, but to her dismay, the coffee table was four steps away. He misjudged the distance, reached out for the table, and missed. As he tumbled to the floor, his chin hit the sharp edge of the table and split open like a sack of grain with a weak spot. The cut was as straight and clean as if someone had sliced him with a knife. Jeff was so surprised he wasn't sure if he was supposed to cry, but Brenda made such a fuss he eventually decided he was hurt badly, so he howled for a few minutes while she got the bleeding to stop. At that point he was ready to go exploring again, but Brenda thought the gash looked quite deep, so to Jeff's chagrin, she hauled him out to the car and drove him to the pediatrician's office.

"It'll leave a smaller scar if we put a couple of stitches in it," Dr. Belnap advised, so Jeff got sewn back together, an experience he didn't agree with in the least. Eventually they had to immobilize him with something called a papoose board—a sort of straitjacket for babies—but he survived the ordeal and was ready to roam again when they let him loose.

After they got home, Brenda called Jerry to tell him the news. He was both shocked and concerned. "Jerry," she said, "don't you know toddlers are naturally accident-prone? We'll have a few visits to the doctor or even the emergency room before we're through with this whole parenting experience."

"You're sure he's okay?" Jerry repeated for the fifth time.

"He's fine, Jerry," Brenda assured him. "Here, ask him yourself."

She put the phone up to Jeff's ear, but he didn't make the connection between the voice inside the funny toy and his daddy, who was big and playful and came home every night as if by magic. He pushed the handset away and crawled off toward his bedroom to find toys.

"Will he have a scar?" Jerry asked. It seemed a shame for someone so new and perfect to have a battle scar so early in the war of life.

"The doctor said it will hardly be noticeable. It's part of life, Jerry. It'll give him personality."

"He's *got* personality—a ton of it," Jerry protested.

"Well, this will just make him even more unique, if anyone who looks so much like his mother can ever be unique."

This quieted Jerry's fears, but he still wanted to come home and see the damage at lunchtime. Normally, Jerry ate lunch with his partners. He'd contracted with a deli truck to stop in the parking lot every day at 11:30. But today he merely grabbed a sandwich and ate it in the car on the way home. He left Nick in charge. Nick, who had never had a job in his entire life, much less any responsibility, had become Jerry's right-hand man. He had blossomed like a wildflower. Everyone liked him, with the possible exception of Bart, who didn't particularly like anyone and who had finally been assigned to run the shipping area, where he could be his own boss and didn't have to work closely with the others. The problem, as Jerry saw it, was that

Bart felt he should be running the whole operation. In fact, he had even pushed this idea to a vote, but his proposition was defeated seventeen to one, with Jerry abstaining.

"Go see your son's stitches," Nick told Jerry. "We'll be fine for a couple of hours."

When Jerry got home, he ran straight to Jeff's room, picked him up to examine the injury, but found it covered by a Band-Aid. This attention was not much to Jeff's liking, though, and he tried to push Jerry away. Eventually, Jerry gave up and put his son down, who immediately found a squeaky rubber toy to chew on.

"I told you he's fine," Brenda said. "You worry too much. Just like you do with your business. You're like a mother hen."

Jerry looked at her and scrunched up his brow. "You really think so?"

"I think you need a vacation, Jerry," she said. "I know *I* do."

This was a new idea to Jerry. In the four years since coming off what he thought was going to be a permanent vacation, he had taken only a random day off here and there. And in the first two years of their marriage, they had gone traveling only once—their honeymoon.

"But what would we do with Jeff?" Jerry asked.

"I wasn't planning on leaving him home," Brenda answered. "I figured maybe he needs a change of pace too."

"Where did you want to go?"

"Somewhere warmer," she said. "I'm tired of winter already, and I'll be even more tired of it by February."

"Is that when you want to go?" Jerry asked.

"Jeff will be walking better by then."

"Better?"

"Oh, didn't I tell you?" she said. "That's how he cut his chin. He walked from the chair to the coffee table and almost made it."

A goofy look crossed Jerry's face, some combination of immense pride mingled with sheer terror, the kind of look parents usually get when their children come home with either a driver's license or a fiancé.

"He walked?" Jerry asked.

"Yeah," Brenda answered.

"Maybe we ought to put pads on the edge of that coffee table and on a few other things."

"He'll be fine, Jerry. You can't protect him from everything. Here, let's see if he'll walk to his daddy."

She took the squeaky toy away from Jeff and handed it to Jerry. Then she propped Jeff up and pointed him in his dad's direction. Jerry knelt down and held the toy to tempt him. Jeff immediately staggered toward Jerry with wobbly steps. Jerry moved backward slowly, and Jeff did a whopping ten steps before Jerry let him reach the toy. Picking him up and swinging him around with a whoop, Jerry looked as proud as any father had ever been.

"By the way," Brenda informed him, "we're going to San Diego."

"San Diego?" In his excitement he'd forgotten about Brenda's idea for a getaway.

"I looked in the classifieds and found a condo on the beach," she said. "An older couple who belong to a time-share thing had a conflict the same week they'd signed up for San Diego, so they had to unload that week. It was a pretty good deal."

"How much?" Jerry asked.

"Five hundred."

"Five hundred!"

Brenda could see sticker shock in his eyes. "It's right on the beach," she said. "There's a pier next to it. You can walk out over the ocean. We can take Jeff to Sea World and the zoo. You'll love it, Jerry."

He was digesting all this slowly, still holding Jeff in his arms.

"You need a break," she told him. "And so do I."

"A whole week?"

"Plus a couple of days to drive there and back."

He mulled it over for a minute. "All right," he said.

"The Homeless Shelter will be fine," she assured him. "Leave Nick in charge. He's twice your age. He's survived forty-five years on the street. He can handle it."

"Okay," Jerry said, and now his mind caught hold of the idea, started to run with it, and he even got a little bit excited. Brenda could see all this in his face and gave him a big hug. Jeff squealed and tried to wriggle in between his mom and dad. He had never seen a hug he didn't want to be part of.

* * *

Bart

Christmas sales were reasonably good, particularly with local retailers who read the story in the *Tribune* and tried a few of the "shelters," hoping people would buy them out of guilt or charity or even the odd chance that they needed a good doghouse or bird hotel. They discovered instead they couldn't keep them on the shelf. Bart was swamped with orders to ship, but he had a hard time getting them out on time. Retailers were calling Jerry, wondering where their orders were. Jerry had to assign Bart a couple of assistants just to get the product out the door, and while Bart reigned over them with an iron fist, he offered little help himself. Jerry decided to let things be until the Christmas rush was over, but he knew he'd have to deal with Bart's increasing aloofness and insubordination. Most of the partners still regarded the Homeless Shelter as a gift straight from heaven, but Bart was different. He acted as if he were the gift and the business was his domain. He didn't recognize any authority other than his own whim, and Jerry was growing weary of butting heads with him.

In the meantime, the week of Christmas rolled around, and Jerry dutifully hauled out Max's old cell phone, charged the batteries, and carried it on his belt. Brenda was a bit nervous when she first saw it.

"Kind of makes you wonder what kind of Christmas we'll have this year," she said. "Life's never dull with a call from Max looming on the horizon, is it?"

"Hasn't been yet," Jerry muttered. His life had been so full and so busy, he wondered if he could handle another major "request" from his secret benefactor. He felt pushed almost to his limit. Granted, his limit had expanded remarkably in the past four years. When he had time to think about how far he had come since that first phone call four Christmases ago, he was amazed. The old homeless Jerry could never have imagined the current Jerry, the one with a wife, a child, and a business of his own now primed to take off if he could keep it from caving in during the post-Christmas slowdown. All because of Max.

"Well," Brenda sighed, "I hope he doesn't have any major changes in the works, unless he wants to give you another million bucks and turn the business over to someone else."

"Don't count on it," Jerry said.

The days passed too quickly, and before Jerry knew it, it was two days before Christmas. All the pre-Christmas orders were out the door, and he announced to his partners that the Homeless Shelter would close on the twenty-fourth for the holiday.

At precisely 9:15 that morning, however, the cell phone rang. Jerry was walking around the shop floor, watching his people clean up after a busy month. He answered the call and walked directly toward his office.

"Max," he said, "is that you?"

"Ho, ho, ho," came the reply.

"How's life at the North Pole?"

"My elves have been working overtime," Max replied. "How have yours been?"

"Busy."

"I've read good things about you in the paper."

"It's all your fault, you know."

"Oh, I just got the ball rolling," said Max with uncharacteristic modesty. "It's you who made the miracle happen."

"That remains to be seen," Jerry answered.

"Oh, you'll be fine," Max laughed, "even if you go on vacation for a few days. You've passed the most difficult part. It will only get easier."

"Easy for you to say," Jerry accused. "You don't have to be here with the worries and the headaches every day."

"That's not in my job description," said Max, laughing again.

"What *is* your job description?" Jerry asked.

"Making life interesting for you."

"So what do you do the rest of the year?"

"Wouldn't you like to know."

"Yes, I would."

"Let's just say I help people help themselves."

"Do you get a good return on your investment?" Jerry asked.

"The best." Max seemed pleased this year.

Jerry wasn't quite ready to hear Max's new request, so he asked, "Where are you calling from, Max?"

"Would you believe the North Pole?"

"No. I was just joking."

"A beach in San Diego?"

"No," said Jerry, a bit exasperated.

"You tried tracing my phone number last year, didn't you?"

"I did. I took a bit of that money you gave me and hired a private investigator."

"I know."

"He came up empty."

"Of course he did."

"The phone company has no record of that number."

"They wouldn't," Max assured him.

"Of course not. It's a cell phone number."

Max laughed again.

"So do you live in Salt Lake?" Jerry asked.

"We're not playing twenty questions," Max told him.

"What are we playing?"

"Life. It's lots more fun."

"So what's going to change in my life this year, Max?"

"Nothing."

"Nothing?"

"Nothing."

"No request?"

"I didn't say that."

Jerry groaned. "You have a request, and it won't change my life any?"

"Aren't you relieved?"

"Am I supposed to be? Oh well, let's have it."

"Don't say no to anybody today."

"What?"

"Don't say no to anybody."

"That's it?"

"You'll be surprised at how hard that is. Think you're up to it?"

Jerry wanted to say no, but didn't. "I suppose so," he said instead.

"Good. So, Jerry, are you still a millionaire?"

Jerry knew he'd spent most of the money and was about to say no, but caught himself. "How am I supposed to answer that?" he said, exasperated.

"Well, are you?"

"If you're counting pennies, yes," he finally answered.

"Very creative," said Max. "Do you hate your wife?"

"I hate canker sores. I hate traffic jams. I hate coconut. But I love my wife."

"Good answer. Are you content with never knowing anything more about me?"

"You devil."

"Well, Jerry, it's been nice . . ."

"We'll have a nice Christmas, Max. You too, okay?"

"And have fun in San Diego. Remember, . . ."

"I know, don't tell anyone no. Just today, right?"

"Right. Bye, Jerry."

The line went dead, and Jerry sat for a while, wondering what Max was up to. Was Ed McMahon going to come calling? Did it have anything to do with Brenda? Or Jeff? With Max, he'd learned, you never knew what lay behind his requests.

After a while he wandered back out onto the floor. Nick was helping Joey and Carlos, a couple of men who had shown some real promise with various saws. They were cleaning up their workstations and doing a little maintenance.

"Hey, boss," said Nick. That was what he always called Jerry lately. "We're almost finished. What do you say we order some pizza and have a Christmas party?"

Jerry thought of Max's request and grinned. "Sure," he said. "You find out what kind everybody wants, and I'll pay for it."

A while later, Nick came back into his office and sat down. "Two supremes, a Hawaiian, and a veggie," he said. "Oh, and one more thing." He plopped a sandwich bag containing a few little white pouches down on Jerry's desk.

"What's that, Nick?" he said. "Powdered sugar to go on the pizza?"

"Even bad mushrooms wouldn't make a topping like this," Nick answered.

"It's . . . it's not . . ." Jerry stammered.

"Coke," Nick stated.

"Where'd you get it?"

"Bart's desk. I saw him snortin' it a week or so ago. He didn't know I was watchin'. I just been waitin' for a chance to search for it when he wasn't there. He went to buy some supplies this morning, so I dug around a bit."

"I wish you'd have come to me before you went snooping," Jerry told him. "It's just your word against his. He'll say you planted it."

"Have him drug tested," Nick suggested.

"Today?"

"Today." Nick looked Jerry straight in the eye. His face was as craggy as the Wasatch Front, but the beard was gone and so was the bandanna he used to wear as a hat. The Homeless Shelter's insurance plan had paid to replace the missing teeth. He still looked like he'd spent years living outdoors, but as a forest ranger perhaps or a land-scaper, not a vagrant.

Jerry had a policy of random drug testing and had contracted with a local lab to actually administer the tests. All he had to do was call and someone would be over in an hour or so.

"It's just a couple of days before Christmas," Jerry argued.

"Listen, boss," Nick answered, "I took a poll around the place. We're all sick of Bart's attitude. It ain't good for business. He's had some strange visitors at his apartment, too. One you won't like at all."

"Who?"

"Josh."

Jerry took this in and mulled it over for a minute. "I think I know what he's got up his sleeve," he said. "We can probably expect a visit from the police any day now."

"Some of the ladies with kids are nervous—for lots of reasons. We want him gone, boss, and this'll do it. He ain't doin' any work, and he's a pain in the neck to deal with."

Jerry wanted to say no, but he knew he couldn't. Besides the random drug testing, he also had a strict policy that any of the part-ners could be tested at any time if another of them saw anything suspicious. He certainly trusted Nick. He didn't think Nick would set anyone up, even Bart. And the story about Josh visiting Bart's apart-ment didn't seem quite so far-fetched.

"Okay," he said finally, "but I want to talk to Bart first. And I want you here."

When Bart returned, Jerry wandered over to the shipping area and asked him to come to his office. Nick was there waiting. The bag of cocaine was still sitting on Jerry's desk, and when Bart saw it, he about jumped out of his skin.

"Have a seat, Bart," Jerry said.

"I'll just stand, thanks," replied Bart.

Jerry sat down behind his desk and picked up the sandwich bag. "Bart," he said, "have you ever seen this before?"

"No," he said flatly, and Jerry knew he was lying. It was written in bold letters all over his face.

"Nick says he found this in your desk."

"Nick would," was all Bart said.

Nick was about to say something, but Jerry shot him a sharp glance, and he clammed up.

"You know the rules," Jerry said.

"I'm a partner here," Bart said. "You can't treat me like this. I'm calling the ACLU."

"Go ahead," Jerry suggested. "In the meantime, I've called the lab, and they're sending someone over this afternoon to administer a drug test. If you pass, you've got nothing to worry about."

Jerry could see Bart's mind churning. A lumberjack cornered by a pack of rabid tree huggers would have been more at ease. Jerry could see in Bart's eyes that he knew he wouldn't pass the test.

"Jerry," he pleaded, "you don't believe Nick, do you? He's had it in for me since the start."

Jerry thought for a moment before answering, and his conversation with Max came back to him. "Yes," he finally said, "I do believe Nick. But I don't think he's had it in for you. He and a lot of others have put up with your attitude and your unwillingness to carry your fair share for some time now. I wouldn't turn anyone out for just that, not if we can correct it. But this is serious, Bart. I'm not going to put up with drugs here. We've got enough problems."

"What if I don't pass the test?" Bart was perspiring even though Jerry's office was a bit on the cool side.

"You're gone."

"You can't do this to me." Bart was getting angry now. "I'm a partner."

"We all play by the same rules," Jerry said.

"I don't want to go back on the street."

"You should have thought of that when you bought this from Josh," Nick said, picking up the bag of coke and tossing it down on the table.

Bart gulped at the mention of Josh's name.

"Where'd you get the money for it anyway?" Nick asked. "None of us are rich enough to afford this stuff. You been stealin' from us, Bart?"

Jerry was shocked by Nick's accusation, but he could read the answer in Bart's eyes.

"Did you steal money from the business?" Jerry asked.

"You can't believe that, can you?" Bart exclaimed.

Jerry wished he could say no, but Max's words were hanging in front of him like a neon sign.

"Yes," Jerry said, "I can."

"You can't let me go," Bart screamed. "Tell me you won't do it."

Jerry couldn't say no. "If you fail the test, you'll have to leave, Bart," he said. "I'm sorry, but this is too serious."

Deep down Jerry was the forgiving type. He believed in second chances or even third or fourth. But he knew on this one issue he couldn't budge. He couldn't set a precedent that would come back to haunt all of them.

"Take the drug test, Bart," he said. "Then we'll see."

"No. I'm outta here. I know when I'm not wanted." He grabbed the sandwich bag from the table before Jerry could stop him and hurried toward the door. Suddenly he turned and stared straight at Jerry, as if a new thought had blossomed in his head. "Just remember something, Jerry," he said in a threatening voice. "I know where you live."

Bart was gone, but his words hung in the air like a dark cloud. Jerry looked at Nick and found absolutely nothing to say.

"I'm sorry, boss," Nick said. "I didn't think he'd go off like that."

"You think he's serious?" Jerry finally asked.

"I wouldn't put it past him," Nick said. "I've seen angry men before, and he's got nothin' to lose right now. If I was you, I'd keep my doors locked."

"You'd better keep yours locked too," Jerry answered. "You're not exactly his favorite friend, you know."

"Listen," Nick told him, "I'll go talk to Sanders, make sure he knows Bart's moving out of his apartment. If he can't get the key from him, we'll have to change a few locks." Sanders was a husky fellow with several rough edges but a good temperament, and Jerry had assigned him to be a combination apartment manager/security man.

Jerry gave Nick some money and left him in charge of the pizza while he hurried home just in case Bart got any crazy ideas. He didn't want Brenda and Jeff to be alone at a time like this. "Don't tell the others," Jerry said as he left. "Just let them know Bart's gone. I think it's just you and me he's mad at anyway."

When Jerry got home, he told Brenda all about his encounter with Bart and the news that Josh had probably been his supplier. She turned away and didn't say anything for two or three minutes.

"You think he's dangerous?" she asked finally.

Jerry was about to say no, but caught himself. "Yes," he confessed. "I'd be lying if I said no. Besides, I'm not supposed to." He then told her all about Max's call.

"How odd," she said. "But he did say nothing in our lives would change this year?"

"Yeah," Jerry answered. "I hadn't thought of that. Maybe there's nothing to worry about."

"Well, if you can't say no today, I'm not going to waste the opportunity." She arched her eyebrows and grinned at him mischievously.

"Merry Christmas," Jerry said. "But we'd still better keep the doors locked for a while till Bart simmers down."

* * *

In the middle of the night, the phone rang. Jerry stumbled out of bed and answered it. It was Sanders on the other end.

"Jerry," he said, "just thought I better call and let you know we had a visit tonight."

"Police?"

"Yup."

"They were looking for Bart?"

"Yup. Glad I moved him out earlier. He was nothin' but trouble."

"You know where he went?"

"Nope. But he was madder than a wet cat."

"What did the police say?"

"They'd heard we had drugs here, in apartment 114—Bart's."

"They find anything?"

"No, but I told 'em that's why we kicked Bart out. We knew he was buying drugs. They said they'd keep an eye out for him, but I could tell they had better things to do."

"Thanks, Sanders," said Jerry. "Get some sleep."

"You too, boss."

* * *

The next morning Jerry opened the door to get the newspaper and noticed something odd on his front lawn. At first he thought it was just a pile of somebody's laundry lying in the snow, but then he noticed a hand poking out one side of the heap. And in the hand was a gun. He closed the door and leaned his back against it.

"Brenda," he called. "You'd better come."

She hurried out of the bedroom. "What's the . . ." she began, then she looked at his face. "You look like you've seen a ghost," she said.

"Worse," he said. "Get your coat."

They walked outside and approached the body carefully. As they got closer, Jerry recognized the coat. The body was all bundled up with a ragged scarf around its neck and a stocking cap covering its head, but it was facedown in the snow, obviously dead and frozen stiff. The hand with the gun had turned white, almost as white as the snow.

"It's Bart," Jerry said, wondering what had happened . . . and what might have happened. "Or at least it used to be. Don't touch the body. I guess we'd better call the police."

* * *

The week after Christmas, the coroner's report came back. The police detective, a portly fellow named, ironically, Dillon Marshall, called Jerry at work. "He died of a heart attack," Marshall explained.

"Keeled over right on your front lawn apparently. You're a lucky man, Mr. Carlson, if what you told me is true. Strange, though. He was only forty-eight. But he did have traces of cocaine in his blood. That could have been a factor."

After the call, Jerry went home and told Brenda what the autopsy had found. She just looked at him and shook her head.

"Want to call Max?" she said.

"Of course I want to call Max," he answered. "But I know just what he'd say: 'Too bad about old Bart, huh? Have a nice vacation in San Diego. Click.'"

"I suppose you're right."

She reached up and put her arms around his neck and held him tight. At that moment, Jeff came toddling out of his bedroom and saw them. He let out a squeal and tried to squeeze between their legs. They each reached down a hand, picked him up, and had a group hug. Jeff couldn't have been more pleased.

* * *

That evening was Christmas Eve, and Jerry and Brenda decided to start a new tradition. They would gather as a little family, read the Christmas story out of the Bible, and eat some of the Christmas goodies Brenda had made during the week to give to neighbors and friends. Jerry went into the bedroom to get the Bible, and when he came out he had an odd look on his face.

"What is it?" Brenda asked.

"You been moving the bookmark and underlining verses?" he asked, already knowing the answer.

"No, why?"

"Look here," Jerry said, handing her the Bible.

It was opened to 2 Kings, to the story of Elisha the prophet, who had been giving strategic information to the Israelite armies in their war against the Syrians. The Syrians were tired of Elisha's meddling in military matters, so they sent an army to rid themselves of this thorn in their side. They had surrounded the city where Elisha was holed up with his young servant, and in the morning the servant awoke early, saw the situation, and cried out in fear, "Alas, my master! how shall we do?"

Elisha's answer was one of two verses Jerry found underlined: "Fear not: for they that be with us are more than they that be with them."

The following verse was also underlined. Apparently the young servant thought his master was one candle short of a menorah, because, as the Bible reported, "Elisha prayed, and said, Lord, I pray thee, open his eyes, that he may see. And the Lord opened the eyes of the young man; and he saw: and, behold, the mountain was full of horses and chariots of fire round about Elisha."

Brenda read the account, looked up at Jerry, and said, "So who is this Max, anyway?"

"I think I'm beginning to understand," Jerry answered, but his thoughts were far away, contemplating a young man who suddenly saw horses and chariots of fire where before there had been only a hillside full of enemies.

sixth christmas

....

Dreams

The incident with Bart made Jerry rethink a lot of things. First, he decided he was spending far too much time away from his family. So in February he took an extra week off, and they not only spent a week in the condo in San Diego, they also drove slowly up the coast and took a week to get home, stopping in Carmel, Monterey, and San Francisco, eventually making it all the way to Agate Beach in Oregon.

The second thing he reconsidered was the whole working environment at the Homeless Shelter. He couldn't afford to let things get as out of control as they apparently had with Bart. He started rotating assignments so that no one was able to build little kingdoms inside the company or start thinking they didn't have to pull their fair share. He also started bringing in specialists to do seminars and training. He realized he had treated these people like children in many ways. He decided, though, if he expected them to behave like adults, he needed to treat them as adults. He had originally intended to have the Homeless Shelter become a place of permanent employment for this handful of homeless people he had rescued from the street. Now he set a new goal—to give them marketable skills as well as life skills so they could leave the Homeless Shelter and move on to bigger and better things if they wanted to. This would enable him to bring in new people and help them get back on their feet. The Homeless Shelter would then become a sort of halfway house for the homeless to help introduce them back into society.

The third matter he rethought was his own role in the company. He decided he'd taken on far too much responsibility and was doing too many things himself. If he hoped to treat his "partners" as real partners and as adults, he needed them to shoulder more responsibility for the management of the enterprise. He even considered making his current position as president a rotating assignment, but thought better of it. Maybe in a few years, after they were more stable and established.

The final thing he rethought was the scope of his goals for the business. He had a year under his belt, and that year had proven to him that the company's products would sell. They had done well in the local market, and he felt sure he could use this as a springboard to the national market. So one day after he got back from sunny California, he hunted down the list of buyers he had found in Max's packet of documents. He figured he may as well start at the top and work his way down, so after consulting with his marketing vice president (Brenda), he called Wal-Mart, the enormous multinational discount chain. After navigating the phone system and talking his way past two or three levels of assistants and screeners, he finally got a buyer on the phone. Not wanting to making the mistake of overselling the product, Jerry opted for an understated approach.

"I've got a couple of products you'll probably want to look at," he said. "We've got an excellent track record locally. I'll send you samples with some newspaper clippings that explain the unique appeal of our products and why they'd do well in the national market."

The buyer sounded preoccupied, but agreed to take a look. A month later Jerry got a call from the same buyer, who, for all he knew, could have been an entirely different person because he was so excited.

"We've got to be cautious," the buyer warned, "so we'll do a test market in some of our stores, but I think it's promising." He then placed an order for so many "shelters" that Jerry almost swallowed his tongue. He knew his eighteen partners could never handle that volume. He'd need at least forty people just to produce the Wal-Mart test market order.

After this response he put the list back in the drawer. He knew only one thing could kill the company now—greed. The one thing he couldn't handle was too much growth. He'd have to take it slow.

The day after he took the Wal-Mart order, he called a meeting for all the partners. "I've got good news and good news and a warning," he told them. That got their undivided attention. "I landed an order yesterday from Wal-Mart."

At first there was silence, then everyone cheered.

"The other good news," Jerry continued, "is that they're going to do a test market in a few of their stores, but they really like the products and think they'll sell well."

Jerry looked into their faces. This was like Christmas in April. These people who had been out on the street a little over a year ago were now providing products to the world's largest retailer.

"The warning," Jerry said, and all eyes narrowed a bit, "is that this test market order is larger than last year's entire output. We'll have to double our workforce and get the new workers up to speed fast."

He could see the partners working out the math and evaluating the challenge. He knew their first thought would be "Why do we have to bring new people in?" They weren't all best friends, but they knew each other and were comfortable with the status quo. Now that Bart was gone, no one caused problems, and they all felt more or less equal. Doubling the workforce meant bringing in a lot of unknown variables. It also meant sharing their profits with people they didn't trust.

"Do we have to?" asked Blake, a fortyish fellow whose wife had left him with more debts than he could pay.

"There's no way you eighteen can handle such a large order," Jerry answered.

"Besides," Nick inserted, "this gives us an opportunity to help some other people who are living like we were."

"But we don't have enough apartments," exclaimed Connie, a single mom.

"I've thought about that," Jerry countered. "I think it's time some of you became more independent. I figured if you're willing, we could institute a dual pay scale. For those of you who would like to go out on your own and get an apartment, we'd pay the extra amount to cover rent and transportation to and from work. That would open up some apartments for the new people. Day care, of course, will still be free."

"What if we don't like 'em?" asked Carlos. "What if we get another Bart?"

"I've thought of that too," Jerry answered. "You pick two representatives from among you, and they'll sit in on every interview. Any one of us can eliminate any applicant for valid reasons."

"Sounds fair," said Carlos. "I'm all for it."

"Let's put it to a vote, then," said Jerry. "But remember, if you vote against it, we'll have to turn down the Wal-Mart order."

By putting it that way, he squelched any dissent. They didn't want to lose the order, even if it meant taking a few risks.

* * *

One pleasantly warm evening in April, Jerry and Brenda were sitting out on the lawn watching Jeff explore the far reaches of the backyard. The sky was fading from twilight's pale blue-grey to the deep indigo of night, and stars were blossoming in the heavens. Jeff had taken a long nap that afternoon and wanted nothing to do with bedtime yet, so they had humored him, seeing how warm the weather had turned, and had taken him outside to burn off some energy.

While their son was getting reacquainted with dirt, dry leaves, and the bare stalks of last year's flowers, Jerry lay with his head on Brenda's lap, staring up at the spring sky and pondering the fortunes of the past few years.

"I remember a day like this at Liberty Park," said Brenda suddenly. "We were lying on the grass, finding shapes in the clouds." She hadn't brought up that day in all the time they'd been married. In a way, he had hoped she'd forgotten it. "I asked you about your dreams."

"As I recall," Jerry said, struggling to keep the emotion from his voice, "you didn't like my answer much."

"I guess I wanted you to be older and a lot more experienced than you were. I wasn't fair to you."

"I really didn't know how to answer you back then," Jerry admitted.

"How about now? What if I asked the same question?" She gazed down at him, and there was no pressure, no expectation that he be anything other than just what he was. It was a look of love and peace—that was all. "I don't know," she said. "I guess looking up at the sky makes me think of bigger things. I wonder about the future, the purpose of life, if there's really an eternity out there, where we go after this life's over. We seem to get so caught up in the tiny details of everyday life. I guess sometimes the bigger picture gets out of focus. Maybe that's why I think it's important to have dreams. I asked you about your dreams that day long ago, and you thought I meant the nighttime ones. Do you dream now, Jerry?"

"Now and then," he laughed. "They're rather strange, but I do remember them now."

"Progress," she teased. "Progress. But what about the other kind of dreams, the kind you weren't very familiar with back then?"

"I don't know," he said. "There doesn't seem to be so much difference between those and the night dreams in my mind."

"Really!" She looked surprised. "What do you dream about, Jerry?"

"Flying, and lights, and fruit, and you."

"That's either really deep or complete nonsense," she laughed, "but what does it all mean?"

"I don't know," he confessed. "All I know is that for a long time all I dreamed about was marrying you. Then you left, and I was afraid to dream. I just survived day after day, and life was pretty meaningless. Then Max rescued me, and I started having real dreams, nighttime dreams, and in a way they started coming true."

"So, what are your dreams about now, Jerry?"

"I have to climb a tall tree to pick the fruit up in the branches, but the branches are too high for me to reach alone. I've got a group of people to help me get there, but they've been difficult to convince. I finally got them to build a human pyramid for me to stand on, but it still wasn't high enough. The last few weeks, though, more people have come to join us around the tree, and the pyramid's getting taller. I've almost reached the lowest branches."

"What's the fruit?"

"I don't know," he shrugged. "But somehow I know it's the best fruit in the world, and I've got to convince the people who are helping me that I'll share it with them if they help me get it."

"You help them, and they help you," she said, almost to herself.

"I guess so," he said.

"That's pretty much what I was dreaming about all those years ago when I told you I wanted to make a difference in the world. You didn't understand, and I didn't know how to explain it."

"Now you don't need to," Jerry told her.

"I know."

They sat in silence for several minutes and watched Jeff examine some acorns he'd found under the tree in the corner of the yard.

"Are you content?" Brenda asked him suddenly.

"Yes and no," he answered honestly.

"What do you mean?"

"I'm content here," he explained, waving his arm at the yard and house. "Couldn't be happier. And I'm pleased with the way things are going for the Homeless Shelter, even though it's a headache some days and a lot of work. But I'm afraid it won't last."

"Max?" she said softly.

"Yes. I just have this fear—I'm afraid I'm going to lose it all. I mean, I wouldn't really be devastated if the business were to go under. I'd feel bad for the partners, but I know I've done my best, and I can always find something else to do. I think I'm pretty marketable now. But when I think about losing you or Jeff," he paused and cleared his throat, "well, it scares me half to death."

"Didn't you know that would be part of the deal going in?" she said.

"Yeah, but that doesn't make it easier."

"Do you really think Max would tear our little family apart?"

Jerry closed his eyes and searched for wisdom somewhere in his heart, some way to explain what he really believed. "I don't think it's Max at all," he said finally.

"What do you mean?" she asked.

"I think Max is just an errand boy," he answered. "I think he'd do his best to make us happy, but I don't think it's up to him. He seems bound by some sort of rules that are made by somebody else."

"Who?"

"Somebody who knows more than Max does."

"Who is Max, Jerry?"

"I think he's my guardian angel, for lack of a better term."

"An angel with a cell phone?" Brenda giggled. "You think heaven's gone high-tech?"

"No, I think Max is just a bit unorthodox, a maverick. Maybe he's an angel with an attitude, a rebellious streak, a bit of personality."

"But you're afraid of him."

"Of Max? No, not at all. I'm just afraid of the one who makes the rules and sends Max out with requests."

Brenda looked over at Jeff and gasped. He was chewing and had mud dripping off his chin. Time for bed.

* * *

Reaping the Whirlwind

By midsummer Jerry had a workforce of forty, and the old warehouse was busting at the seams. Still, they managed to fill all their orders, and the cash started rolling in. A little free newspaper publicity in the cities where the test market was going down didn't hurt, and sales were solid if not spectacular. Jerry had his hands full, but he also had Nick and a couple of the new partners who showed real promise in their leadership ability.

One day in early August, Jerry looked out his office window and noticed that the sky was incredibly dark even though it was only noon. Thundershowers had been forecast for the day, but this looked like a nasty one. He gazed up into the gathering gloom, and the clouds suddenly took on a pale-greenish tint.

"No," he whispered to himself, "it can't be. Not in Salt Lake." Brenda, who was a farm girl from Nebraska, had told him how two tornados had come close to their farm. She'd described the strange, greenish shade of the horrible, dark clouds preceding the two twisters. Jerry ran out onto the factory floor and saw several of the partners gazing up at the high windows on the south side of the building.

"Stay away from the windows," he yelled. "I think we're going to have some wind."

No sooner had he spoken than a big gust hit the side of the building. Everyone hurried toward the center of the floor. Through the high windows, they could see papers and leaves and other debris swirling in the air. Jerry's ears felt funny, almost like he was underwater, and suddenly a window gave way and glass came raining down on the lathe where Carlos had been standing just moments before.

The sky outside got even darker, and the sound of small objects hitting the west wall echoed through the building. It lasted just a couple of minutes, then it was gone.

After a few moments, Jerry and Nick ran to the door and out into the parking lot. Just a couple of blocks to the east, a dark funnel cloud was churning its way toward downtown Salt Lake. They looked in morbid fascination at this powerful force of nature that could tear up man-made structures, shred trees, toss cars around, and snuff out life. In a few minutes the twister was out of sight. Several other people had followed Jerry and Nick outside, and now they looked around at their immediate surroundings. Two cars were in the parking lot, as well as the business's truck. They looked like they had been victims of a drive-by shooting. Windows had popped when the air pressure dropped rapidly. Tree branches were strewn about. And then they looked down the street and realized they had been on the very fringe of the damage.

North of the factory, the street looked like a war zone. Trees were toppled, buildings had lost a lot of brick, and some of those falling bricks had dropped onto cars parked next to the buildings. Power lines were down, and people stood dazed, in shock, not knowing what had happened or what to do. Fortunately, Jerry thought, the apartment building with their day care center was south of the factory, out of the path of destruction.

"Nick, come with me," Jerry yelled. "People may be hurt. Let's see if we can help."

Then he turned to Carlos, who was staring wide-eyed at the mess in the parking lot. "See if the building's damaged other than the one window," he said. "Get people to clean up a bit. I'll send Nick back if we need more help."

Carlos seemed to wake up at the sound of Jerry's voice and started organizing people. Nick and Jerry walked slowly up the street, avoiding any downed power lines and keeping an eye out for injured people. When they reached the center of the tornado's path, they stopped and stared at the house that had taken the most damage. A good deal of brick had fallen from the upper story, the car in the driveway was totaled, and almost all the windows looked as if a dozen vandals had held target practice with slingshots.

"Poetic justice, I'd say," Nick suggested. It was Josh's house.

"Let's see if anybody's hurt," said Jerry.

They knocked on the door. No answer. Nick tried the knob. It turned with a squeak, and the door swung slowly open.

Nick looked at Jerry and shrugged. "Do we go in?" he asked.

"Anybody home?" Jerry yelled.

They heard nothing for a minute, then a weak reply came faintly from somewhere inside. "Yeah, I'm here. Can you help me?"

They made their way carefully through front part of the house. It looked like a bomb had gone off. Glass was everywhere. So were paper and dirt and leaves. In a back room, a toppled bookcase was on the floor. A pair of ankles and feet poked out from under one side. Josh Monk's shoulders and head stuck out the other. A groan escaped him. "Can you get this thing off me?" he gasped.

Jerry and Nick took hold of the bookcase and stood it upright. Josh groaned again and rolled over onto a handful of the books that lay scattered about. When he saw who his rescuers were, he closed his eyes and shook his head.

"Any broken bones?" Nick asked.

"I don't think so," Josh said with a grimace. "I'll just be sore for a few days. Thanks for the help."

"You need to take a look around," Jerry suggested. "Your house looks like it got shelled."

Josh limped out the door and wandered around the yard. "What on earth?" he kept repeating.

Jerry and Nick checked some of the other buildings, but everything seemed to be under control, so they walked back to the factory.

"It might be poetic justice," Jerry said to Nick, "but I think I smell an opportunity here."

"What kind?" Nick asked, a hint of displeasure in his voice.

"What if we were to help Josh put his place back together?"

"Are you nuts?" Nick exclaimed.

"Of course, but I'm thinking this might be a way to defeat an enemy with kindness."

Nick thought for a few moments. "Maybe you're right," he said. "It's probably worth a try, but I doubt it'll work."

"We've got some cash coming in. Let's see what we can do."

* * *

The freak tornado, the largest ever seen in Utah, gathered power as it went through downtown Salt Lake; it tore part of the roof off the Delta Center, blasted apart the tent that was housing an outdoor retailers convention, just missed Temple Square, and toppled a construction crane on the Mormon Church's latest construction project, the colossal 21,000-seat Conference Center. Then it headed up through the Avenues, tearing roofs off houses and blowing up power transformers, until it finally hit the mountains northeast of the city and disappeared. It caused a good deal of damage and kept everyone talking for several weeks.

All the partners at the Homeless Shelter were drained by the close call. Jerry knew no one would get much done the rest of the day, so he sent them home to watch accounts of the disaster on the TV he'd bought for the day care center. He called Brenda to tell her he was okay, then settled in at his desk to plan the reconstruction of Josh Monk's old brick pile.

Josh was speechless when Jerry and Nick showed up the next day to offer their help. They could tell he wanted more than anything to turn them down, but they also knew he couldn't afford to. He admitted that he'd somehow managed to cancel his homeowners' insurance, even though the bank required it, so there was no way he could pay to repair all the damage. Finally he agreed to let them help put his place back together, but it was obvious he was none too pleased about it.

So for the next month, Jerry sent a crew of five up the street every day, and slowly Josh's house began to resemble the ugly, old edifice it had been for at least twenty years. When the work was all finished, Josh swallowed his pride and made a courtesy visit to the Homeless Shelter to sing a painful tune of gratitude.

Not two weeks later, however, a For Sale sign appeared on Josh's front lawn. Jerry walked over to see what was up, knocked on the door, but no one answered. He took the realtor's name and number down, called when he got back to the factory, and was told the house had been repossessed by the bank.

"Do you know where the former owner went?" Jerry asked.

"No, I was hired by the bank to sell the place," the realtor explained. "Haven't spoken at all with Mr. Monk. He didn't leave a forwarding address."

* * *

Another Envelope

On the homefront, Jeff was growing like a weed and was at that stage where he was into everything. One day Brenda came into the living room and discovered her own little tornado had spread powdered cocoa all over the carpet and furniture. A week later, the same thing happened with the flour canister. The next day, much to Jeff's chagrin, she invested in childproof latches for all the lower drawers and cupboards.

"That'll teach you, you little pest," she scolded, but the next day he pushed a chair over to the counter, clambered onto it, and pulled everything he could reach out of the cupboards. Brenda soon put latches on the upper cupboards, and Jeff discovered how much fun it was to unload the refrigerator. At that point, Brenda threw her hands in the air and put Jeff in his room for a couple of hours. When she finally went in to check on him because he had been so quiet, she found he had unloaded all the clothes from his dresser drawers and was sitting atop the pile like the king of the hill.

When she called Jerry in exasperation to complain, he laughed and said, "He'll grow out of it."

"Yeah," she replied, "but in the meantime, one of us is going to spend a couple of years locked in a padded room—and it isn't going to be me."

* * *

Actually, this phase didn't last very long, and by December Jeff had moved on to scribbling on the walls with crayon. It was all Brenda could do to keep up with him. In the meantime, she had joined a neighborhood Bunco group that met once a week to play the game and gab—more of the latter than the former—and when she heard the others tell their own horror stories, she realized her little destroying angel really wasn't so bad. She hadn't had oil-based paint spread all over the sofa or found her toddler eating old cat food yet.

Brenda wondered whether it would be safe to decorate for Christmas, given Jeff's propensity for making a colossal mess of anything he touched. But in the end, her love for the season overcame her fear of bedlam and ruin, and she went ahead and decorated. And by some strange quirk of nature, Jeff didn't touch her decorations. He was fascinated by them, but all he would do was sit and stare at them for long stretches of time. Even the gifts under the tree remained untouched. It was as if the holiday spirit held him spellbound.

* * *

Jerry started carrying the cell phone on December 18, and on the twentieth, about midmorning, it rang. He was in the middle of a staff meeting, but excused himself quickly and wandered out into the warehouse portion of the building to talk.

"Hi, Max," he said.

"How's business?" Max asked.

"Couldn't be better," Jerry replied.

"Oh, but it will be," Max assured him.

"Max," Jerry said, then paused.

"Yes, Jerry?"

"What happened to Bart?"

"I hear he suffered a heart attack."

"On my front lawn? With a gun in his hand?"

"I must admit, it *was* an odd place to have a heart attack."

"The timing was a bit suspicious too, wasn't it?"

"I suppose. Maybe he saw a ghost."

"What did he see, Max? Some chariots of fire?"

"Oh, I doubt it."

"Did he see you perhaps?"

"Why would that give Bart a heart attack? Good-looking guy like me?"

"I don't know. Maybe you're not so good-looking. How would I know? Maybe you're really ugly. Maybe you're an alien."

"Maybe I am."

"What, your spaceship only comes to earth once a year, around Christmastime?"

"Something like that."

"You expect me to believe you?"

"No," Max laughed. "But I'd be interested, Jerry. What *do* you believe?"

"I don't know what to believe anymore, Max. You're either my guardian angel, or those paranoid best-sellers about conspiracy theories and secret organizations that know everything about everybody are on to something."

"Don't believe everything you read, Jerry."

"So, are you an angel?"

"My mother probably wouldn't say so."

"Who is your mother, Max?"

"Wouldn't you like to know?"

"Of course I would. So, tell me, Max, do you have a belly button?"

"That's getting kind of personal, don't you think?" Max suggested. "But I'll tell you this—I don't have any birthmarks."

"What a relief," Jerry said sarcastically. "For a minute there, I thought you were just a voice in my imagination. So, can I see you sometime?"

"I can't show myself to unbelievers," Max stated.

"What if I say I believe?"

"I still can't show myself."

"Why?"

"Time's not right."

"Will it ever be?"

"Maybe."

"How will I know when it is?"

"You'll know."

"Gee, thanks."

"Don't mention it."

"So why did you call this year, Max? Just to teach me patience?"

"I'm doing a pretty good job, don't you think?"

Jerry didn't answer.

"You'll be getting another envelope in a day or two," Max told him.

"What's in it?"

"You always ask such obvious questions, Jerry."

"Okay, what color is it?"

"Blue."

"Blue? So what's in it?"

"A surprise."

"How . . . how utterly surprising, Max."

"I know you don't like surprises."

"Sorry to disappoint you."

"That's okay. How's Jeff?"

"He hit the terrible twos early, I think."

"Good for him. How's Brenda?"

"Fine. Exasperated. Losing her mind. Take your pick."

"Good. Well, have a nice Christmas, Jerry."

"You too, Max. Talk to you next year."

Jerry put the cell phone down and shook his head. He wondered what would be in the envelope this time.

* * *

Two days later, when Jerry got home from work, a small blue envelope was resting on his dinner plate.

"It's got another key in it," Brenda informed him.

Somehow Jerry wasn't surprised. He picked up the blue envelope, tore open the end, and tipped it. A key slid out into his hand. He held the envelope up and blew into the open end. It puffed out, but nothing else was in it.

"Just a key," he said. "With numbers stamped on it."

Brenda took it from him and examined it. "I think it's to a safe-deposit box," she said.

"Hmmm," Jerry replied.

"Wonder what's in it."

"I wonder what bank it's at."

"I'll call around tomorrow," she said.

* * *

The next day was the last workday at the Homeless Shelter before the Christmas holiday, and again, all the orders had been shipped, so the partners spent the day cleaning up and partying. At about three o'clock Brenda called.

"Sorry I'm so late," she said, "but Jeff didn't want to go down for his nap until two. Anyway, I called a couple of banks. Didn't take long. The box is at the downtown First Federal Bank. They're only open until noon tomorrow."

"We can go in the morning," Jerry told her. "I don't have anything else to do here before the holiday."

So the next morning, the three of them headed out in Jerry's truck for the bank. First Federal's main branch was on the corner of Broadway and Second East. Jerry parked in a lot behind the building, and they made their way to the lobby. A pretty receptionist with bottle-blond hair asked them if she could help. Jerry showed her the key and said they wanted to look in their safe-deposit box. She called for Martha Burnham, who apparently worked in the safe-deposit box area.

After a minute or two, Martha emerged from an elevator in the corner of the lobby and approached them. She was about fifty, dressed impeccably in a navy suit and a multicolored scarf, wore her silver hair short, almost like a man's, and had a smile full of perfectly straight, white teeth.

"So you want to open your box," she said without introducing herself.

"If we could," Brenda answered.

"Let me see the key," she said. She took it from Jerry and read the number, then handed it back. "One of our larger boxes, I see. Follow me, please."

They followed Martha to the elevator, descended two floors, and stepped out into a waiting area with a small privacy room on either side and a doorway at the rear through which they could see a wall of safe-deposit boxes.

"Wait here," she instructed, then disappeared through a door just to the left of the elevator. A moment later she returned with a key.

"Two keys, as you surely know," she explained, "yours and the bank's, are required to open the box."

They followed her into the room at the rear of the waiting area and found themselves surrounded by metal walls lined with boxes.

Martha walked straight to the spot she desired, inserted her key, turned it, and motioned for Jerry to do likewise. He put the key in the other lock, turned it, and looked at Martha. She slid the box out of its slot. It looked to be a foot square and about sixteen inches deep. She handed it to Jerry. "You can go into one of the privacy rooms to look at the contents," she said. "Take anything you like or put new items in," she said. "But if you add anything, I'll have to check it, you know, to make sure it's nothing dangerous."

"Fine," Jerry said, "but while we're opening the box, could you look up our records? I'd like to see them to make sure everything's still current."

"Certainly," she said, and pointed them toward one of the privacy rooms.

When they were alone at last, Jerry removed the lid from the box and looked inside. It was just a plain, dark blue cardboard box, the kind envelopes come in, but Jerry just stared, not believing his eyes. Brenda looked up at him, wondering why he didn't take the box out. Then she noticed the tear trickling down his cheek. She reached out and took his hand.

"What is it, Jerry?" she asked.

He wiped the tear away with his free hand, then said, "Here, I'll show you." He pulled the box out and removed the lid. It was full of photographs. He picked up the top one and handed it to Brenda.

"Jerry," she said, "if that's not you, it's your twin brother. But who's the woman?"

"My mother," he replied.

"That man's your dad?"

"Yup."

"If he had a mustache, I'd swear it was you."

"This box is the only thing I was really sorry to leave behind," he said, "but I didn't dare take it with me, and I didn't have anyone to give it to."

"So how'd it get here?"

"I have no idea," he said. "I know Max paid off my credit cards, and he must have turned the Explorer back in to the dealer. But I didn't know he'd saved this."

"I have a question," Brenda said.

Jerry looked at her but didn't say anything.

"If he knew you were heading out to throw your life away at the start, why did he let you spend three years on the street? Why didn't he save you at the beginning?"

"I think I know," Jerry said pensively. "And I think Max knew what I know now—this is the only way it could have worked out. Without losing my life, I never could have found it. Besides," he added with a grin, "I think he had to give you three years to come to your senses."

"Gee, thanks," Brenda said, and kissed his cheek. "Let's take this box home and look through it. There are some people here I need to get acquainted with."

They left the privacy room and found the ever-efficient Martha waiting for them. "Here's the paperwork," she said.

Jerry took the documents and looked through them. "I signed it," he said to Brenda, "or at least it looks like I did, and I paid for ten years in advance. But the address listed is our current address."

Brenda whistled softly to herself. "What do you know?" she said.

"What did you expect?" Jerry handed the papers back to Martha and carried the box to the elevator.

* * *

That evening, Christmas Eve, after Jeff had gone to bed, Jerry and Brenda sorted through the contents of the box. Not only did it contain all the old photographs Jerry had saved when he'd cleaned out his parents' house, but it also had a few important documents such as his birth certificate and his Social Security card. It was a special Christmas. In a way, Jerry felt his parents were there with them.

The snapshots brought back all sorts of memories that had been crowded out of his mind, first by the numbing blankness of his years on the street and then by the busyness of his current life. Now they came creeping back into his mind, and he told Brenda about each picture. There were vacations to Disneyland, Mount Rushmore, and Bryce Canyon when he was a youngster; birthday parties and hikes in the canyons and Little League baseball games. All this and more. For Jerry it was almost like reliving his childhood, and for Brenda the pictures and their accompanying memories filled in empty spaces in the life that had joined hers, spaces she hadn't been able to fill because Jerry had forgotten the events and faces occupying those spots.

When they finally finished looking through the photographs in the box and enjoying the memories they evoked, Brenda put her arms around her husband and kissed him.

"Well," she said, "I think I like this Max."

seventh christmas

....

Second Chance

The Wal-Mart test market had gone well. Not spectacular, but enough bird- and doghouses were sold to persuade the giant retailer to place a sizeable order for the next year. Jerry had to lease another building down the street and turn it into a warehouse and shipping center. He rounded up twenty more partners, bringing the total to sixty. He also found a single mother at Del Greco's Downtown Mission who had been a bookkeeper before life had taken some mean twists and turns. Her name was Avalon, and she was able to take over the accounting from Brenda, who kept more than busy splitting her time between being a mom to an energetic two-year-old and generating publicity for the Homeless Shelter's products.

Jerry had taken one step back from managing the day-to-day production. He found he just couldn't do it all, so he left production in Nick's increasingly capable hands and focused his efforts on the larger picture—finances, long-term planning, and what most companies would call "human resources." Jerry found the term repugnant, so he referred to it as "people services."

In April he and Brenda left little Jeff with some neighbors who had a son his age and got away from everything and everyone for the first time since their brief honeymoon. They spent a week on a cruise ship in the Caribbean and came back tanned, rejuvenated, and ready to slay dragons and conquer kingdoms. Or at least Jerry did. For three days after returning, Brenda, who had been a bit seasick on the cruise, felt as though the earth were rocking back and forth under her feet.

The neighbors who had tended Jeff assured her this was normal for many people who hadn't gotten their land legs yet and it would pass in a day or two.

May rolled around, and Brenda was still feeling a bit queasy. She was quite sure it wasn't delayed seasickness, but she did believe it had something to do with the cruise. A visit to the doctor confirmed her suspicions, and that night at dinner she had some news for Jerry and little Jeff.

"How would you like to have a little brother or sister?" she asked Jeff.

"Brover," he said matter-of-factly.

"Is this an announcement?" Jerry asked.

"I suppose so," Brenda answered.

Jerry beamed at her and gave her a big hug. "You sure you don't want a sister?" he asked Jeff.

"Brover," Jeff insisted.

"Brover it is, then," Jerry answered. "See what you can do about that, Brenda, okay?"

"Sure," she said. "Whatever my two masters want."

"When's the due date?"

"Jeff's birthday."

"You're kidding."

"Do I look like I'm kidding?" she said.

"No," he admitted, "you look like you're going to throw up."

"I'm going to lie down for a few minutes," she said. "Could you make sure Jeff eats all his broccoli?"

* * *

In September, Jerry had five of his partners give him their two-week notice. They had offers at regular businesses and had decided to leave. Jerry was happy for them of course, and this was exactly what he wanted for them, but he was still sad to see them go. That also meant he had to go to Del Greco's Downtown Mission and recruit some new partners. The reverend had this down to a science now. He put Jerry and the partners' two representatives, Nick and Marci, in a room upstairs and had ten people scheduled one after another.

The first was a young man who had run away from home. He looked barely seventeen. What he needed, Jerry decided, was to go home, apologize to his parents, and get a job at McDonald's. They were hiring, he knew, and the kid was too immature to be out on his own. Jerry gave him a piece of his mind and sent him on his way. He figured the kid had about a week more of rebellion in him before he'd come to what few senses a seventeen-year-old might possess.

The second applicant was a fifty-year-old, laid-off project manager with a manufacturing background. He had grown teenagers who were working and making it on their own, but he couldn't find work. Manufacturing was being replaced by high-tech in the Utah economy, as it was elsewhere in the country, and jobs were scarce, especially for fifty-year-old men without college degrees. He'd been out of work for a year, but on the street for only a couple of months. His name was Frank Hampton, and he was married. He and his wife, Lola, had been sleeping in their old Dodge Caravan, which they parked in Del Greco's small parking lot. Frank burst into tears when Jerry told him he was exactly the man he'd been looking for. Nick and Marci agreed. They could always use someone with a good, solid manufacturing background.

Jerry was jotting down some notes about Frank when the next applicant came in and sat down. He knew something was up when Nick cleared his throat rather loudly. He looked up and almost fell out of his chair.

"Hello, Jerry," the man said.

"Hi, Josh. What brings you here?"

"I'm homeless," Jerry's old nemesis said.

Jerry was suspicious, of course. "Why'd you leave your place over by our factory? I mean, we helped you with all the repairs."

"Ran out of money," Josh answered with a shrug. "The bank foreclosed on the old house. Since then I've been living on the street. It's tough, Jerry. You don't know how tough it is."

Jerry didn't say anything. For a brief moment he wondered if this was a setup. A couple of years ago, he wouldn't have put it past Josh to stage something like this. Try to get hired, then sabotage the business from within. But something in Josh's eyes was different. There was none of the old swagger, not even a hint of the vindictiveness left.

He looked tired. Rock bottom, end of the rope, and all the other clichés seemed to fit the image in front of Jerry. He had become rather adept at reading eyes, and in Josh's he saw two things: a weary hope and, right behind that, suicide. They were as plain to read as his greasy, unkempt hair and the stains on his shirt.

Jerry still didn't answer.

"I need help, Jerry," he said, and Jerry could tell how hard this admission was for him.

Jerry glanced at Nick.

"What can you do?" Nick asked him.

"I can learn," Josh answered.

"What were you doing when you lived down the street from us?" Nick asked.

"Selling coke, a little crack, anything to make a buck."

Jerry sighed audibly and shook his head, but still didn't say anything.

"Selling but not using?" Marci asked, skepticism dripping from her voice.

"Never did," Josh answered, looking down at his shoes. "With me it was all about money. I made some big mistakes with my dad's business, and I wanted to make back what I'd lost. I didn't want to be labeled a loser my whole life." He paused here and laughed uneasily. "But look at me now."

"You never used the stuff yourself?" Marci asked, still not satisfied.

"Never," Josh said, and Jerry could see in his eyes this was true.

"You just pushed it, got other people addicted?" he asked.

"They were already addicted," Josh claimed. "I just sold 'em what they needed."

"Was Bart already addicted?" Nick asked.

"Yeah. It wasn't hard to pick him out. He was hungry for it."

"So you fed his addiction and then called the cops," Marci accused. "Who were you trying to put out of business, yourself or us?"

Josh hung his head. "Maybe both," he confessed. "Listen, okay, I knew my life was going down the drain. I couldn't stand to see you and Brenda so happy. I figured it might make me feel better if I pulled you down with me."

"And now?"

"When you people came after the tornado and helped me out," Josh said, "I realized what a scum I was. I stopped pushing dope, and after that the money ran out really fast. That's why the bank foreclosed."

"What other work have you done since Lumenescent went under?" Jerry asked.

"Nothing," Josh said, shaking his head sadly. "I mean, who would have me? I ran my dad's business into the ground. Some resumé, huh?"

"What have you been doing since the bank kicked you out?"

"Begging for change, hanging out here at the shelter, sleeping in doorways and parks. But you wouldn't understand."

"I wouldn't?"

Josh looked up at Jerry.

"I lived that way for three years, Josh." He paused and let these words sink in.

"When?"

"After your dad fired me."

Josh was speechless. "Three years?" he finally stammered.

"Three."

"I'll never make it that long." He hung his head again.

Jerry looked at him long and concluded this was probably true.

"I don't know," Jerry said to Marci and Nick. "What do you two think?"

"I can't help but wonder what he'll do when he gets a bed to sleep in and three meals a day," Marci answered. "When his suffering's over, will he start hatching his nasty little schemes again? I'd love to believe people can change, but with this one I'm not so sure. Can anyone as rotten as he was completely leave his old habits?"

"Good question, Marci," Jerry said. "I can't help but wonder the same thing."

"But he ain't tough enough to make it on the street," Nick observed. "If we don't help him, he'll be dead before the end of the year. I say we give him a chance, but I don't think we can do that without having the partners vote on it. And it would have to be unanimous."

"Okay," said Marci reluctantly. "But it has to be unanimous."

"I'll do anything you want," Josh promised. "Anything to get off the street."

"No," said Jerry. "Not anything. Anything is what you were doing to stay off the street before. You'll do right and you'll live by the rules, or you'll be on the street again so fast you won't know what hit you."

Josh nodded, then got up to leave.

"Be at the Homeless Shelter factory tomorrow morning," said Nick. "I believe you know where it is. We'll let you introduce yourself and make your case."

"Josh," said Jerry as he headed for the door.

Josh turned around, and there were two dollars in Jerry's outstretched hand. "Bus fare," he said. Josh took the bills silently and left.

* * *

In the end, the vote was indeed unanimous. These people knew something about second chances and were willing to give Josh one—but only one. They let him know if he caused any trouble, he'd be out on his ear.

* * *

Money

By Christmas, two things were obvious. Brenda was going to be greatly relieved to have the pregnancy end—she had been nauseated for most of the past eight months—and the Homeless Shelter was going to be in the black in a major way. Orders kept flooding in, and Jerry's partners were, for the most part, productive and happy. He'd come to the conclusion that the best way to motivate new partners was simply to pair them up with the established ones and have them learn by watching. Sales were strong, costs were under control, and the future looked bright.

On December 18, Jerry came down with a nasty cold and decided to stay home from work. Brenda was miserable and said she could use a little help with Jeff anyway. But about 10:30 in the morning, the phone rang. Brenda answered it and handed it to Jerry.

"Jerry, Jerry, Jerry," came the familiar voice. "What are trying to do, ignore me? The cell phone's not on."

"Max!" Jerry exclaimed. "Sorry. I'm sick today and didn't even think of it."

"Well, take some cold medicine and get yourself on over to work."

"Is something happening there I need to know about?" he asked, suddenly concerned a disaster may have occurred.

"Well, you'll never know if you don't show up."

"Can't I just get some rest?"

"Get some rest after Christmas. Today you need to be at work."

"You called just to tell me to go to work?"

"No," Max sounded impatient. "You also need to make sure you say yes to anything anyone proposes today."

"That's it?"

"What do you expect, a major miracle every year?"

"Sorry, Max. By the way, thanks for saving my pictures."

"Don't mention it. You weren't thinking very clearly back then, you know."

"Yeah, I suppose you're right."

"Of course I'm right. Have I ever been wrong?"

"How should I know? I haven't known you forever."

"Just get to work, okay? You need to be there by 11:00."

"All right, all right. But tell me one thing . . ."

"No, Jerry," Max sounded impatient. "Just get to work."

"Okay," Jerry said. "Have a nice Christmas, Max."

"You too. Bye."

Jerry hung up the phone, looked at Brenda, and shrugged.

"Sounds like I'd better get to work," he said.

"Ohhh," Brenda groaned. "Of all the silly things he could ask."

Jerry felt like death warmed over and looked about as bad as he felt. He hadn't showered or shaved. But as he looked at the clock, he knew he'd barely make it by 11:00 if he left right then. He grabbed his coat from the closet, blew Brenda a kiss, and headed for the door.

"Call me when you find out what's so urgent!" she yelled as he ran out the door.

*   *   *

Jerry screeched to a stop in the parking lot, checked his watch, and ran for the door. It was eleven on the nose. He yanked the door open, rushed into the front office, and looked around. Everything appeared as normal as could be. He hurried to the factory floor, pushed the door open, and peered inside. The partners were going about their work as if nothing were amiss. Nick was standing next to a tall stack of lumber, writing something in a notebook. He glanced up when he heard the door open.

"Hey, boss," he yelled, "I thought you were sick today."

Nick took three steps toward Jerry, and suddenly there was a loud thud. Lance, who had been moving something with the forklift, had accidentally backed into the stack of lumber. The top bundle toppled off and landed right where Nick had been standing a moment before. He jumped out of the way and barely escaped getting hit. Jerry stared at him, and he stared at Jerry. Nick, usually unflappable, started shaking like a leaf.

"If you hadn't come in the door just then," he said, "I'd be a pancake."

"You'd be dead," Jerry told him.

"Man," Nick exclaimed, "your timing couldn't a been better. I didn't think you were comin' in today."

"I wasn't," Jerry told him. "I think your guardian angel must be looking out for you." *Thank you, Max,* Jerry thought. He knew he could go home now, but since he was there, he decided to stay, at least for a couple of hours.

* * *

Just after lunch, Nick came into Jerry's office with his two foremen, Bill and Skip, and Marge, who was currently assigned to run the shipping department.

"What's up?" Jerry asked. His head was throbbing, and his sinuses wanted to explode.

"You look awful, boss," Nick told him. "You oughta go home."

"That's the plan as soon as I get a little paperwork finished. What can I do for you?"

"Well," Nick said, shifting his weight from one foot to the other and back again, "we been talkin'."

"Good," said Jerry. "What've you been talking about?"

"We got an idea."

"Who's we?"

"All the partners."

"You've all had the same idea? Great minds must think alike."

"Well, at least ours do, I s'pose," said Nick with a grin.

"Let's hear it, then."

"Now, don't misunderstand," Nick began. "We know even though you call us partners and all . . ."

"You *are* partners," Jerry assured them.

"I know," Nick continued, "but, I mean, this is really *your* business. It's your money that got it started and all . . ." He paused here, and Jerry didn't say anything, so he went on. "You've never acted like you was in this for the money."

"I'm not," Jerry told them. "We just need to stay profitable to stay in business."

"Well," Nick hemmed and hawed, "we was thinkin' this is going to be a pretty good year."

"It is. I'm very pleased with the way things are going. But where are you going with this, Nick?"

"Avalon says we'll probably turn a profit, after taxes, of near half a million this year."

"Yes, that's what she's projecting."

"Well, have you thought about what you're goin' to do with all that profit?"

"I've given it some thought," Jerry answered.

"Well, so have we." Nick paused and looked at his cohorts as if for moral support. "We got a proposal."

This got Jerry's attention. "Let's hear it," he said. "I'm all ears."

"Well, first off, we need some repairs and some capital improvements on the old factory here," he said. "We figured if you put maybe a couple hundred grand into improvements, that would fix things up for this year."

"I'd considered that," Jerry said.

"Avalon did some other projections," Nick continued. "She figures next year might be twice as profitable as this year."

"It could be," Jerry agreed. "Orders are increasing all the time. So?"

Nick fidgeted a little with his hands. "We want you to know, boss," he said, "we ain't in this for the money neither. We don't need to get rich. You pulled us in off the street, and we can't tell you how grateful we are."

Jerry could tell how difficult this was for Nick, but he let him continue.

"After the capital improvements," Nick said, "the rest of the profit's yours, of course, and we don't have any right to tell you what to do with it."

"No, it's not," Jerry assured him, "and yes, you do."

"Well, we don't see it that way."

"If there's any profit, you people have created it," Jerry told him.

"Well," Nick said, "we know how generous you are, but we don't want you givin' us the rest of the money as profit sharing or bonuses or anything."

"Then what am I supposed to do with it?"

"Well," Nick said, "we got figurin' if you wanted to split up maybe fifty grand among us partners as a year-end bonus, we wouldn't necessarily argue. Now, we don't expect it, mind you, but we wouldn't argue. Any more than that, and we'd give it back."

"So what am I supposed to do with a quarter of a million dollars?"

"Hang on to it for a year," Nick said. "Put another two hundred grand into improvements again next year, split up another fifty grand for bonuses, and you've got a million bucks in the bank. We'd love to tell you to just retire, but we know you wouldn't, so we're proposin' that you take that money and give it to somebody who can start up another business like this one. Fund another business to get people off the street."

Jerry's head had stopped pounding. He looked at Nick and smiled. "Nick," he said, "I think that's a wonderful idea. I was wondering what we'd do if we started earning lots of money. I was maybe going to donate it to the shelter, but I think you're right. Like they say, a hand up is better than a handout."

Suddenly Jerry remembered Max's phone call, and he knew this was exactly what Max wanted him to do with any excess profit. He'd have to find someone, though, who had an idea and who would use the money as he had done. That would be the hard part. Of course, chances were, it suddenly occurred to him, next year's phone call from Max just might include the name of someone who was right for the job.

After Nick and his cohorts left—quite pleased, Jerry thought—he called Brenda and told her what had happened.

"That Max," was all she could say. "So much for my mansion on the hill."

* * *

Later that afternoon when Jerry went home, Brenda put her arms around his neck and kissed his cheek.

"I've got something to show you," she said.

She pulled him into the bedroom, sat him down on the bed, and picked the Bible up off the nightstand.

"After your call, I just figured Max might have left us a little message again," she said. "Actually, I guess the message is for me." She laughed with guilty delight. "Here, see for yourself."

She placed the book on his lap, and there, underlined in red pencil, were the words, "For we brought nothing into this world, and it is certain we can carry nothing out. And having food and raiment let us be therewith content. But they that will be rich fall into temptation and a snare, and into many foolish and hurtful lusts, which drown men in destruction and perdition. For the love of money is the root of all evil."

eighth christmas

The Fall

It had been an eventful year. Megan Anne Carlson was born at two in the morning on January 10, a healthy baby girl with a head full of dark, wispy hair and a dimple in her left cheek.

"Sisser?" Jeff said, a puzzled expression on his face when Jerry picked him up from the neighbors who had tended him while his sister was being born.

"Yes, a baby sisser," Jerry assured him.

"Brover?" Jeff suggested.

"No, a sisser. Megan."

"Maygun?"

"Yeah, Maygun."

* * *

In June they flew back to Nebraska to let Brenda's parents get better acquainted with their grandchildren. The McDonalds had come out to Salt Lake twice during the winter since Jeff's birth, but this year they suggested Jeff might like to have some fun on the farm in the summer. Plus, this would also give them the chance to meet their new granddaughter. The trip was an enormous success. Jeff had the time of his young life, riding horses; chasing chickens; helping Grandpa drive the tractor; making friends with Ralph, the old farm dog; and generally running free all over the open spaces surrounding the old farmhouse. It was as if he had found his element, and when the time came to leave for home, he didn't want to go.

"Please, Mommy," he pleaded, "can I stay wiff Grampa?"

"We'll come again, dear," she promised, and he broke into a terrible, sobbing wail. "No" was not a word he had learned to relish.

The new little sister also made a quite an impression on him. For some reason, the new baby fascinated him. Jerry and Brenda hadn't seen or heard of anything like it. They'd been warned that Jeff would be jealous and might turn into a spoiled little brat in his efforts to compete for attention, but the exact opposite was true. Megan brought out the best in Jeff. He would sit for long stretches, far longer than a four-year-old's longest attention span, and just stare at the baby. Now and then he would reach out and put his finger in her palm, and she would grab it and hold on for dear life.

Jeff was fascinated with every new thing little Megan learned. When she began rolling over, he would roll with her. When she learned to giggle, the two would lie on the floor together and have giggling contests. When she started crawling, he was right by her side on hands and knees, and when she started pulling herself up to furniture, he was amazed and encouraged her to walk.

While all this was happening at home, sales were rolling in at the Homeless Shelter, and by August, when Christmas orders began to appear, it was evident they would beat Avalon's sales projections by almost fifty percent. There were still conflicts now and then between partners, but for the most part things rolled along harmoniously. Josh, Jerry's most obvious worry, had not given them any trouble at all—yet. *So far, so good,* Jerry would tell himself, but deep inside he still wondered how long the change would last. Actually, Josh was getting quite good at cutting out some of the more difficult parts on the jigsaw and was visibly pleased at having learned a new skill—and also at having a roof over his head. But every now and then, he got a look in his eye that scared Jerry. It reminded him too much of the old Josh.

During the first half of the year, six more of Jerry's partners accepted offers to work elsewhere for substantially higher wages. This was exactly what Jerry had hoped for, but there was sadness on both sides when these people left. Jerry replaced them, however, with newly rescued souls from Del Greco's mission, and the company marched along almost as smoothly as if there had been no turnover.

In September, the mayor of Salt Lake presented Jerry with a special humanitarian award and made him honorary mayor for a day. After accompanying the real mayor to a city council meeting, helping him preside over the groundbreaking for a new strip mall, eating catered food at a fund-raising banquet, and hearing complaints about everything from road construction to liquor laws, Jerry decided politics was definitely not in his future. And anyway, to be honored publicly for something he felt was actually Max's doing embarrassed him. The last thing he wanted was public attention—even though it always pushed sales higher—because he still felt *he* was the primary beneficiary of everything Max had done.

In fact, everything had been so perfect for so long, it almost didn't surprise him when Brenda called one cold day in late October with a note of panic in her voice.

"Jerry, come quick," she blurted out. Then her voice broke, and she sobbed into the phone, "We're at the hospital. Jeff fell down the stairs. He's in surgery."

"Surgery!" Jerry exclaimed. "What's wrong with him?"

For a long moment, Brenda couldn't make any words come. Finally she stammered, "He broke his neck. Please hurry."

Jerry rushed out the door without his coat and shattered all the speed limits on the way to the hospital. He parked and ran through a thin, biting rain to the main door. At the front desk, he asked quickly where Jeff's surgery was taking place and ran up the stairs to a waiting room on the third floor. There he found Brenda hugging little Megan tight, tears streaming down her cheeks. Megan wasn't crying, but looked eager to get down on the floor and go exploring. She couldn't understand why Mommy was so upset. Jerry sat down next to Brenda and wrapped his arms around both of them.

"Oh," Brenda sobbed, "I'm so glad you're here."

"Calm down if you can," he said. "Tell me what happened."

"Jeff was building a . . . a Lego castle," she said, taking a deep breath every few words to keep from losing control. "He was so proud of it. . . . He wanted to show me and came running down . . . the stairs. He tripped . . . and I saw him. He landed funny . . . and didn't

get up. I could tell he was hurt bad. His head was twisted . . . at a
horrible angle. He was conscious . . . and he didn't even cry. He said
he couldn't move. . . . I didn't dare touch him, so I called 911. The
paramedics brought him to emergency . . . and the doctors took one
look and took him straight to surgery."

"What did the doctors say?"

"It looked real bad. . . . They were concerned . . . I could tell."

Jerry held her tight and didn't say anything. He didn't tell her
about the dream he'd had the night before, nor would he ever, he
decided. He had finally made it to the lowest branches of the tree.
The human pyramid was high enough for him to barely reach a
branch. He had hoisted himself up onto it and was reaching for
another when his foot slipped and he toppled backward. Falling
seemed to take forever, but he hit the ground awkwardly, and
suddenly he couldn't feel a thing. His head worked fine, but he
couldn't feel his arms or legs. In a way he felt lighter than air, but in
another way he felt as heavy as death. There was no pain, but there
was also no sensation at all. It was as if he'd been cut off from life. In
fact, physically he felt just as he had emotionally all those years on the
street. The pyramid quickly came down, and the partners gathered
around him. "You almost made it, Jerry," they said. "It's going to be
so much harder now, but have faith. You can still make it." And now,
once again, he felt somewhere deep inside just as he had felt in the
dream—numb and helpless.

After what seemed an eternity, a doctor in surgical gear came
through the door and approached them. "Would you come with me,"
he said kindly. "I'm David Metcalf, the neurosurgeon who operated
on your son."

They followed him out the door and down the hallway to a small
consultation room. Dr. Metcalf was a tall, balding man with a salt-
and-pepper goatee and frizzy hair that poked out around his ears like
overused Brillo pads.

"Your son's name is Jeffrey?" he asked as he closed the door
behind them.

"Jeff," Jerry answered.

"Well, Jeff's had a bad accident," Dr. Metcalf pronounced somberly.
"We rushed him into surgery because he was having trouble breathing

and the break was so severe it was putting a great deal of pressure on the spinal cord. We've stabilized his spinal column and taken most of the pressure off, but there's still a good deal of swelling. The good news is that he's breathing on his own now. He shouldn't need a respirator."

"And the bad news?" Jerry asked.

"I'm afraid your son is a quadriplegic," Dr. Metcalf stated. "There was simply too much trauma to the spinal cord. Unless monumental advances are made in the future, he will spend the rest of his life in bed or in a wheelchair." He paused to let this sink in. "I know this is incredibly difficult," he said, "but your lives have just changed more than you can understand. Life will never be the same for you. This is permanent, and you need to come to grips with it. Now, in a while Jeff will wake up, and you need to be there. I know it's hard, and the first reaction is to deny reality, but you need to help him face the future with a positive frame of mind. For his sake, you need to make the best of this." He paused again, then continued. "Now, I'm sure you have a million questions, and there will be a time to answer them. But first you need to come to terms with what I've just told you and prepare yourselves to see your son. I'll leave you here for a few minutes to talk and to console each other, but I'll come to get you in a while, and when I do, you need to be brave for Jeff. You need to help him make this difficult transition from an active little boy to someone who will never walk or run or jump or even feed himself again. And you need to be encouraging. He needs you to be positive."

With that, the surgeon reached out, squeezed their hands briefly, smiled a grim smile, and left them alone in the room.

Brenda buried her face in Jerry's shoulder and cried silent tears. Jerry sat and stared at the wall, not seeing anything but a future that would now never happen. He saw with his mind's eye Jeff at the farm just a few months ago, how completely joyful he was, and he saw that this would never happen again. Jeff might visit the farm again, but he would never run through the fields, never help his granddad on the tractor, never pet old Ralph again. Jerry saw himself wanting to play catch with his son in the backyard, but now there was no one to throw the ball to. And then he saw the bike they had found on sale at Wal-Mart and had bought for Christmas and hidden at the Homeless Shelter. Of course, they would have to take it back. These and a thousand and one other thoughts raced through his mind, but he had to put them away. He couldn't afford to wallow in self-pity. He had to be strong for his son, his dear little Jeff, who meant more to him than life itself, and who now needed him to be positive and full of hope.

He looked down at Brenda, and as she looked up at him with tearstained cheeks, he said, "We'll be okay."

She took a deep breath, wiped the tears away, and then said, "I know. But it will hurt. What do we tell him?"

"The truth, I guess."

After a while, Dr. Metcalf returned. "Your son's waking up," he said softly. "Are you ready?"

"We are," Jerry answered grimly.

They found Jeff in a room by himself. He had some sort of contraption around his shoulders and head. Jerry assumed it was to immobilize his neck when they had to turn him. They sat down in two chairs that had been moved next to his bed. He looked up at them groggily and tried to smile.

"I'm thirsty," he said.

Brenda looked up at Dr. Metcalf. "He can suck on a piece of ice," the doctor told her and motioned for the nurse who was monitoring Jeff to go get a cup of ice.

"I can't feel anything," Jeff said.

"I know, honey," Brenda said. "You had a bad accident. Do you remember falling down the stairs?"

"Kind of," he murmured.

"You hurt your neck, Jeff," Jerry told him. "It took all the feeling away so you can't feel your arms or legs."

"Will I get better?" he asked.

"Probably not, honey," Brenda answered, and her voice quavered. "But we'll take real good care of you."

They watched as his little four-year-old mind processed this information, and they wondered what his reaction would be. Would he scream or cry or refuse to accept the truth? "I love you, Mommy and Daddy," he said eventually. Then he closed his eyes. "I'm so tired," he said. "I want to sleep."

He closed his eyes for a minute, then opened them again. "I had a dream," he said. "I was flying in a funny airplane. It was cool." He then closed his eyes and fell asleep.

By now it was late in the day, and Megan, who had sensed something was wrong and had behaved like an angel, started to whine.

"She's missed her nap," Brenda said. "We need to take her home."

"Why don't you go now for a while," Dr. Metcalf suggested. "You can come back this evening. We'll take good care of Jeff. The next few days are going to be busy, though. We'll need to train you to take care of him once he comes home."

"And when will that be?" Jerry asked.

"Probably a few weeks. We need to have his vertebrae heal a bit, then you can probably handle him at home."

Megan was fussing even more now, so they kissed Jeff good-bye and left him for a while.

Jerry and Brenda hardly spoke a word on the way home, but each knew what the other was thinking. Was Max going to start taking back what he had given?

When they got home, Megan was already asleep in her car seat. Brenda put her in her crib, and when she came out to the kitchen she found Jerry sitting there, staring at the wall with unseeing eyes.

* * *

Last Call

That evening, Jerry and Brenda drove back to the hospital. A sitter was staying with Megan. Jeff was awake and alert when they arrived and was watching *Rugrats* on the TV in his room. He was still too young to understand much of the humor, but he was laughing anyway, his eyes glued to the tube.

"Hi, Sport," Jerry said, trying to sound upbeat.

"Hi, Daddy," he answered. "We gotta get cable."

"Oh?"

"Have you ever seen *Rugrats*?"

"Afraid not, boss."

They watched the show until it ended, then Jeff said, "Scratch my chin, Mommy. It itches." Brenda reached out and gently scratched his chin, then left her hand resting softly against his cheek.

Jerry hadn't thought yet of all the simple things his son would never be able to do for himself. He looked into Jeff's bright blue eyes.

"The nurse said I could have ice cream," Jeff exclaimed. "Can I have some now?"

Jerry pressed the nurse button and waited. He tried to smile, but all the while he was sick inside. He almost couldn't bear to see his son in this condition. What Brenda was feeling he couldn't even fathom.

The nurse came, and then the ice cream did, and when Jerry had spooned the last of it into his son's mouth, Jeff asked if they would read a story to him. Brenda had brought some of Jeff's favorite books, and they read four of them. Then they watched TV for a while longer until Jeff was tired again.

He yawned, then said, "I'm gonna walk again, Daddy."

"How do you know, Jeff?" Jerry asked tenderly.

"I just know. I dreamed I was walking in a big forest."

Jerry didn't say anything. *Of course, you can do anything in your dreams,* he thought.

Just then, the nurse came in to get Jeff settled for the night.

"You just yell if you need anything, Sport, okay," she said. "I'll be right out here. We'll send your mom and dad home now so they can get some sleep too, but they'll come back tomorrow."

"He'll be okay, Mr. and Mrs. Carlson," she said when they were out in the hallway. "We'll take good care of him. And tomorrow we'll start training you for when you take him home." At these words Jerry felt an emptiness inside as deep and wide as the Grand Canyon.

* * *

The next few days were like a bad but persistent dream. Jerry and Brenda saw little change in Jeff except that he started to get impatient with his inability to move, and the training pounded home the reality that his condition was not only permanent, but that it would change their own lives forever. Jeff would be dependent on them for virtually everything he needed—until the day he died. The doctors and nurses had been kind and patient, but at the same time brutal in their honesty and unyielding in their insistence that Jerry and Brenda fully accept the reality of their situation. They fostered no hopes for even a partial recovery of any mobility and didn't allow the grieving parents to live one second in a wish-world of their own making.

After a couple of weeks, both Jerry and Brenda were emotionally drained and weren't sleeping well at night. It seemed almost more than they could bear. Everywhere they turned they saw reminders of the life Jeff would never have. Every child running or playing or just walking down the sidewalk spoke pain to their souls. A therapist at the hospital met with them daily, but she was as unencouraging in her "reality therapy" as the doctors and nurses.

Still, in spite of all the hopelessness that surrounded them, an odd thought had been taking shape in the back of Jerry's mind, an idea he dismissed at first as mere wishful thinking. But as time passed, this thought became as persistent as the medical professionals' denials, as if it were fighting not against reality but against their sterile, scientific definition of reality. Indeed, it was the thought of life itself, of the reality Jerry had experienced firsthand over the past seven years. The miracles of his own life were at odds with the facts the doctors and nurses fed him daily. And as time passed, the incongruence between the two views grew and expanded beyond all reason until Jerry felt his head would burst. This notion was an unreasonable, irrational thought, but then so had been the story of his life since that eventful day when he had found the cell phone in the bushes on South Temple Street.

He hadn't said anything to Brenda about what he'd been thinking. He knew it may have been nothing more than his brain denying the stark reality of their predicament. If so, he couldn't afford to drag her down to despair if nothing came of it, but still he couldn't let go of the thought. Or rather, the thought wouldn't let go of him. It was taking control of his mind, and this worried him. He wondered if he was losing touch with sanity.

Then one night, two weeks after the accident, Jerry dreamed again and found himself lying flat on his back on the forest floor. He couldn't move, and there was still no feeling in his arms or legs. Suddenly a voice spoke from behind him, a voice he hadn't heard in his dreams for a long, long time now.

"Don't be afraid, Jerry," Max said. "Your head's fine, and so's your heart. Have faith. All things are possible to those who believe."

Suddenly, pain like fire shot through his body from head to toe. He wanted to scream, but was afraid he'd wake Brenda. Somehow in the dream he knew his screams would be real screams in the silence of their bedroom. Still, he felt as if he'd been thrown into boiling oil. And yet the pain was thrilling in a way because he could feel it.

He woke up with a start and sat up in bed. The room was dark and silent except for Brenda's gentle breathing. The pain was gone except for a strange tingling in his fingertips and an echo in his mind, but Max's words still rang in his ears. Jerry lay down again, but sleep stayed far away. Finally, he picked up the Bible from the nightstand and carried it out into the kitchen. He turned on the light, poured himself a glass of grape juice, and sat down at the table. Using the bookmark, he opened the Bible and found, to his surprise, that a different page was marked than the one he and Brenda had been reading right before turning out the lights earlier that same night. Several new verses were carefully underlined in red pencil. Jerry read them with wide eyes.

"And Jesus stood still, and commanded him to be called. And they call the blind man, saying unto him, Be of good comfort, rise; he calleth thee.

"And he, casting away his garment, rose, and came to Jesus.

"And Jesus answered and said unto him, What wilt thou that I should do unto thee? The blind man said unto him, Lord, that I might receive my sight.

"And Jesus said unto him, Go thy way; thy faith hath made thee whole. And immediately he received his sight, and followed Jesus in the way."

* * *

In the morning Brenda found Jerry in the kitchen fixing breakfast. She walked over to him and put her arms around his waist

"How did you sleep?" she asked.

"Not at all—after the dream."

"What dream?" she asked, concern in her eyes.

"Max spoke to me. He said to have faith." He paused while this sank in. "I'm going to call him."

She didn't say anything for a moment, then said, "Won't he ask for everything back?" Jerry could hear fear in her voice.

"Let's talk about our options," he suggested.

"What do we gain by calling?" Brenda asked.

"Well, I'd say we need a miracle. If Max really is what I think he is, maybe he can do something."

"Do you really think he would? Isn't this just part of the deal, that you have to give everything back? Isn't Jeff's accident just the first payment?" A hint of bitterness tinged her voice.

"Maybe," Jerry admitted. "But we don't know that. We'll never know if we don't call. I'd hate to turn my back on a miracle just because I was afraid to take a risk."

"But if you call, won't he ask for everything all at once? You only have this one call left."

"I've had a strange thought that's been pestering me ever since the accident," he admitted. "For some reason I just can't believe Jeff's going to spend the rest of his life this way. Something won't let me. And look at this," he said, handing her the Bible. "The bookmark was here when I woke up."

Brenda read the underlined passage and closed her eyes.

"Somehow it just feels right," Jerry said.

"I know. But I'm afraid." Brenda started to cry, and Jerry held her tight. "It's hard to be rational at a time like this," she said after a few minutes. "I wish everything weren't so hard."

"I know," Jerry said, "but it seems that's just how life is."

"Oh, Jerry," Brenda exclaimed, "what do we do?"

"There's a chance he won't ask for everything," Jerry suggested, trying to sound hopeful. "He's invested too much in my life. I can't believe this is just some silly game he's playing and that when I make the third call I lose everything. That would be absurd, and I don't think Max is absurd. Unpredictable, yes, and a bit mischievous perhaps, but not absurd. And I don't think God is either. I don't think He just plays with people's lives and jerks them around for no reason."

"So what happens if we don't call?" Brenda asked.

"Jeff lives his life as a quadriplegic. And we never know whether we could have helped him. I'd be willing to give up everything, go back onto the street and sleep under a tarp in the canyon again, if I could give Jeff his future back."

"I know you would," Brenda told him. "And I would too."

They stood silently for some time, holding each other and hanging on to tattered shreds of hope.

"I think you're right," she said finally. "We've got to trust him."

After breakfast Jerry got the cell phone out. He had charged the battery during his sleepless hours. He knew he could call Max on the house phone, but somehow it just didn't feel right. He punched the numbers, then sat down at the kitchen table. On the second ring he heard a click, then a familiar voice said hello.

"Hi, Max," Jerry said.

"This must be urgent, Jerry. It's only November."

"It is." He didn't know quite how to begin, so he just blurted it out. "Jeff fell and broke his neck."

"So I heard. I'm sorry," said Max.

"He's paralyzed."

"Yes, that often happens with such injuries."

"We need a miracle, Max."

"What do you think I am, Jerry?" came the gentle reply. "A genie?"

"No, Max. I think you're better than a genie. But what I think doesn't matter, does it?"

"So you don't think I'm an alien anymore?" Max laughed. "Or Big Brother? Or a secret agent?"

"Aliens and Big Brothers can't help me, Max, and neither can the CIA. But I believe you can."

"You know the deal, Jerry," Max answered. "This is your third call. There will be no more calls—from you or me."

"I know." Jerry swallowed hard. "And I know the other part of the deal."

"Are you willing to give up everything, Jerry? All for your little boy's health?"

"Of course I am, Max. I'd give my own life if necessary."

"Oh, you've already done that, Jerry. Many times over."

"What do you mean?"

"Jerry," Max answered, "you remember Abraham in the Bible?"

"Sure. Some of the details are a bit hazy, but I remember."

"Well, sometimes it's the willingness and not the sacrifice that's important."

"So will Jeff be healed?" Jerry asked.

"That's not for me to decide now, is it?" Max answered. "Just have faith, Jerry."

"So how will I know?"

"You never did like surprises, did you?"

"Never did, never will."

"Then I'll wish you a merry Christmas in advance, since I won't be calling this year to give you your annual surprise. See you around, Jerry."

"Will you, Max?"

"Who knows, Jerry. I might see *you*, but you'd never recognize *me*, would you?" Max laughed again. "One last thing, Jerry."

"What?"

"Throw that old phone away. Get yourself a new digital one. That one's so old and outdated, you know, you look like a guy watching black and white TV."

Jerry shook his head and smiled as the line went dead. He took one last look at the phone, then tossed it in the garbage can. Brenda looked at him with questioning eyes.

"I won't be needing it anymore," he explained.

"So, what did Max say? Will Jeff be healed?"

"He didn't say. He just said to have faith."

* * *

The Impossible

The next day, Jerry and Brenda spent the morning with Jeff. He seemed in good spirits and not overly frustrated with his inability to move. They figured that he was finally getting used to it. Or maybe he didn't really understand that he was supposed to be this way for the rest of his life. Or maybe his simple, childlike faith was all he could see. Or maybe it was the dreams he'd been having. He claimed he would certainly walk again.

For the next week, nothing happened. The doctors wanted to keep him in the hospital a little longer than they had originally said, ostensibly so that Jerry and Brenda could learn all they needed in order to take care of him at home. But Jerry wondered if perhaps the doctors were unwilling to send Jeff home yet because his parents seemed unable to deal with the reality of his condition. They spent most of each day with him, and the doctors and nurses continued to hammer home the fact that Jeff would never walk, never roll over by himself, never lift a finger. But every night when they went home, they tried to encourage each other.

"Are we crazy to keep on hoping? Are we crazy to believe?" Brenda asked.

"Yes," Jerry answered, "but what other choice do we have?"

"Max didn't promise he could do anything. He just told you to keep on believing."

"Maybe that's what we're supposed to do. Maybe if we don't believe, it won't happen."

"Okay," Brenda sighed. "I'll go on believing as long as you do, but the nurses must think we're a bit loony by now. Jeff keeps telling them he'll walk again, and we go right along with him. They must think we're refusing to deal with reality. Are we?"

"Yes. But that's what faith's all about, I suppose."

They had been reading from the New Testament every night, and what struck them was how often Jesus told people it was their faith that made them whole. It was almost as if the use of His power depended on whether people believed in Him or not. In fact, in His own hometown He couldn't perform many miracles, He said, because of the unbelief of the people. Jerry and Brenda felt they were walking on thin ice and that every step might plunge them into the freezing depths, but they just kept inching along, holding onto each other, holding onto hope.

* * *

On the eighth day after the call, more than three weeks after Jeff's fall, they were in his room with him, and Brenda was absentmindedly rubbing his feet. A nurse walked in to take his temperature and check his heart rate, and Brenda moved her chair to be out of the nurse's way.

"Don't stop, Mom," Jeff said. "That feels good."

Brenda pulled her chair back to his bedside and reached out for his feet, then stopped.

"What did you say, Jeff?"

"Don't stop rubbing my feet. It feels good."

She pinched his toe.

"Ouch!" he yelled.

Jerry was at Jeff's bedside in a flash. "Can you feel your fingers, too?" he asked, and rubbed Jeff's hand.

"Not so good. They feel like ice."

"But you can feel this?" Jerry asked, rubbing harder.

"A little bit."

By now the nurse had fled the room in search of Dr. Metcalf, and soon Jeff's bed was surrounded by a whole team of medical skeptics.

"There's got to be an explanation," Dr. Metcalf said. "Sometimes there's phantom pain involved, like with an amputated limb. His brain might be trying to convince itself the feeling is still there, but I'm sure he won't be able to move his fingers or toes."

In response, Jeff pulled a face and with great effort wiggled his big toe.

"Well I'll be," Dr. Metcalf exclaimed. "I've never seen anything like this. Not with this type of injury."

"You don't believe in miracles?" Brenda asked.

"Only medical ones."

"O ye of little faith," Jerry chided. "You know what? I think we ought to do an x-ray of Jeff's neck."

Finally Dr. Metcalf agreed, and when the film came back, all he could do was scratch his head.

"This isn't the same injury I operated on three weeks ago," he said.

"No," Jerry agreed, "it probably isn't."

Within a week, Jeff had full feeling in his body and was learning to walk and use his hands again, since his muscles had forgotten how to respond to signals from the brain. A week later he walked out the hospital door to the bewildered cheers of the medical staff and went home with his parents.

The day after Jeff's homecoming, Jerry went back to work. He hadn't been there much since the accident, and lots of things had piled up on his desk. He sorted through the mail first, throwing away the junk—mostly credit card applications—and opening the rest. The monthly bank statement was there. He opened it and glanced at it with little interest. Then something caught his eye. A withdrawal had been made—actually, a large CD had been closed out and the cash withdrawn—in the amount of one million dollars and change. He stared at the numbers on the statement for a minute, scratching his head. Then he had an idea. He called the bank and asked who had made the withdrawal. "Why, you did, Mr. Carlson," the answer came back.

Jerry sat at his desk for a long time, wondering what Max had used the money for. Eventually he turned his attention back to the pile of unopened letters, and there on the top was one with no return address. He opened it and found inside a handwritten note in a neat, bold cursive.

Jerry, it read, *with God nothing is impossible, but if one thing comes close, it's transferring money from the future to the past. You can't imagine the headache this has caused me. I'll leave you to puzzle over the details, though, and how to explain this to your partners! Max.*

Jerry put the note back into the envelope, stuffed it into his shirt pocket, and walked out onto the floor to see how the Christmas rush was going.

* * *

Christmas

The week before Christmas seemed a bit lonely to Jerry. Even though he had thrown the phone away, he half expected Max to call on the home phone. But the call never came. Max was true to his word. But as Jeff's health continued to improve, Jerry knew the benefit was well worth the price.

Christmas morning arrived, and when Brenda and Jerry finally allowed Jeff downstairs to see what Santa had brought, they grinned at his squeals of delight. There by the tree he found a new bicycle and, of course, a helmet. He wanted to go out and learn to ride it that very minute, but Jerry had to disappoint him. There had been snow during the night, and besides, Dr. Metcalf had strictly forbidden any such activity for at least three months. So Jeff had to be content with sitting on the seat and letting his dad wheel him carefully around the house.

Jeff finally tired of this—long after Jerry was ready for a rest—and decided he wanted to see what other gifts he had under the tree. He wasn't disappointed. But he also took great interest in what the others received, particularly Megan. She wasn't old enough to understand the whole concept of Christmas, but had a great time ripping the paper off gifts, even if they weren't for her. One particularly large box, however, caught her attention.

"It's for you, Meg," said Brenda. "Go ahead and open it."

She and Jeff attacked the paper, and suddenly a picture of a tricycle emerged from the wreckage.

"Look, Meg," screamed Jeff, "a bike for you too! We can ride together this summer."

Jerry gave Brenda a necklace she had wanted but thought was too expensive. "Oh, you shouldn't have," she scolded when she opened it, but she also took it out of the box, put it on, and appeared in no mood to return it to the store.

Jerry found a small package under the tree with his name on it. When he opened it, he laughed. It was a new digital cell phone, much smaller than the old one Max had given him years before.

"The battery on this one lasts almost forever compared to the Max phone," said Brenda, "but I doubt that you'll get as many interesting calls on this one."

"If you call me on it," he answered, "that's good enough for me."

When all the other presents were opened, they found one last package behind the tree against the wall.

"What's this?" Brenda asked. "We don't have any paper like that. Is it from the partners?"

"I don't think so," Jerry replied. "Let's see who it's for."

Jerry searched the package and finally found something written in faint ink in one corner.

"It's for you, Jeff," he said.

Jeff took the package and turned it over, and when he did they heard the sound of something with many pieces rattling inside. Jeff tore the paper away, and there in his hands was a box Jerry had seen before.

"Look!" Jeff yelled. "It's a plane just like the one in my dream."

ninth christmas

∙∙

The Last Surprise

At 2:30 in the morning on Christmas Day, Brenda went into labor. Jerry woke up Avalon, who had spent the past few days in the extra bedroom next to Jeff's in anticipation of the event. She had become Jeff's favorite baby-sitter over the past year and was there to stay with Jeff and Megan while Jerry and Brenda rushed off to the hospital.

"Just go," she told them. "We'll be fine here."

Jerry helped Brenda out to the new van they had purchased in anticipation of having one extra passenger. And they hardly made it to the hospital before their third child, a seven-pound, five-ounce boy, made a rather rapid entry into mortality.

It had been an easy pregnancy, and when they finally placed her new son in her arms, all wrapped up in a new baby blanket, Brenda looked up at Jerry and smiled. "Well," she said, "what shall we name him?"

They had talked about every name under the sun, but hadn't been able to agree on one. "Shall we let Jeff decide?" Jerry suggested.

"That's a dangerous idea," Brenda said. "We could end up with anything from Darth Vader to Buzz Lightyear."

* * *

When Jerry went home later that morning to open presents and then to bring the kids to the hospital to see their new brother, they were excited.

"Can I really hold him, Dad?" Jeff asked.

"Brover, brover, brover," squealed Megan.

When they finally marched into Brenda's room in the maternity wing, Jeff was grinning from ear to ear.

"Where is he, Mom?" he asked.

"He's sleeping in the nursery," Brenda replied. "We'll have the nurse go get him."

Eventually, the nurse brought their new little baby in and handed him carefully to Jerry. Jerry sat down in a chair next to Jeff and gently placed the baby on his lap. Jeff was thrilled, and the baby made an expression the nurse would claim was gas, but one Jerry would have described as pure bliss.

"So what do you think we ought to name him?" Brenda asked Jeff.

"You mean you don't know?" Jeff exclaimed.

"We haven't decided yet," Jerry answered.

"But his name's Max," Jeff said.

"Max?" exclaimed Jerry. He didn't think he'd ever mentioned Max to Jeff.

"Yeah, Dad," Jeff said, "the man in my dream told me."

Jerry and Brenda looked at each other with arched eyebrows.

"Brenda," Jerry finally said, "something tells me the ride's not quite over."

"Merry Christmas," she replied.

about the author

· ·

R. K. TERRY is a writer and magazine editor. He has also been a small business owner, a literary agent, and a faculty member at BYU's Marriott School. He is the author of *Economic Insanity: How Growth-Driven Capitalism Is Devouring the American Dream* and *Away with Stereotyped Mormons! Thoughts on Individuality, Perfection, and the Broad Expanse of Eternity*. He resides in Orem, Utah, with his wife and four children.

EXCERPT FROM
TIMELESS MOMENTS

CHAPTER ONE

Vietnam
July 1972

The smell of fuel, jungle, and death surrounded the seven soldiers as they walked across the mist-covered tarmac and climbed aboard the Huey helicopter.

Their orders were exact, their mission top secret.

Low-hanging fog cloaked the landing zone as the helicopter lifted off, but a few moments later the craft broke into the clear. Vietnam, even in war, was scenic with its green jungle, thickly forested mountains, and slashes of silver rivers crisscrossing the terrain.

About four miles from X-ray, their assault landing zone, the pilot, Bryan Randall, gave the signal, and the helicopter dropped down to treetop level to fly nap-of-the-earth on the final approach. It wasn't even daylight and already, 105mm artillery pounded the area below them. Startled birds took flight as the Huey roared along at 110 miles per hour.

Dalton "Mac" McNamara's stomach tensed. The cornflakes he'd had for breakfast roiled and rumbled inside of him. He always felt this way before a mission, but today it was worse. Wondering if he would be fortunate enough to defy death yet one more day, he drew in several slow, calming breaths. Still, the question nagged at the back of his mind.

Mac sensed that the most critical part of the operation was coming—the drop. The timing had to be perfect. Not close. Not almost. Perfect. The choppers had to get in, get out, and get gone—otherwise they were an easy target. If everything didn't go precisely as planned, the enemy would be waiting when the Hueys came in. That wasn't the greeting any of them wanted. Not today. Not ever.

Still two minutes out. Below, smoke and dust flew from artillery fire where broad, low-rolling plains were dotted with trees thirty to fifty feet tall and interspersed with a few old Montagnard farm clearings and dry streambeds. There were no villages. No people. Just the enemy, shells, and hatred.

With the precision of months of training and the experience of battle, the operation continued, on time and on target. The small, tightly knit band of men was a reconnaissance group, part of the Fifth Special Forces Group out of Nha Trang, South Vietnam. At great risk, these men managed to bring in critical information that saved the lives of many American soldiers—yet often at the expense of their own. The area they were to enter was crawling with Viet Cong. The trick was to find them, close in, track their position, strengths, capabilities, and hopefully their intentions, then get out.

Mac and his men prepared themselves for the drop into battle. They had seconds, not minutes, to get out so the Huey could get back in the air. No one spoke, but the look in everyone's eyes told Lt. McNamara that they were brothers; they were a team. They would fight together, and if necessary, die together.

Randall gave the signal as they touched down, and in a split second, following Mac's lead, the men jumped out of the Huey and ran for cover. No one moved and no one breathed as the *whump whump whump* of the chopper roared away from them, then drifted further away. Tense, the men waited, a collective prayer in their hearts for Randall and his crew not to be shot down as they flew out.

Straining, they listened as an eerie stillness settled in. In the distance, several explosions shattered the silence. Smoke and gunpowder hung in the moist, tropical air.

Clinging to the last moments of peace, Mac glanced at each of his men before giving the signal. He knew it was impossible for them to land without notice, but hopefully the Viet Cong weren't aware of their exact location. The quicker they moved out and evaded the enemy, the safer they would be.

Staying low, hidden by elephant grass, the seven men crept toward an island of trees a hundred yards away. Mac paused a brief moment to listen, wishing for the sound of gunfire. The artillery would indicate the position of the enemy. But the silence remained.

Creeping stealthily, they arrived at the cluster of trees. Again, Mac and his men watched and waited, their movements unnoticed and nearly invisible.

After waiting for what seemed like an eternity, Mac nodded his head, and they walked toward the mountains. The early morning sun, hot and blazing, turned the moist jungle terrain into a steaming sauna. Sweat trickled down Mac's forehead and cheeks, trailing a path down his neck and between his shoulder blades. Brush and vines grew so thick that at several points, every step had to be carved out with a machete. Progress was slow and arduous, but progress just the same. They hoped to reach the appointed spot before nightfall.

Mac knew their route like the back of his hand. He'd studied the map, memorizing every hill, stream, and boulder. Yet knowing what they were headed for didn't bring him any comfort. The tree line ended up ahead, where they would cross several hundred yards of open field before they could disappear into the dense mountain foliage. If they made it across that field, the rest would be easy.

Sinking low in the brush, they inched their way to the edge of the clearing and looked out. The hair on the back of Mac's neck stood up. Something didn't feel right, and he motioned for them to stop.

Mac felt the other men watching him, waiting for his signal. Three of them would cross the field while the others covered for them. Once those three were safe on the other side, the other four would go.

Chambers, the recon platoon radio operator, nodded toward the clearing, but Mac shook his head. He couldn't explain it, but something told him to wait.

Just then, a rustle in the bushes across from them caught their attention. A young Vietnamese boy no more than sixteen years old stepped into the clearing wielding an AK-47.

Mac held his breath and watched, unsure if the boy was Viet Cong or not, since not all of them wore uniforms. Just as he suspected, several other soldiers no older than the first followed, heading straight at them. Mac now knew they were indeed VC.

Chambers eyed Mac, who remained motionless. If anyone moved, it would give away their position. If they fired, they would attract every Viet Cong soldier within a mile. No, it was better to wait.

Willing the enemy to turn and head west, Mac felt his heart pound in his chest. He didn't want to fire, but if the VCs got much closer, he'd have to.

Brady, the man to Mac's left, shifted his weight. A twig cracked, the noise magnified by the tension in the air. The VCs halted, drawing their weapons as they scanned the bush.

Mac's heart stopped.

Peering directly at their hiding spot as if they could see through the trees, the three young soldiers trained their gun barrels directly at Mac and his men, who remained frozen in their positions.

Mac knew if he and his men opened fire at such close range, the VC soldiers wouldn't know what hit them, but he resisted the signal until the last possible moment. Blowing their cover would defeat their mission and probably cost them their lives. He wasn't ready to make that call.

The men beside him flinched, their muscles taut and ready, their nerves sparking with the instinct to fire. Still they waited.

Just then, someone shouted from across the clearing where several other VC soldiers motioned for the three young men to join them. Mac expelled air from lungs that were ready to burst.

Two of the soldiers immediately retreated, but one narrowed his gaze and studied the bush. Suddenly, he exclaimed something in Vietnamese and raised his AK-47.

Mac's split-second decision to fire was one he'd regret for the rest of his life.

At the signal, Chambers quickly fired and shot the soldier. Just as Mac had feared, a dozen more VC emerged from the trees and pelted them with bullets. Two of Mac's men went down while the rest of them continued firing at the advancing troops.

A bullet whizzed passed Mac's head, but he continued firing. He heard a hollow thud as another one of his men went down.

"Jackson's hit!" Chambers yelled. Mac glanced down to see Jackson's helmet in front of him with a bullet hole in it. Mac kicked it out of the way, reeling from the gruesome sight.

Another man went down—Beckett, the youngest man on their team. From the very day Beckett had joined his team, Mac had felt protective of him, almost like he was a kid brother. Mac was close to all his men, but Beckett was young—too young to be killing people. The boy had already lost a brother in the war. No family deserved to lose two.

Mac grabbed the M-79 grenade launcher lying next to Beckett, whose arm and chest were both bleeding freely.

"Help," Beckett called to him, lifting his bloodied arm toward Mac.

Chambers grabbed the M-79 from Mac and launched a grenade. Mac tore off his shirt and wrapped it tightly around Beckett's arm. "You're going to be okay," he shouted over the din. Grabbing his M-79 again, Mac took aim and pulled the trigger, but nothing happened. He opened the feed cover, flipped the gun over, and hit it on the ground, jarring the shells loose. Debris had caught in the ammo belt. Mac flipped it right side up, slapped the ammo belt back in, slammed the feed cover, and began firing again.

Even though they were getting pummeled, the men in Mac's group who were still standing held off the NVA troops, and one by one, the enemy dropped.

The rat-tat-tat-tat of an enemy machine gun mowed down the foliage in front of them, taking Chambers, who screamed in pain as he writhed on the ground. Mac looked at Chambers, whose shoulder had been hit. Bullet fragments had also shredded the side of his face.

Raging anger filled Mac, and he fired, taking out two of the advancing troops, leaving only four or five standing. "Hang in there, Chambers, we've almost got 'em!" he yelled.

Mac heard a shot and glanced over to see Brody Thorpe fall backward without a whimper.

"I'm out of ammo," Sinclair hollered, throwing his M-60 on the ground and grabbing another one. He immediately began firing, taking out another soldier from the NVA—the North Vietnamese Army.

Then, out of nowhere, Mac felt a hot stinging in his head. A wave of nausea washed over him, and he knew he'd been hit. Still, he continued shooting, wondering why he wasn't feeling any pain. Another bullet whistled past, hitting the tree behind him.

"Lieutenant Mac," Sinclair yelled. "You okay? There's blood—"

"I'm fine," Mac yelled. But he spoke too soon. Right as the words left his mouth, a stick grenade passed through the trees and exploded at his feet. Mac reached down to his right leg and touched grenade fragments, suddenly feeling like he'd just touched a red-hot poker, sizzling his hand. He collapsed back as agonizing pain worse than anything he'd felt in his entire life consumed him.

A North Vietnamese soldier plowed through the trees and stumbled over some of the dead men on the ground. Mac gripped his gun, but it was Sinclair who fired, putting a full magazine through the enemy soldier before he went down.

Mac heard Vietnamese voices coming toward him. The three NVAs charged through the trees and began kicking at the American soldiers on the ground. Opening one eye just a slit, Mac saw the men removing guns, ammunition, watches, and other valuables from the American soldiers. Lying still, Mac prayed the North Vietnamese soldiers would just take what they wanted and leave them for dead.

Mac watched as they searched Beckett, then kicked him hard in the ribs. Beckett's body jackknifed with the blow, then stilled.

Certain the young boy was dead, Mac fought the urge to scream. Then he stopped. One of Beckett's eyelids fluttered, and the boy made eye contact with him.

A prayer of gratitude flashed through Mac's mind, as well as a plea for the rest of his men.

But the NVA soldiers had other plans. After they'd taken what they wanted, they made sure all of the Americans were dead by shooting a few extra rounds into their bodies. Mac's heart sank. All of his men were gone, and most likely he was next. If only he hadn't given the signal to fire, maybe that young Viet Cong soldier would have moved on. Maybe he wouldn't have discovered them hidden in the bushes.

His muscles tensed, waiting for the final bullet that would take his life. Mac's only thoughts were of his buddies. They'd fought together, and now, they would die together.

Yet the bullet didn't come. Mac waited, then saw the NVA soldiers leaving.

Confused, Mac wondered why they hadn't put a bullet through him. Was his injury so bad that they took him for dead?

He watched them leave, and just when he thought it was safe, one of the NVA soldiers unexpectedly turned. Mac closed his eyes, but not before they saw one another. Mac tensed. He was certain that it was over. His moment had come.

But he wasn't that lucky.

The soldier shouted an order to the other two men who were with him. They stopped, turned, and approached Mac with murder in their eyes. Fear claimed him.

Take me, God, he begged. *Death is better than prison.*

Just as the prayer escaped his lips, the men grabbed his arms and legs and jerked him off the ground, causing a horrific pain in his leg.

He panicked. This wasn't right. He wasn't supposed to get captured; his men weren't supposed to get killed. He was supposed to seek out the NVA and radio their location back to the base. Hundreds of American soldiers' lives depended on this information.

NO! Mac wanted to scream. He knew what happened in North Vietnamese prisoner of war camps, and he knew he'd rather die now than spend years rotting away in a camp, inhumanely tortured and stripped of all dignity.

Realizing he wasn't wearing his helmet, he squirmed to find it and received the butt of a rifle in his ribs, several of them cracking with the blow.

Mac cried out in pain, wondering how much more he could bear. Leaving his buddies and helmet behind, God's grace finally fell upon him as he passed out.

* * *

Mac woke up in excruciating pain. Where was he?

Disoriented, he took several shallow breaths to get a grip on the pain and a bearing on his surroundings. The last thing he remembered was being dragged by North Vietnamese soldiers away from his company, who all lay dead amidst the trees, but here he was, in the middle of a field somewhere with the sound of artillery flying all around him.

His mind processed the situation slowly. Maybe the NVA had been attacked or ambushed, and in their effort to combat the enemy, had left him for dead. Either way, he knew he was one lucky soldier. Maybe. He was in the middle of enemy territory. He was as good as dead. He didn't know how serious his other injuries were, but the chance of using his leg was slim. But he wasn't going to lie there to be used for target practice. If he was going to die, he was going to die trying to survive.

He reached to his side and discovered that he still had two or three frag grenades, a smoke grenade, and two or three hundred rounds of ammo, but his M-16 was gone. He felt around his waist and located his canteen and a small mirror.

As his mind cleared, he realized that the first thing he needed to do was get out of the open. His chances of survival were better in the trees.

Crawling army style, he dragged himself slowly, elbow by elbow, through the grass. Any movement could bring artillery and mortar his direction, so he held his breath and proceeded cautiously.

Eyeing a clump of bushes, he crawled over to it, planning to wait until he was concealed before he assessed his wounds and came up with a plan.

Several times he froze as the sound of enemy voices carried on the air. If he were spotted, there certainly wouldn't be any second chances. Yet each time, the voices rose and then faded. Still, he wouldn't breathe easy until he found cover.

With muscles tensed and trembling, he pulled himself the last few feet before snaking his way through a low opening in the branches and finding space to sit.

Sweat poured down his face, neck, and back. The unbearable heat and thick humidity made breathing difficult, yet in the shade, he was able to find some reprieve. He couldn't get a good view of his leg wound, but judging by the blood, pain, and gaping hole, he knew it wasn't good.

Ripping the sleeve off his shirt, he fashioned a bandage to help stop the bleeding and to lend some support to his knee. Hopefully, even if he had to limp the entire way, he would now be able to move on foot.

He waited several hours for the siege of battle to move away from his position, and then, using a dead branch for support, he slowly, painfully, got to his feet.

Wincing as he put weight on his injured leg, he moved a few steps and stopped. The base of the mountain was five to six hundred yards in the distance. He had to cross through a patch of tall elephant grass to get there.

Keeping his head down, he hobbled his way through the grass, noticing that each step actually seemed to become less painful.

After a hundred yards he stopped again. Artillery suddenly sounded from the treetops, and before he dared take another step, the grass in front of him started to move, suddenly parting to reveal a NVA soldier.

With razor-sharp reflexes, Mac threw a frag and a smoke grenade and cut sharp to the left, his heart pounding faster than the bullets flying overhead. He dragged himself as fast as he could, away from the explosion of the smoke grenade behind him.

Without looking back, he headed for the mountains and soon came to a stream. There he waded upstream for a hundred yards to conceal his route, stumbling on the slippery rocks, filling his canteen along the way, and gulping in all the water he could hold. He found a rocky bank where he could exit without leaving a trail, and he hobbled across a valley where he could have a clear view of his back trail. Once there, he took a break, concealed in the brush.

For now he was safe, as he noted that the sound of battle was receding to his rear. But he knew as night closed in that he needed to find a place to hide.

A constant prayer ran through his mind, a plea for guidance, help, wisdom, strength, and protection. Mac knew he couldn't get more isolated than he was right now. He was alone yet not alone, for he was surrounded on all sides by North Vietnamese soldiers who wouldn't think twice about killing him.

But he was on his own. There was no one to help him. No one but God.

He'd been in battle enough to know deep down just how much courage he had. He'd experienced feelings of sheer terror, and of bravery beyond belief. In any given situation, he knew that he would sacrifice his life for any of his men. He'd prepared himself to die, and he was at peace with death.

But that was not how it had happened. Each and every one of his men had been slaughtered right before his eyes. He'd heard their cries, seen them gasp for their last breath. And here he stood, living and breathing. It seemed cruel and unfair.

Not that he wanted to die. But he didn't know how he would ever live with the memory of those last moments with his friends . . . his buddies . . . his brothers.

An ache filled his heart, rending it in two, until the sound of artillery started closing in on the mountain. He scrambled between two large trees and crouched low, scanning the surrounding area for a place to hide.

Locating an area near another tree where thick grass grew, Mac hobbled over and settled in for the night. He shivered against the damp night air, trying as best as he could to keep ants and bugs out of his wounds. A throbbing in his head upset his stomach, and with each drink of water he threw up. In misery he lay there, looking at the stars, thinking of his men. They'd depended on him, and now they were all dead. All because of him. All because of one decision he'd made.

Mac couldn't help but second-guess those last few moments before he'd given the signal to open fire. Would the North Vietnamese soldier have seen them hiding in the bushes?

He would never know, and he was afraid the question would haunt him for the rest of his life. The images of his buddies, bleeding and dying, were indelibly etched into his memory.

The next morning, he woke up and lay there, listening. In the distance, helicopters landed and took off. United States choppers flew over him, and he tried to signal them with his small mirror but had no luck. He heard gunfire between him and the site where his men still lay.

Staying low and hidden as much as possible, he climbed to the top of a hill and found a large log, which he used for cover. Another battle soon ensued, and he found himself caught in the middle. The artillery and mortars continued until dark and on through the night. Mac covered himself with brush and leaves, trying to conceal himself. Between the ants, the cold, and the sound of artillery, he didn't get much sleep that night either, but he knew he was close to the American landing zone, which gave him the hope of rescue.

Daybreak greeted Mac with a shower of artillery that sprayed all around the slope where he hid. When it quieted down, he began moving toward the landing zone, crossing a wide, shallow creek and rocky terrain until he finally approached the perimeter of the landing zone where he knew he would be recognized as an American soldier.

When he broke into the clearing, the landing zone was empty. In shock, Mac realized that the Americans had pulled out and abandoned the site.

An empty despair replaced his earlier hope. He wondered by how many hours—or was it only minutes?—he had missed them. They'd been there throughout the night, and he'd been so sure that they would still be there this morning. But they were gone, and he was still on his own.

With shoulders slumped and a weariness born of a lack of food and sleep, Mac revisited his plan. He hadn't come up with a Plan B, so certain was he that Plan A would work. But it hadn't, and now he was back to the drawing board.

Closing his eyes, he balanced on his left foot to take weight off his injured leg. It had begun to stink, and he knew the wound was infected. He didn't allow himself to dwell on it—there was nothing he could do until he found help—but he feared the damage was severe. At least he could limp. He'd be dead by now had he been unable to walk.

A rustle in the brush behind him sent a bolt of fear through Mac's body. He froze, straining to hear any further sound, praying it was nothing. But the furious beating of his heart and the dread that filled him left no room for hope.

Slowly he turned his shoulder, then his head . . . and looked straight into the barrel of a Vietnamese patrol soldier's gun. Behind that soldier were five others with their sights set on Mac.

He'd almost made it. But the eyes staring back at him had no mercy, no compassion. Just hatred. And he knew that he was just about to discover what purgatory really was.